# DANGEROUS

## BOOK FIVE

*Silence*

O'CONNOR
BROTHERS

# RHONDA BREWER

# Dedication

*This book is dedicated to all the victims of human trafficking and their families. This book is a work of fiction but sadly there are people who live this for real. May God watch over each and everyone of them.*

# Acknowledgements

There are so many people who made publishing this book possible and saying thank you just doesn't seem enough.

As always thank you to all the authors who I consider friends and mentors. Special thanks to Michelle Eriksen, Abbie Zanders, and Amabel Daniels for their constant support and help. To my dedicated beta readers, Jackie Dawe Ford, Nancy Arnold-Holloway, Mayas Sanders, thank you so much for the support and constant encouragement. To my readers, you are the reason that I continue to do this.

Last but certainly not least, thank you to my husband, Danny who gives me the inspiration for the romantic heroes I write and encourages me every day. To my two children Laura and Colin, both of you show me everyday how proud you are and how much you love me. That gives me even more encouragement to keep doing what I love. To my beautiful granddaughter, Emma. You may not be old enough to read yet but your smile gives me inspiration to keep going. I love all of you.

# Chapter 1

*Twenty-seven years ago,*

*Mrs. Carter brought the new boy to the front of the class. Michael O'Connor was anxious to meet a new friend, but the lady next to the kid was distracting him with the way she moved her hands. The new boy watched her while Mrs. Carter spoke.*

*"Class, this is our new student, Lyle Earle." Mrs. Carter smiled at the class like she always did. She was the best teacher in the world and the prettiest too.*

*"Hi, Lyle," The students shouted.*

*"Boys, this is Mrs. Earle, and she's Lyle's mom. She's going to be coming with Lyle every day." Mrs. Carter said.*

*"Why?" Bobby Tucker always asked way too many questions.*

*"Well, you see, when Lyle was born, he couldn't hear like you*

*and me." The teacher explained.*

*"Why?" Bobby asked again.*

*Mrs. Carter never got annoyed with Bobby, but Michael sure did. Bobby was one of his friends, but it still bugged him the way he always asked tons of questions.*

*"Bobby, not everyone is the same, it's what makes everyone special. Lyle has to use his hands to talk. I'm sure you've been watching Mrs. Earle moving her hands." Mrs. Carter said.*

*"Uh huh." Bobby nodded.*

*"That's a special way to speak with someone who can't hear. It's called sign language." Michael stopped listening to Bobby and concentrated on Mrs. Earle and the way she made all the different movements with her hands. It seemed like one of those dances they did in that movie his grandmother liked with that Elvis guy.*

*"He's weird." Ernie Marsh whispered from behind Michael.*

*"He's not." Michael didn't like Ernie because he picked on most of the boys in the class. He'd probably pick on girls too if it weren't an all-boys school. Michael wasn't afraid of him, and he made sure Ernie knew it.*

*"Is too, he can't even hear." Ernie snarled. "That's stupid."*

*"Just because he can't hear don't make him stupid," Michael spoke a little louder than he probably should have because the next thing he heard was Mrs. Carter's soft voice.*

"Michael, we don't say stupid." She swirled her finger in a circle which meant to turn back around in his seat.

"Sorry, Mrs. Carter," Michael dropped his head.

"Do you want to tell me why you said that word?" Mrs. Carter asked.

"He said the deaf kid was stupid," Ernie shouted.

"I did not. You did." Mike yelled.

"I didn't," Ernie yelled back.

"Boys, that's enough. Michael, and Ernie, I want both of you to follow me outside the class." Mrs. Carter pointed to the door.

Michael never got in trouble in class. It was all Ernie's fault. Now Mrs. Carter would probably call his mom and dad, and he'd end up with no dessert. It probably meant he wouldn't get to go fishing with Grandda over the weekend either and he'd miss out on Nanny Betty's homemade bread. Ernie was a jerk.

"Now, boys, what happened in there wasn't very nice. Ernie, I've told you many times not to say mean things. I'll be calling your father today." Mrs. Carter stood in front of them with her hands on her hips. "Ernie, go back in the classroom and pull out your special notebook. I want you to write I am sorry twenty times, and I'll get it at the end of the day."

Mrs. Carter opened the door, and Ernie scuffed into the classroom with his head down. When she closed the door, she *crouched in front of Michael and took his hands.*

*"Michael, I'm surprised at you." He couldn't look at his favorite teacher. "Do you want to tell me why you yelled and called Lyle stupid?"*

*"I didn't call Lyle stupid. I told Ernie that Lyle wasn't stupid just because he couldn't hear but Ernie said he was." He felt awful that Mrs. Carter would think he could be as mean as Ernie and he couldn't stop the tears.*

*"Michael, don't cry." Mrs. Carter pulled a tissue out of her pocket and gave it to him. "I didn't think you would say something like that. Why don't we move you to the other side of the classroom and you can sit by Lyle? Maybe you can help him settle in the class."*

*"He can't hear me." Michael didn't know how to do the hand language.*

*"That's why his mom's here. She's going to help us talk to Lyle and help him talk to us" Mrs. Carter smiled.*

*"Can she learn us how to do the hand language?" Michael asked.*

*"If you want to learn sign language, I'm sure she can teach you some." Mrs. Carter smiled again. "You've got a very big heart, Michael O'Connor. You're going to make some lucky young lady very happy when you grow up."*

*"Thank you, Mrs. Carter." Michael smiled.*

When they entered the classroom, Mrs. Carter quickly changed the seats and put Michael right behind Lyle and across from Bobby. Ernie kept sticking his tongue out at Michael for the rest of the day, but he didn't care.

While they ate lunch, Michael sat with Lyle and Mrs. Earle. It was easier to talk to Lyle than he thought it would be. Everything Michael said, Mrs. Earle would sign and then she would tell Michael whatever Lyle signed. Lyle even showed him how to spell both their names with sign language. It was so cool.

After Lunch, they played outside in the sandbox. Mrs. Earle had left them to play, but Michael learned he and Lyle could play together without even talking. If Michael wanted to say something to Lyle, he would act it out. It was fun until Ernie started to destroy the roads and hills they made with the sand for their trucks.

"Stop, Ernie," Michael shouted and stood in front of Lyle.

"If you play with the dummy then you're a dummy too." Ernie kicked the dirt.

"You better stop." Michael fisted his hands at his sides.

"Dummy," Ernie made a face and kicked dirt at Lyle.

"I warned you already, stop," Michael shouted louder.

"Dummy, dummy." Ernie pointed between Lyle and Michael and kicked dirt at Lyle again.

The dirt hit Lyle in the face and looked like it had gone into his mouth. Lyle jumped up and spit on the ground. Now Michael was mad. He remembered his mom and dad gave them three chances to behave themselves and decided he should do the same.

"This is your third chance. Stop kicking dirt at Lyle." Michael growled and clenched his fists tighter. If Ernie was going to be mean, Michael would teach him a lesson.

"What are you gonna do, dummy? Shake your hands at me." Ernie pushed Michael, and he fell on his butt.

Michael jumped up and lunged at Ernie pushing the bigger boy to the ground. Michael punched Ernie in the nose then stood up and turned around, but Lyle was gone. Before he could look for his new friend Ernie grabbed him around the feet and knocked him down to the ground. Michael and Ernie rolled around the ground punching whenever one of them would get on top.

Michael and Ernie got yanked apart when someone grabbed Michael by the collar of his shirt. He looked up and swallowed hard.

Father Wallace.

"Boys, both of you march yourselves straight into my office." The priest was scary when he was angry, and from the look on his face, Father Wallace was more than a little mad.

Michael sat on the bench in front of the Principal's office waiting for his mom and dad to arrive. He was in so much trouble when his parents got there. Ernie's dad was in the room with Father Wallace, and Ernie and Michael cringed every time he heard Mr.

*Marsh's raised voice.*

*"Michael Francis O'Connor, what's wrong with you?" His mother whispered when she sat next to him on the bench. She always used his full name when he or his brothers were in trouble at home.*

*"Now, Kathleen lets wait until we chat with Father Wallace." His father gave him that look he gave when he was disappointed, and that didn't sit well with Michael.*

*"Dr. and Mrs. O'Connor, thank you for coming." Father Wallace walked out of the office, and Ernie walked out behind his father. Michael knew Ernie didn't have a mom, but he didn't know what happened to her. "You too, young man."*

*Michael sat between his parents with his head hung down. His school pants were dirty, and the knee had a huge hole. That wasn't going to make his mom any happier.*

*"Michael, I've heard Ernie's side, and now I want to hear yours." Father Wallace sat back in his chair with his hands clasped in front of him. He was a great principal and didn't yell like the last one, but Michael had never been in trouble before, so he didn't know what to expect.*

*"Ernie kept kicking sand at Lyle. I gave him three chances to stop because mommy and daddy always give us three chances, but he wouldn't stop. He was picking on my friend." Michael finished talking and dropped his head. "He just wouldn't stop."*

*His head snapped up when he heard Father Wallace chuckle.*

*Michael glanced up to see his dad with his hand over his mouth, but his mother still looked upset.*

*"What do you say to that?" Father Wallace smiled at Michael.*

*"There's never a reason to use your fists, Michael. Isn't that what Uncle Kurt is teaching you in Karate?" His mother pointed at him.*

*"Mrs. O'Connor, I agree, but Michael's never been in trouble before. He's the first one of your boys I've ever seen in my office." Father Wallace said.*

*"Considering there are six of them here I'd take that as a good percentage." His dad laughed but stopped when his mom glared at him.*

*"You have one more boy starting next year, right?" Father asked.*

*"Yes, A.J." His mom said.*

*Michael shifted in the chair because he still didn't know what punishment he was going to get. None of his brothers got in trouble in school and from the way his mom tapped her foot he was in big trouble.*

*"Michael, I want you to apologize to Ernie tomorrow, and he will apologize to you." Father Wallace stood and shook hands with his dad. "I understand you were protecting the new boy but as your mom said, fighting is not the way."*

*Michael nodded and glanced up at his dad. His father didn't seem as mad as his mother, but that didn't mean he wasn't in huge trouble when he got home.*

*"I'm sorry for getting in trouble." Michael looked up at his mom.*

*Her face softened, and she cupped his cheeks with her hands and knelt in front of him.*

*"You know we love you and I'm proud you stood up for someone who couldn't stand up for themselves but next time take your friend and walk away. Okay?" His mom kissed his cheek.*

*"Yes, mommy." Michael jumped off the chair and wrapped his arms around her.*

*"Since the day is almost over, you can take Michael home." Father Wallace said.*

*"Can I go say goodbye to Lyle?" Michael asked.*

*"He's in class right now, but I'll tell him for you." Father Wallace said.*

*On the way home, his mom and dad talked about the trip to his grandparent's house. It was a long drive, but Michael and his brothers always had so much fun when they were there.*

*"I'm gonna learn sign language so I can talk to Lyle," Michael told his parents as he tried to force himself to stay awake.*

*"That's great honey." His mom said.*

*"He's cool." Michael yawned, and his eyes drifted closed. Yep, he and Lyle were going to be best friends.*

*Present day….*

Mike took a sip of his rum and let the dark liquid sit on his tongue before swallowing it. It burned as it slipped down his throat, but it was a good burn. It was the first time he'd been out with his friends in a while, and although he wasn't into the club scene much anymore it was good to shoot the shit with them

They'd dragged him in, and out of so many bars on George Street, he didn't even know which one he was in at the moment. He scanned the huge crowd from his perch wondering why the hell he was there in the first place. The clubs weren't as much fun as they used to be.

The three men showed up at his office and never even gave him a chance to stop at home to change out of his suit. So now he sat in a bar with the collar of his shirt open and the tie hung loosely around his neck. The bastards got to dress in comfortable jeans and t-shirts.

George Street spanned three blocks in downtown St. John's. Lined with bars, pubs, and restaurants, it was popular among the party crowd. It was only a hop, skip and jump from his apartment building, and there were nights he could hear the pumping sound of the music if he opened his fourth story window. Most weekends the street swarmed with people, and during Mardi Gras, it was wall to wall party animals.

At one time, he, his two younger brothers and their friends would spend every chance they could get hopping from club to club. He'd usually end the night with a girl spending the night at his place, or he'd go to hers. Now, most of the girls were jailbait or too drunk to talk. He'd even noticed his two younger brothers weren't partying as much anymore.

Yeah, George Street had lost its appeal, or maybe he was just getting too old for this shit. At least at thirty-two, he felt that way.

Ernie, Bobby, and Lyle were his best friends through school. He and Ernie had a rocky start, but Mike found out why Ernie had such a rough time. His mom had run off, and his dad had begun to date Lyle's mom. Around grade four Ernie's father married Lyle's mom, and that's when Ernie changed. He was excited to have a brother, and by the end of the year Ernie, Lyle, Bobby, and Mike were inseparable.

They grew up in Hopedale, played on the same baseball team, spent summers at the beach chasing girls and graduated high school together. That's where their time together got less.

Mike finished his law degree in Toronto and moved back to Newfoundland as soon as he could. When Lyle graduated, he moved to Burnaby, British Columbia and worked as a teacher at the school for deaf children. Ernie was a firefighter in St. John's and Bobby was a paramedic. They shared the apartment with Mike, but because of their schedules, it was hard to hang out and even more challenging with

Lyle.

They'd all learned sign language so they could communicate with Lyle. It also came in handy when you were in a loud club and couldn't hear anyone speak.

"It's so good to hang out together." Ernie signed.

"I don't remember the last time I was on George Street." Lyle signed.

Even though he couldn't hear the music, he was able to feel the vibration and had no problem getting out on the dance floor. March wasn't typically the month Lyle came home but it was his mother's sixtieth birthday, and he came back to surprise her.

"You need to come back home more often." Bobby signed.

"I know, that's what mom keeps saying. She's lonely since Peter died. I've applied to the School for the Deaf here but not sure if they are hiring right now." Lyle signed.

While his friends discussed their lives, Mike scanned the bar. The high tables and stools made it a lot easier to scope out the bar. He fully expected to see one of his younger brothers in the place but then again, they were probably at one of the bars in Hopedale. He glanced toward the bar and his gaze locked with a raven-haired beauty smiling at him

It wasn't unusual for women to notice him. Not that he was conceited or anything, but from experience, he was aware women found him attractive. Of course, most women considered Lyle, Ernie, and Bobby appealing as well. With four of them sitting together it wasn't any wonder the beauty and her two friends were eyeing their table.

"Look at that there goes O'Connor reeling them in with that pretty boy smile." Ernie chuckled as he signed what he was saying.

"Hey, he's not the only one with a pretty boy smile." Lyle grinned.

Mike rolled his eyes and glanced back to where he'd seen her. He was disappointed to see her talking to a man. The guy was a little shorter than Mike and chunky. Mike was ready to cut his losses when he saw her try to pull her arm away and it got his attention.

"Hey, you're losing your touch, Mike. She's moved on." Bobby nudged him, but when the guy grabbed her again, Bobby noticed. "Whoa, that's not right." All four men were on their feet in seconds.

"I got this, guys." Mike signed and rounded the table.

"Just sign if you need us," Ernie yelled.

While he squeezed his way through the crowd, he never took his eyes off her. Her back was to him, but the other two women looked terrified as the guy pinned her against the bar. People seemed to close together, making it harder to get around them, and it pissed him off. He didn't want to start a fight in the club, so he needed to quickly come up with something to get the guy to back off. If that didn't work, Mike would move him.

"Come on, baby." The guy slurred. Great, the dick was drunk. "Just one little dance."

"I'm waiting for my boyfriend." Mike could hear the tremor in her voice.

"I don't think you're telling the truth." The guy dipped his head, and the woman turned away.

"He'll be here any second, and he's not going to like you pawing me." She tried to push the guy away again.

"Hey dude, you want to get your hands off my girl," Mike shouted as he stepped next to them.

"Your girl?" The guy sized Mike up and down but didn't back away.

"Yeah, my girlfriend. Now back the fuck off." Mike stepped closer as she glanced back and forth between him and the asshole.

"It took you long enough to get here." One of her friends picked up on Mike's plan right away.

"Yeah, we've been waiting for you for over an hour." The other friend tapped her finger on her watch.

"Sorry, got stuck at the office." Mike didn't know what else to say, but he was glad they were quick to catch on.

"Shouldn't leave a beauty like this alone in a bar, buddy." The guy slowly stepped back and held up his hand. "Sorry." He staggered away.

"Are you okay?" Mike asked.

"Yes, just a little embarrassed. Thank you for doing that." Now that he was closer to her, Mike could see her hair wasn't black but a dark brown. She tucked a piece of it behind her ear and looked at him through her lowered lashes.

*So fucking cute.*

"My pleasure, but you know since I'm your boyfriend now, you've got to join my friends and me at our table." Mike tapped her chin lightly with his finger.

When she lifted her head to look at him, he forgot how to breathe. She had the most beautiful eyes he'd ever seen, and he couldn't tell if they were brown or black. He just knew they were incredibly mesmerizing. She was petite but certainly not without curves. She looked to be about a foot shorter than his six feet one inch, and she had to tip her head back to look up at him.

"You know I should be furious at my boyfriend for being late." Her smile revealed a little dimple in her left cheek.

"You really should, but I'm so cute you can't stay mad at me." Mike flashed a smile.

"Oh, dear God, you're not one of those are you?" One of her friends gagged.

"I guess you girls should join us to find out." Mike glanced at the other two girls but quickly brought his gaze back to those big beautiful eyes.

"Don't you think we should at least know each other's names." She pressed her finger against the middle of his chest.

"I can get by with just calling you, beautiful," Mike wrapped his hand around hers and pressed it against his chest.

"Oh, and what do I call you?" She grinned.

"Anything you want, but I usually answer to Mike." He said.

"As much as I would love to be called beautiful, I think it would be better if you called me Billie." Mike lifted her hand to his lips and kissed her palm.

"Since your drunk friend over there is staring; I don't think he'd believe I was your boyfriend if we shook hands." Mike linked his fingers with hers and led her toward the table. Ernie shook his head and gave Lyle a twenty-dollar bill.

By the time they made it back to the table, Ernie had grabbed some extra chairs for the ladies and pulled two tables together to make more room. Lyle, as usual, held himself back. Even at thirty-two, he felt self-conscious around people he didn't know.

"Let me do the introductions, I'm Ernie, this is Bobby and that guy there is Lyle," Ernie said aloud and signed at the same time.

"I'll introduce the girls, I'm Billie, this is Dana, and the one next to you is Abbie," Billie said and to Mike's surprise signed.

"You know sign language?" Mike glanced around at his friend's shocked expressions.

"Yes, my best friend and her daughter are both deaf." She signed everything perfectly, and he was sure his heart did a flip-flop in his chest.

"Guess, we can't do any secret conversations there, Mikey." Bobby laughed.

For the next couple of hours, Mike kept her close to his side not only because of the creepy guy still watching from the other end of the bar but because it felt right. He especially enjoyed holding her close as they danced but her sweet honey scent drove him crazy.

"You're a pretty good dancer for a suit." She wrapped her arms around his neck and gazed into his eyes.

"A suit?" He chuckled and pushed a stray piece of hair back from her cheek.

"You know lawyers, businessmen, bankers and such." She ran her finger down around his neck to the hollow just below his Adam's apple.

"I don't always wear suits." Mike swallowed hard as she swirled her finger down his chest where his shirt was open slightly.

"I'm sure you don't. I wouldn't be surprised if you told me you were a model." She dropped her head and licked her lips. The sight made his dick twitch, and he wanted nothing more than to drag her out of the club and up the road to his apartment.

"I'm no model." Mike lowered his lips to her ear and whispered. "You're making me jealous."

"Jealous?" She tipped her head back and looked up at him.

"You get to lick those luscious lips, and I haven't even gotten to taste them." Mike gazed into her eyes, and it was as if someone struck him in the chest because he wanted nothing more than to kiss her right there in the middle of the bar.

"Would you like a taste?" Her hot breath blew across his ear, and he shivered with need.

"More than I want to breathe." Mike brushed his lips against her ear. He held this woman that he'd known less than two hours in the middle of a crowded club and it was as if they were the only two people in the room.

"Kiss me." Her voice came out in a soft whisper.

Mike locked his gaze with hers as he lowered his head. First, a gentle brush of his lips against hers. Soft and warm. Again, he brushed them against hers, and she sighed. She threaded her fingers through the hair at the back of his head and tugged him toward her.

"That's a peck, not a kiss." She grinned.

"I guess I need to try again." He laughed.

Mike pressed his lips softly against hers and inhaled deeply as his tongue glided along the crease of her mouth. She opened to him and met his tongue with hers. She tasted like the strawberry drink she'd been sipping on. He never liked the fruity drinks, but on her tongue, it was the best thing he'd ever tasted.

He knew he needed to stop before things got out of control. A small part of his brain reminded him they were in a public place, but when Billie pressed her body against him and moaned into his mouth, he thought he'd come in his pants.

"Hey, do we need to pour some cold water on you two?" Mike growled when he heard Ernie shout next to him.

"If they keep that up you may need to pour cold water on me. Whoa, that was the hottest kiss I've ever seen." Mike reluctantly pulled his lips away from Billie's when he heard Abbie's voice.

When he turned his head, their friends were dancing to some fast pop song that he didn't like, but he hadn't heard it until that moment. He didn't even know how long he and Billie had been making out, but he didn't give a shit.

"Umm… I think that got away from us for a minute." Billie smiled.

"Maybe a little bit." Mike took her hand and tugged her toward the patio deck exit.

"You do realize it's February?" She giggled as he pulled her outside.

"Yes, but I need to cool down a bit." Mike pulled her into his arms and grinned. "Although, having you this close is not helping."

"I know this sounds like bullshit, but I don't come downtown to hook up." She tucked her arms in front of her and snuggled into his chest.

"It didn't enter my thoughts that you did." Mike knew from the moment he locked his gaze onto her that Billie wasn't one of those women.

"I just wanted to make sure you knew that." She smiled and again it took his breath away.

"I can't say the same but I haven't hooked up in a while and to be honest there's something different with you." He couldn't put his finger on it, but Billie wasn't like the girls he usually took home.

"Are you saying I'm the type of girl a guy brings home to meet mom?" She chuckled.

"Yes." Mike didn't laugh because for the first time in his life it's the way he felt.

"And how often have you used that line, Mr. Lawyer man." She fisted her hands in the lapel of his shirt.

"Never." He stared into her eyes, and it felt as if his whole body started to vibrate.

"Shit, that's my phone." She stepped back and pulled her cell from her front pocket. "It's my friend." She didn't put it to her ear but began to type frantically, and her face turned white as a sheet.

"Everything ok?" Mike didn't like the expression on her pretty face.

"I'm sorry, I need to go. Now. It's my friend. She's…., I'll call you." Billie disappeared through the door.

It took a second for him to realize that she had no way of calling him. He hadn't given her his number nor did he have hers.

"Shit," He grumbled as he hurried into the club seconds after she did. He scanned the room, but he couldn't see her anywhere. He glanced towards the table where they'd all been sitting. His friends were still there, but the girls were gone.

"Hey, where are Dana and Abbie?" Mike asked Bobby once he'd squeezed through the crowd.

"Billie came in, and before I knew what happened, they were gone," Bobby shrugged his shoulders.

"Abbie said something about a friend being in trouble," Ernie leaned over the table.

"Billie got a text that freaked her out. She left before I got a chance to exchange numbers." Mike plopped down in the chair.

"Just look her up on Facebook." Lyle signed.

"I would if I'd been smart enough to get her last name." Mike sighed.

The three men stared at him for a minute before they burst into laughter. Mike didn't see the humor in the situation.

"You had your tongue down her throat, and you didn't even get her last name?" Bobby laughed.

"Fuck off; I didn't think she was going to run off so fast." He plowed his fingers through his hair.

"You win some you lose some. It's just funny to see Mr. Homerun strike out." Ernie laughed, and Mike flipped him the bird.

Ernie had dubbed Mike Mr. Homerun because, in their early days downtown, Mike never left alone.

"I just hope their friend is okay." Lyle signed.

"They all looked pretty concerned," Ernie's expression turned serious.

"You didn't by any chance get either of the other girl's last names?" Mike immediately regretted the question when they started to laugh again.

"Sorry, buddy, guess she's the one that got away." Ernie slapped Mike on the shoulder.

There was no way he'd be able to find her. Then again, the name Billie wasn't a typical name for women. He might have to enlist his sister-in-law to track Billie down.

# Chapter 2

"I'm telling you, Billie, she's never going to get away from that idiot," Dana put her tray on the table.

They sat next to the window in the hospital cafeteria. Since Dana was a nurse, they'd meet her for lunch because it was easier for Abbie and Billie to leave the office then for Dana to get away from the hospital.

"What do you want me to do?" Billie groaned as she picked at her fries. "I've tried telling her to stay away from him, but she keeps letting him come back. Then she ends up in the same position. She has to text me to call the police because he's hitting her again."

Billie Carter loved all her friends, but she was particularly close to Peggy. When Billie was ten, Peggy moved in next door with her family. Peggy Butler was eight, an only child and born deaf but Billie clicked with her from day one.

Even though there were alternatives for hearing impaired, Peggy wasn't eligible for implants because she didn't have an auditory nerve. It meant hearing aids or Cochlear Implants would not work because the device couldn't pass the message to her brain.

Peggy started to teach Billie sign language when they met. It was great because they could communicate and most people didn't understand what they discussed.

Peggy was the one who gave her the nickname Billie because it was easier to spell for the little girl, and the name stuck. Soon the only one to call her Belinda were her parents and grandfather. Although, there were times they would let the nickname slip as well.

At school, Billie would keep a close eye on her friend to make sure nobody picked on her. Dana and Abbie took a quick liking to Peggy, and the four girls would hang out all the time. Peggy was two years behind them in school, but they always managed to spend lunch together.

Peggy was eighteen when she got pregnant with Chloe and Billie, Dana, and Abbie stood by her through the whole thing. The little girl's father was not in the picture and Peggy would never talk about him. It was the only secret she kept from Billie.

"We've all tried to get her away from him. I honestly don't see what she sees in him. He's got a face like a boiled boot." Abbie cringed.

Billie shuddered because Abbie's description of Eugene Wilks was accurate. He was Peggy's current boyfriend, ten years older and seemed to think what he said was law. He gave Billie the creeps.

"She needs to start coming downtown with us. Maybe she could find a hottie like Billie did last month." Dana grinned.

"Yeah, too bad she didn't get his last name before she locked lips with him." Billie felt the heat rise in her cheeks and Abbie laughed.

"Or at least get his phone number for Christ sake." Dana threw her hands up.

"Well, I hadn't planned on running out on him, but when Peggy texted, I didn't think." Billie rested her elbows on the table and put her chin in her hands. "He was hot, wasn't he?"

"They all were." Dana sighed.

"You know we should kick the shit out of Eugene ourselves just for fucking up our night." Abbie slapped her hand on the table. "We could change that song by the Dixie Chicks to Eugene instead of Earl."

Billie almost choked on her water when Abbie began to sing the song and inserted Eugene where the name Earl should be. Abbie Martin was the type of girl that made you laugh and told you what she thought whether you wanted to hear it or not.

"So, we have two things to do," Dana said.

"What's that?" Billie asked.

"Hunt down Mr. Hottie and his friends and find a tarp for Eugene." At first, Dana looked dead serious, but the quirk of her lips had Billie and Abbie laughing hysterically. They really were the best friends in the world.

Billie pulled her Blue Kia Rio into her parent's driveway. It was the one thing she'd missed when she lived in Labrador, and the other lesson, she was not cut out to be a Social Worker. Especially, when she had to walk into someone's home and remove their children. Sure, it was for the good of the kids, but it broke her heart when they'd cry.

Billie's parents were surprised since it was all she'd ever wanted to do, but like the incredible parents they were, they supported her. They had even offered her old room until she decided what she wanted to do. She loved them but living under their roof again would drive her crazy. Once a person got a taste of independence, there was no going back.

When Billie returned to St. John's, Abbie hired her right away. Abbie owned a small real estate company, and although Billie thought being an assistant would be boring, Abbie made it fun. Billie planned to apply for her real estate license, but there was a lot to learn before she took that step. At the moment, she was content and making decent money.

She got out of her car and headed up the front walkway and gave a friendly wave to her mother's neighbor. Rita's family lived next door for as long as Billie could remember and they played together as kids. As they got older, they drifted to their own groups of friends.

Rita moved away after university and returned home a couple of months earlier to care for her aging mother. She didn't have any brothers or sisters, and Mrs. Fifield had lost her husband a few years before.

Billie felt sorry for the young woman. She wasn't much older than Billie and didn't seem to get any time to herself since she'd returned. Although, every time Billie saw her she always greeted her with a smile and a wave.

"Hey, Mom," Billie called from the front foyer.

"Belinda, I wasn't expecting you today." Her mother came out of the kitchen wiping her hands on her apron. Margaret Carter had two things in her life that she loved, teaching and preparing meals. Since she retired from teaching, cooking had become an obsession.

"I was on my way home and decided to drop in." Billie hugged her. "Where's Pop?"

"He had a doctor's appointment, so your brother took him." Her mother rolled her eyes, and Billie laughed.

Frank Carter didn't allow women to go to his doctor's appointments in case he had to take off his clothes. Although, when he had a bad fall a few years before he didn't mind the nurses giving him sponge baths and Billie was sure he had a little crush on his physiotherapist Stephanie.

"Who took him, Philip or Matt?" Billie asked

"Philip this time. Matt had to work." Her mother motioned to the kitchen chair as they entered.

Billie was the youngest of the family, and her two older brothers never let her forget it when they were kids. They also terrorized her boyfriends in high school which was probably why when she brought someone home to meet the family, the relationship usually ended. Of course, she wasn't afraid of either of them and made sure she returned the favor when they'd bring girls home. Maybe she was the reason neither of them was married.

"By the way, your grandfather's party is a go. I even got in touch with Stephanie. She's bringing her husband, and she just found out she's having another baby." Leave it to her mother to get the scoop on Stephanie. She was a little nosey sometimes.

"That's a few months, away, but that's great. I'm sure Pop will love to see her." Billie poured herself a cup of tea from the teapot her mother placed on the table and snatched a freshly baked muffin from the plate. "Not sure he'll like her husband though."

"I agree. I think Frank was a little smitten with her." Her mom sat down at the table and sighed.

"Something wrong, mom?"

"I heard Peggy is back at the women's shelter again."

"Yes, it's the fourth time in the last couple of months, and they told her she could lose Chloe if it happens again." Billie had been there to interpret for the social worker all four times.

"That poor girl is so desperate for affection since her parents passed and now she can't shake that terrible man. I don't understand it." The crack in her mother's voice had a lump form in her throat.

Peggy's father was a fisherman and died when the boat went down during a storm. Thankfully they'd found everyone on board, but nobody survived. Peggy was only seventeen years old at the time. Her mother was so distraught that Peggy stayed with Billie's family for a couple of months, but less than a year later her mother died. Billie's dad said Peggy's mom died of a broken heart, but she'd gone into cardiac arrest and didn't make it to the hospital in time. Peggy remained in their family home because she was eighteen.

"I wish that jerk would just leave her alone. I mean he's already got her head so screwed up I don't know if she'll ever get over it." Billie growled.

"I was such a lucky woman to find your father." Her mother sighed.

"Yes, you were." Billie and her mother both jumped at the sound of her father's voice. She hadn't heard him come into the house.

"Bill, you startled me." Her mother giggled as he buried his nose in her neck.

"Just making sure you don't have some young stud here." He laughed.

"Oh honey, there's not a stud in the world that could hold a candle to you." Her mom smiled.

"You two are so cute." Billie chuckled.

It didn't bother her when her parents were affectionate with each other. Her brothers hated it, but Billie always thought it was great that even after almost thirty-seven years they were still attracted to each other.

"I'm glad to see my little pumpkin too." Her father leaned over the table and kissed the top of Billie's head.

"She must be missing mommy and daddy." Matthew's voice boomed as he sauntered into the kitchen.

"I certainly wasn't missing you." Billie poked him when he sat next to her.

Matthew was the youngest of her two brothers and the biggest pain in the ass. He worked for a construction company, and although he didn't work out, he was in decent shape. He and Billie had the same dark brown hair and dark brown eyes thanks to their mother's Portuguese. Philip had the dark eyes, but his hair was closer to their father's brown. Although, their skin wasn't as dark as her mother's they did have that tanned appearance.

"So, when are we going to meet the new boyfriend?" Matthew raised his eyebrow, and Billie furrowed her brows. "Oh right, you don't have one." He slapped his hand on his thigh and let out a loud laugh.

"And where's your girlfriend?" Billie tapped her finger against her lips. "Right, you don't have one." Matthew wrapped his arm around her neck and gave her head a rub with his knuckle.

"God, will you ever grow up?" Billie squealed and pinched his side to get him to release her.

"He's about as mature as he's going to get," Philip grumbled as he pushed her grandfather's wheelchair into the kitchen.

"Bite me," Matthew snapped.

"How are you doing, Pop?" Billie ignored the rest of the insults going back and forth between her brothers to kiss her grandfather and help him out of his jacket.

"I'm doin' just dandy, pussycat." He grinned. "It's good to see you."

"Since everyone's here, why don't I throw some burgers on the grill and your mother can make some of her famous double baked potatoes and salad. It's been a while since we had supper together." Her father said.

"You're going to barbecue? In April? With snow still on the ground?" Billie laughed.

"April, June, October. It's always a good time for a good old barbecue." Her father pulled on a jacket, toque, gloves and headed out through the back door.

"He's insane." Billie shook her head.

"Nah, it's no big deal. One time when you guys were little he actually cooked burgers in a snowstorm." Her mother laughed.

Billie rested her arms on the table and glanced around. She was so lucky to have such an annoying but loving family. They teased each other but were always there when someone needed them.

A lump formed in her throat when Peggy's tear-stained, bruised face flashed in her mind. Peggy and Chloe had no family. The only people she had were Billie, Abbie, and Dana. Of course, the whole Carter family would do anything for Peggy, but she would never ask or accept for that matter.

"What's up, sis?" She felt a gentle hand on her shoulder.

"I just zoned out there for a minute." Billie smiled at her brother, but from the raised eyebrow she knew Philip wasn't buying her answer.

"You want to take a walk?" That was his answer to everything. Philip always told her he did his best thinking when he walked and although she would never admit it to him, she'd found herself doing the very same thing when she needed to clear her head.

"It's a little chilly out." She sighed as she sat back in the chair.

"Best time to walk." He pulled her chair away from the table and leaned down so he could whisper in her ear. "Plus, Matt will have to help with the dishes."

Billie jumped to her feet and pulled on her jacket. Matt looked back and forth between her and Philip but before he had a chance to say anything her mother ordered him into the kitchen to help with the cleanup.

"You two take your walk, and we'll have tea and dessert when you get back." Her mother waved them off. Billie giggled as Matt flipped them the finger before he disappeared into the kitchen.

Outside the wind had a bite to it, but as they walked down toward the lake, she forgot about the chill and just enjoyed the beauty of Quidi Vidi Lake. They'd been walking for about ten minutes when Philip spoke.

"How's Peggy doing?" He asked.

"I spoke to her this morning, and she swore she was done with him. She wasn't taking a chance of losing Chloe." Billie linked her arm into her brothers.

"You don't believe that, do you?" He cupped his hand over hers.

"No, she's said it more times than I can count, but he keeps coming back." Billie sighed.

"Maybe Matt and I could have a chat with this guy," Philip suggested.

"It wouldn't work. He'd just take it out on her."

"Men like that make me sick," Philip stopped on the bridge.

"Me too, big brother." Billie rested her head on Philip's shoulder, and they watched the waves crash against the shore.

"So how's the love life." Philip chuckled a few minutes later.

"Ready for the life support to be unplugged." Billie laughed.

"Cool, same as mine." Philip wrapped his arm around her shoulder and kissed the top of her head. "I'm sure there's some guy just waiting for you out there."

The words had the blue-eyed hottie from the bar popping in her head. The only things she knew about him was his name was Mike, he was a lawyer, and his kiss made her knees weak. If Peggy hadn't texted her that night, she'd probably have gone home with him. That thought both scared and excited her. It was a good thing she didn't get to know him more. It would probably ruin the fantasy man she'd made him out to be in her dreams.

Billie pulled into the driveway of the small house she rented a couple of blocks from her parents. She'd stayed later at her parent's then she'd intended, and forgot to leave on her porch light. She grabbed the flashlight out of her glove compartment because the front of her house was pitch black at night. She needed to get the landlord to put some motion sensor lights placed on the walkway.

Billie got out of the car and hurried to the front entrance. She used her Fob to lock her car as she made her way to the door. She slid her key into the lock and turned it, but a loud crash from inside had her jump back. She almost tripped over her own feet as she ran back to her car. She unlocked it, jumped in and locked it again while she fumbled in her purse for her phone.

She'd never had such a difficult time tapping three numbers in her life as she was having at that moment. She took a couple of deep breaths and tried again, but a knock on her car window made her scream, and her phone flew across the car.

At first, she didn't recognize the face in the window, being that it was dark and her heart was about to jump out of her chest.

"Billie, are you okay?" She sighed when she heard Matt's gruff voice.

"I think there's someone in my house." She stepped out of the car.

"Get in the car and lock the doors." He grabbed the flashlight from her hand and jogged toward her front door.

"Let me call the police, Matt," Billie called out.

"Get in the car." He ordered right before he disappeared into the house.

Billie did just that and grabbed her phone from the floor. She'd managed to punch in nine one one but hadn't sent the call. Her finger hovered over the call button as she glanced back to where her brother entered the house.

"Damn it, Matt," Billie glanced down at her phone.

It seemed forever since Matt entered the house. What if someone was inside and they'd hurt him? Maybe worse. She didn't even give it a second thought when she tapped the talk button.

"Nine one one, what's your emergency?" the operator answered.

"I think there's an intruder in my house, and my brother just went inside, but he hasn't come out." Billie hadn't realized she was trembling until she almost dropped her phone again.

"What's your address?" The operator replied.

Before she could answer Billie saw someone exit and come toward the car. At first, she wasn't entirely sure it was Matt. At least not until she saw the flashlight in his hand.

"My brother just came out. Can you hold on a second?" She didn't give the operator a chance to reply as she threw open the car door and stepped out.

"You left your kitchen window open." He growled. "Anyone could have gotten in there, but thank God it's only a cat."

Billie let out a huge breath and leaned back against the car. She glanced down at her phone and remembered she still had an emergency operator on the line.

"I'm so sorry for wasting your time. My brother is here, and said it's just a cat that got in through an open window." Billie chuckled a little embarrassed for her overreaction.

"Are you sure everything's okay?" The operator asked.

"Yes, I'm so embarrassed." Billie glanced up at her brother who looked about ready to kill her.

"It's okay." The operator said, and Billie ended the call.

"Thanks for checking." Billie tried to walk around Matt and head into her house.

"Belinda Carter, you've been told more times than I can count to make sure all your windows and doors are locked before you leave your house." Matt grabbed her arm and spun her to face him.

"Yes, Matthew, I know. I was in a hurry this morning, and I must've forgotten to close the window before I left. I always open it to put milk out for this stray cat who hides under my back step." Billie pulled her arm away and grabbed her things from the car.

"Well, it seems your stray cat decided to move inside. He's sleeping on your counter, and there's a broken bowl on the floor." Matt followed her into the house.

"Great, now I won't have to worry about the poor thing freezing to death." She wasn't thrilled with the cat in her house. Not that she didn't like cats, but she didn't know if the cat was tame or if it had some sort of disease.

"Take the thing to a shelter," Matt grumbled.

"Is there a reason you're here?" Billie groaned when she entered the kitchen she spotted the black and white cat perched on her counter like he owned the place.

"Mom asked me to drop off the container of leftovers you forgot. I put it in the fridge by the way."

Billie turned to thank him, but the cat began to hiss and growl. The fur on his back stood up, and he slowly stalked toward the window. Billie glanced at Matt. He shrugged his shoulders as he eyed the cat.

"Hey sweetie, what's wrong?" Billie spoke softly as she slowly moved closer.

"Careful that thing doesn't fly at you," Matt whispered.

"He sees something." Billie stood on her toes to look out through the window. It was completely black, but she didn't see anything at first. Then, something moved, and she jumped back against Matt.

"There's someone out there," Matt shouted and ran out of the house.

"Call the police. Now." He yelled.

Billie did just that.

# Chapter 3

Mike smiled as Keith dropped to his knee and proposed to Emily Bradshaw. Keith was so obviously head over heels in love with the cute hairdresser that a blind man on a galloping horse could see it. Keith was the fourth of his older brothers to snag a fantastic woman. Was he the next in line?

*Fuck no.*

That thought had to get out of his head because when he thought about spending his life with someone, there was only one woman that came to mind.

*Billie!*

How was it possible to not be able to get a girl out of his mind that he'd known less than two hours? It was stupid, and he was obsessed with her only because he never got to know her better.

"You don't even know her last name," Mike muttered to himself.

"I love that song." Isabelle chuckled behind him.

This was just what he needed. His cousin Isabelle was probably the only one in his family that knew Mike well. She was also the only one besides Sandy, that knew about the cute girl that scampered out before he had a chance to do anything but kiss her. Oh, what a kiss it was. He still got hard when he remembered how her lips molded perfectly with his.

"Of course you do." Mike shook his head.

"Or were you referring to your night with Cinderella?" Isabelle climbed onto the stool at the bar. She'd started to call Billie Cinderella because of the way she disappeared into the night. The problem was at least Prince Charming had a glass slipper to track down his mysterious beauty.

"This is not the time or the place to discuss that." Mike scowled at her.

"Has Sandy had any luck?" Isabelle wasn't going to drop it.

"No, and I told her not to bother. It's just one of those things." Mike leaned his back against the bar and rested his elbows on the top.

Jack's Place was a small pub and restaurant owned by his Aunt and Uncle. Also, Isabelle, Jess and Kristy's parents. Kurt O'Connor was more of a silent owner because being the superintendent of Hopedale's division of the Newfoundland Police Department; he didn't have much time to tend bar or cook. That was his wife's job, and Alice loved it.

"Maybe you should talk to Aunt Cora," Isabelle giggled.

"Let's leave cupid out of this." Mike laughed.

His father's younger sister had a reputation of bringing couples together or at least knowing when they were meant to be together. She'd even been dubbed Cora the Cupid, but Mike took all that with a grain of salt. No matter how often she was right.

"Looks like Keith finally got his Princess." Mike turned at the sound of the gruff voice. Dean Nash otherwise known as Bull stood off to the side of the bar as if he was hiding from something.

"Skulking in corners now are we." Isabelle teased the huge man.

"Nope, just dropping off a little gift for the happy couple before I head out of town again. It's a family affair, and I don't want to interrupt." Bull put the large wrapped present on the bar and turned.

"If you weren't such an idiot you'd probably be part of the family." Isabelle sighed.

"I think I'm too old to adopt," Bull called over his shoulder as he ducked out through the door.

"He's still avoiding Kristy, I see." Mike chuckled

"Do you know he gave Keith a card to give her to congratulate her on graduating nursing school?" The annoyance in his cousin's voice was evident.

"Why didn't he just give it to her himself?" Mike sat on the stool next to her.

"Who the hell knows? That guy is driving my sister crazy, and I've told her to forget about him and look for someone else." Isabelle sipped on a glass of water the bartender put in front of her.

"Maybe it's for the best." It was kind of hypocritical to say since he couldn't get a particular brown-eyed beauty out of his mind.

"Are you staying in Hopedale tonight?" Sandy giggled as she linked her arm into Mike. His sister-in-law looked like she had a few too many of those fruity drinks his aunt had been passing out.

"Depends on what time I get out of here." Mike helped her as she struggled to climb on the stool between him and Isabelle.

"Aren't you breastfeeding?" Isabelle laughed when Sandy almost fell off the second time.

"Not at the moment." Sandy pulled out her shirt and looked down. "Nope, no baby sucking down there."

Mike almost choked on his soda.

"I mean, are you suppose to drink when you are breastfeeding?" Isabelle sighed.

"Of course, if I didn't drink I'd get dehydrated." Sandy looked at Mike and hiked her thumb over her shoulder. "What is wrong with her? People have to drink water, and juice whether they are breastfeeding or not." Sandy sighed. "Isabelle, people need to stay hydrated." Sandy hiccupped.

"Alcohol, Sandy, Alcohol." Isabelle groaned.

"Sure, what are ya drinkin'?" Sandy grabbed Isabelle's glass and sniffed it. "That's water. You can't get drunk on water." Sandy shook her head and slouched in her seat.

"Oh, dear, God." Isabelle slapped her hand over her face and sighed.

"Churchie, are you ready to go home now?" Ian wrapped his arms around Sandy's waist, and she leaned back against him.

His brother Ian probably had his hands full for the rest of the night. Mike felt a twinge of jealousy as he watched the way Sandy's face lit up when she looked at Ian. Not that he wanted Sandy. It was what they had. Between the two of them, they had four children. Ian had two little girls that he had with a former girlfriend, Sandy had a daughter from a previous relationship, and they had little Alexander a couple of months back.

Mike found himself beginning to crave what his older brothers had. Someone to spend their lives with and families. It wasn't something he'd ever thought he wanted, but over the last few months, he felt that ache for it. Ever since the night, he met Billie.

"I'm a little drunk, Doc." Sandy giggled.

"I think you might be." Ian laughed.

"Mike, I can keep looking." Sandy poked Mike in the shoulder with every word she said.

"Nah, don't worry about it." Mike flicked his gaze to Ian. He'd told Sandy not to say a word to anyone, but Ian was her husband. They probably didn't keep things from each other, but from the way Ian raised his eyebrows, it was evident he didn't know anything.

"She could be the one." Sandy leaned closer to Mike as if she was going to whisper, but she was shouting.

"Forget about it, Sandy." Mike pushed her back against her husband. "She's losing it. Time to take her home, bro."

"Something you want to talk about, Mike?" Ian asked as he helped Sandy off the stool.

"Nope, all good." Mike chuckled. "Do you need a hand getting her out to the truck?"

"I'm good but if you need an ear, call." Ian waved to everyone as he practically carried Sandy out of the pub.

"She's gonna be sick as a dog tomorrow." Marina laughed.

"Her dad has the kids so at least she won't have to deal with them in the morning." Stephanie placed some empty glasses on the bar.

The two sisters were terrific and were also married to the oldest two brothers. John fell in love with Stephanie when the family hired her as his physical therapist. Stephanie got him back on his feet after he hit a moose on the highway.

Marina and James fell in love while James was keeping her safe from a crazy ex-husband. Well, it was her ex-husband's twin brother, but that was such a crazy situation it's a wonder any of them came out of it with their heads on straight.

Both couples had incredible kids, and they were still adding more. Stephanie was pregnant, and from what Mike had overheard, Marina and James were trying for another. They had three boys but wanted to try for a girl.

Now it was Keith's turn to begin a new chapter in his life. Emily was ideal for his brother and kept him on his toes. The feisty redhead recently had her own brush with danger but came out of it into Keith's arms.

After the party, Mike stayed behind to help his aunt Alice clean up the pub. He wasn't the only one to offer, but since his two younger brothers, Nick and Aaron had to work the next day, Mike told them to head home. The last thing they needed was to be tired while on duty.

Mike decided to spend the night at his parent's house instead of driving back to St. John's. It made his mother and grandmother happy to have him home for a night.

"Mike, you don't seem yourself tonight?" His mother helped him clear one of the booths.

"Just tired, mom." He lied.

"Dat's cause yar always makin dat long drive ta town. Mikey should be livin' here in Hopedale." His grandmother grumbled as she carried way more than a woman in her late seventies should lift.

"Nan, let me carry that out back." Mike tried to grab the two garbage bags from the tiny woman. He should've known Nanny Betty wasn't going to let him.

"Doncha be so foolish, I'm not handicapped." She snatched the bags out of Mike's hands.

"I know, Nan. I'm just acting the gentleman as you and mom taught me." Mike smiled at her.

"Oh, he's good." Alice chuckled. "Kurt and Sean wouldn't have even thought to say that."

For some reason, his uncle Kurt and his father always put their feet in their mouths when it came to Nanny Betty. They still tried to get her to slow down and take it easy only to be told in no uncertain terms to back off.

"That's my boy." His mom smiled.

"Ya don't fool me, Mikey, but I'll let ya take dis anyway." Nanny Betty seemed to be amused by his comment as well.

At a little after two in the morning, Mike finally settled into the old room he shared with Nick and Aaron as kids. It was still set up in the same way. Three twin beds separated with night stands. He could have taken one of the other rooms that used to belong to his older brothers, but he was feeling nostalgic and just wanted to sleep in his old bed.

He stripped down and crawled under the old homemade quilt. The bed was comfortable enough, but Mike was no longer a little boy, and he'd been sleeping in a King size bed for the last eight years. Still, he relaxed and looked up. There it was, the window, and he could see the beautiful starry sky he used to gaze at before he'd drift off to sleep as a kid. It was something the city didn't have, and he never realized how much he missed it.

"Nan's right. It's time to move back to Hopedale." Mike sighed and tucked his hand under his head. "Nothing's keeping me in St. John's. It's only a ten-minute drive to work in the morning and home in the evening."

Now he needed to find a place to live. He sure as hell wasn't moving back in with his parents and Sandy's sister had bought Ian's old house. There was the old ranch house on the corner behind Keith's property. It needed some repairs and upgrades, but he had the savings to do that. He'd invested the money his grandfather had left him and made some serious cash that was doing nothing but collecting dust in the bank.

It wasn't like he couldn't do the repairs himself and if he ran into anything he couldn't do, he'd enlist his brother. Keith owned a security firm but he also had a construction company, and he was pretty handy too. All of his brothers were no slouches when it came to that sort of thing.

The thought of moving back home and buying a house would have made him panic at one time but not anymore. He was ready to settle down. As odd as it was, it was all because of Billie. The day he met her changed him. Made him want to stop being an overgrown boy and become an adult.

"Yeah, not bad it only took me thirty-two years and two hours with Billie to figure out it's time to grow up." Mike chuckled to himself.

Maybe one day he'd see her again, and they'd spend more than two short hours together.

# Chapter 4

"I dropped by today, and again that fucking window was left open." Matthew stomped around her kitchen as he waved his hands over his head.

Billie dropped her head on the table and groaned as she listened to her brother rant for the third time about how she didn't think about her safety. How whoever had been at her house the week before could have been a serial killer.

"I'm not aware of any serial killers on the loose in St. John's at the moment," Billie mumbled without lifting her head.

"Don't be a smart-ass." Matt slammed his hands on the table making her jump.

"For heaven's sake, Matt. I was gone for twenty minutes to pick up some milk." Billie had kept the stray cat and ran out of milk.

"Oh, so criminals wouldn't break into your house in that case." Matt rolled his eyes.

"Why are you here anyway?" Billie got up from the table and grabbed a banana off the counter.

"I'm starting on a new project on Monday, and I wanted to let you know that I won't be in town during the weekdays." He seemed to calm a little.

"Cool, where are you going?" She loved her brother, but he was seriously getting on her nerves the way he was hovering since she'd had the intruder.

"Hopedale, one of my bosses relatives is renovating an old house. It's free room and board while I'm out there as well as my pay." He plopped down in one of the chairs.

"I'm sure Pop will miss you." Matt still lived with her parents, and he usually played cards with their grandfather in the evenings.

"I'll miss him too, but I need to get some cash together and get my own place. My baby sister is living on her own, and I'm still living in my old room." He sighed.

"Plus, you can't have women over at home." Billie laughed.

"Yes, cause I've got such a full love life." He snorted, but the expression on his face told her someone was on his mind. "I see you still have a knack for changing the subject."

"I do," She popped the last of the banana in her mouth.

"Seriously, Billie. I'm worried about you." That hit her in the heart.

"I'll be fine, and I'll be more careful about securing the house when I leave." She moved behind him and wrapped her arms around his neck.

"I know you're an adult, but you're still my little sister, and I love you." Matt rested his head against hers.

"And I love you for that, but you're really a pain in my ass." She giggled.

"It's a big brother's job." He laughed.

"I'm such a lucky girl to have two big overbearing brothers." She stepped back and put her hand over her chest.

"You're a brat, that's for sure." He shook his head.

"Wait, did you say Hopedale?"

"Yeah, why?" He raised an eyebrow.

"I'm pretty sure that's where Stephanie lives." Billie had gone to coffee with the physical therapist a couple of times when her grandfather first started therapy.

"Yes, she does. Stephanie is married to my bosses brother." Matt sighed and shook his head. "You get me off subject every damn time."

"Well, if you see her tell her I said, hi." Billie motioned to the front door. He'd taken the hint that it was time for him to leave.

Billie appreciated her brothers wanted to protect her, but she was sure the intruder was not looking to kill her. Something told her that whoever it was, they didn't want to get caught and probably wouldn't be back. Still, she did make sure to lock all the doors and windows at night and when she left for work.

Then there was Cougar. The black and white cat was like a guard cat, and it seemed he decided to move in. Since he appeared set on living with Billie, she brought him to the veterinarian to ensure he was healthy and had him neutered. That didn't please the large feline, but he quickly forgave her when she cooked him some fresh salmon the day he came home.

Cougar was a fitting name since he sounded like one whenever anything moved outside the window. The wind blew, Cougar immediately growled and jumped on the window ledge. It helped Billie feel more at ease. Who was scared of burglars when she had Cougar, the guard cat?

Matt did seem a little over the top with the whole situation. At least more than usual. Something about the intruder bothered him, and it wasn't just about her safety. Maybe Philip had some idea why her usually laid-back brother seemed so on edge.

When she thought about it, Matt started to drop by her house more often shortly after Peggy's former boyfriend got arrested the first time. The same night she had to leave the bar to help her friend. Maybe he was worried the asshole would come after Peggy's friends.

Monday morning always seemed to come way too fast. It didn't help that she'd spent most of the night before awake because of nightmares. She finally gave up around five in the morning after she woke from a dream of Eugene stood over her with a gun pointed at her head. She blamed Matt. If he hadn't dropped by, yet again, to remind her to keep her place locked she would probably have had the kind of dream she enjoyed. The one where she got hot and heavy with the sexy Mike. She'd never tell anyone about those dreams because it was crazy to be still fantasizing about a man she'd been with for less than two hours.

"Did you get the file on that house on Anspach Street?" Abbie shouted from her office as Billie shrugged out of her jacket.

"Good morning to you too." Billie opened her laptop and plopped down in her chair.

"Hard weekend?" Abbie chuckled from the doorway of her office.

"Just didn't sleep much last night," Billie grumbled.

"Why is it I get a good eight hours of sleep and spend an hour on my makeup and still look like hell and you get no sleep, wear little to no makeup, and you look like that." Abbie propped her hip against Billie's desk.

"Yes, I look freaking fantastic." Billie rolled her eyes.

"Is this about Peg?" Abbie's expression changed to one of

concern.

"No, I just had one of those nights." Billie lied.

"Have you talked to her lately?" Abbie was probably just as worried as everyone else.

"Not since Friday. She's still at the shelter, but I'm going to go by there today after work." It was strange to not hear from Peggy all weekend.

"It was bad this time. Dana said that her eye was swollen shut." Abbie shook her head.

"Chloe was so scared." Billie couldn't get the image of the little girl curled into a fetal position under her bed.

"If Peggy doesn't get her head out of her ass and stop letting him in she's going to screw up that baby's head." Abbie sighed.

"We don't know what it's like to be in that situation. How do you get out of something like that?" Billie rested her chin on her fist.

"I've got no idea."

The day went faster than Billie expected. Abbie invited Billie to join her and Dana for supper, but Billie wanted to see Peggy and Chloe. Peggy looked so beaten the last time Billie saw her and not just because Eugene had hit her. It was as if Peggy could see no way out. At one point Billie thought Peggy was about to tell her something, but she stopped right before one of the shelter workers walked in.

Billie pressed the buzzer on the main door to the shelter. They kept the building very secure to ensure the safety of the women, and children inside. She pulled her coat tightly around her as a brisk wind blew around her. For a place that was supposed to make people feel safe the entryway was creepy as hell.

She was about to push the buzzer a second time when the door came open. Billie grabbed the handle and was ready to thank whoever opened it but stopped when she saw who walked out.

"Matt?" Billie stepped inside, and he walked back inside with her. "What are you doing here?"

Her brother looked like he'd got caught with his hand in the cookie jar. It wasn't that he didn't know Peggy, but it wasn't like they were close friends.

"I just dropped by to see… to make sure… had to check on Chloe." Matt stammered as he continued to avoid eye contact with Billie.

"Is everything okay? Did Peggy call you?" The first thing that popped in her head was Philip's suggestion that he and Matt have a chat with Eugene.

"No, I just wanted to check on the kid." Matt sighed. "They're family."

That statement made sense, but Matt never seemed to show an interest in Peggy or her daughter. He wasn't rude to them, and his sign language skills were limited.

"Are you finished giving me the third degree now?" He grumbled as he pushed open the door.

"Geez, who put the stick up your ass?" Billie rolled her eyes as he waved and let the door slam shut behind him.

"Can I help you?" Billie turned toward the voice. An older woman stood just inside the security door.

"I'm Billie Carter. I'm here to see Peggy and Chloe Butler." Billie smiled.

"Was that your husband that just left?" The woman asked.

"What? Matt? God no. He's my brother." Billie laughed.

"Oh. Well, come in." The woman's expression seemed to go from worry to relief.

"Was he rude?" Billie had to ask because the woman looked almost concerned.

"No, not at all." She turned and motioned toward the large room on the left side of the hallway. "They're in the playroom."

Billie stood in the door for a few minutes. Peggy was curled up on the chair with Chloe on her lap watching something on an Ipad. Neither of them noticed Billie, but she studied them carefully. Peggy's bruised eye was turning yellow now, and the cut on her cheek was healing. Her arm was in a sling because Eugene had twisted it so hard he'd strained her shoulder. She was lucky he hadn't snapped her arm.

As if Chloe sensed her, the little girl looked up and grinned. She jumped from her mother's lap and ran to Billie waving her hands. Billie caught her in the air as the little girl launched herself into Billie's arms.

"She really doesn't like you at all." Peggy laughed as she signed.

"I know," Billie responded.

Chloe frantically signed how excited she was to see Billie and that Matt had brought her an Ipad to watch movies and Facetime everyone. Billie didn't show it, but she was a little shocked her brother would give such an expensive gift to Chloe.

"I was surprised to see him." Peggy signed when Chloe zoned into something on the Ipad again.

"I ran into him on the way in." Billie saw an expression pass over Peggy's face that surprised her.

"Do you want a coffee or something?" Peggy stood up and walked over to the table in the corner of the room.

"No." Billie watched her friend slowly walk away from her. It was evident she was still sore from her injuries, but there was something else.

"Why are you looking at me so weird?" Peggy sat next to her

and placed her coffee on the table in front of her.

"Is everything okay?" Billie didn't know what was going on, but something wasn't right.

"I'm just great. I'm healing from getting the hell beat out of me and living in a shelter and don't know where I'm going to go after this. I can't go back to my house. So yeah. I'm wonderful." Even in sign language, there was no problem seeing the sarcasm.

"You know what I mean." Billie shook her head.

"I know. I just don't want to stay here anymore. I feel like I'm in jail and Chloe misses going outside." Peggy signed.

"I have an extra room. Why don't you move in with me?" Billie said it before she even considered anything else.

"I can't impose on you like that." Peggy smiled and rested her head back against the couch.

"You're not imposing. It will only be until it's safe to go back to your house and I have a huge backyard for Chloe." Billie hated to see her friend so sad.

"I'd have to check with C.P.S., but if you're sure about this, I'd be so grateful." The spark of hope in Peggy's eyes was all Billie needed to see.

"Okay, you talk to them, and we'll see if we can get you out of here by the weekend. I'll go by your house and get some things for both of you and put them away at my place." Billie's eyes filled with tears when Peggy wrapped her uninjured arm around Billie and sobbed.

Billie drove home humming along to the radio pretty pleased with herself. She still wondered why her brother had told her he would be out of town all week but ended up at the shelter bringing Chloe a pretty pricey present. Something was off with him lately, but he wouldn't talk about it to anyone.

Since Peggy's house was on the other side of town, Billie went there first. She piled what she could into her car and get Matt and Philip to help over the weekend. Eventually, Peggy would go back to her house, but until Eugene was no longer a danger, Peggy and Chloe would be safe with Billie.

She'd tried to call Matt and give him the news, but apparently, his phone was off. So Tuesday she left work early and drove the ten minutes to Hopedale. She'd called Stephanie to see if she was home because she wanted to drop by and see her. Billie really liked Stephanie and was thankful that she'd helped Billie's grandfather when he'd broken his hip.

Luckily, Stephanie had an appointment in the morning and had taken the day off work. She seemed excited to hear from Billie.

Billie had never been to Hopedale before, but as she drove into the town, she glanced around. Like most small towns outside the city, the houses were set back off the narrow roads and surrounded by trees.

It was lovely and made her seriously think about moving out of the city.

She followed the directions that Philip gave her to find Matt. He'd called Matt's boss to find out how to find her brother. When she pulled into the long driveway, she gasped. The large ranch house was white with a deck running right around it. The road ran around in a circle and with enough room to park at least a dozen cars next to the few trucks that were already there.

Matt stomped out of the house as she pulled up to the entrance with a huge smile on her face. That faded when she saw the rage in his eyes.

"Are you out of your fucking mind?" Matt shouted into the window of her car.

"Nice to see you too, Matthew." She snapped. "It's not that long a drive, and I've had my license for…"

"I'm not talking about coming out here. I'm talking about the danger you're putting yourself in by letting Peggy and Chloe move in with you." He rested his hands on the window opening, and his knuckles turned white.

"Oh for Christ's sake, Matt. Eugene is not going to come within five feet of my house. Plus he's in jail, and when he gets out, he has a restraining order to stay away from them." Billie threw her hands up in the air when he growled at her.

"So what are you going to do when he gets out of jail and comes looking for her. Throw the piece of paper at him." He snapped.

"Everything okay here." Billie turned her head to see a very large red-haired man heading toward them.

"Fuck." Matt closed his eyes and stood up.

"Hey, Keith. Everything's fine. This is my little sister, Belinda." Matt stepped back from the car as Billie opened her door to get out.

"Nice to meet you." Keith held out his large hand, and Billie felt very small when he completely covered her hand with his.

"You too." Billie smiled nervously. Matt's boss was incredibly sexy with his beard, black T-shirt pulled tight across his chest, and the way he wore his jeans should be illegal.

"He's engaged, sis," Matt whispered and chuckled.

"Shut up." She elbowed her brother.

"I just dropped over to check on things." Keith scanned the house.

"We found some water damage in the master bath, but the guys are tearing that out now. The HVAC guys were in and checked out the air quality and gave us the go ahead. I was surprised because it's an older house."

While Matt chatted with his boss, Billie looked around the

property. Pine trees surrounded it on three sides, and a line of them practically hid the house from the road. The house appeared in good shape considering it looked at least fifty years old. Since she'd been working with Abbie, she'd come to appreciate the beauty of real estate.

"Are you selling this?" Billie blurted out.

"No. My brother bought it. He's tired of living in the city, so he hired us to renovate." Keith explained. "Gave the ass a good deal too."

Billie laughed. It seemed Keith had the same type of relationship with his brother as she had with hers.

"Aren't younger siblings a pain in the ass." Matt hitched his thumb over his shoulder toward Billie.

"I don't know. If my younger brothers were as cute as her, I think I'd deal with it." Keith winked at her.

"Hey, dude. You're engaged." Matt pointed his finger at Keith.

"Engaged, not blind." Keith pointed back. "I bet he terrorizes you doesn't he?"

"So much that I'm thinking about seeking therapy." Billie exaggerated a sigh.

"I don't have sisters, but I have four female cousins that are like the sisters we didn't want, and now I have three sister-in-laws. So including my fiance, the women are starting to outnumber the men."

Keith laughed.

"That's right. Stephanie's your sister-in-law." Billie remembered Matt telling her.

"You know Steph?" Keith asked.

"Remember I told you she was Pop's physiotherapist." Matt pulled a hammer out of his tool belt.

"Oh yeah." Keith nodded.

"I'm going to go see her after I talked to Matt." Billie got back in her car.

"Easy as pie to find the house. Turn left at the end of the driveway and drive to the end of Knob Lane. You'll be on Hart Street. Turn right and drive straight down to the beach. Turn right, and they are the last house across from the beach." Keith told her.

"Thanks." Billie started her car. "I'll talk to you later, Matt."

"I'll call you when I get back to Keith's place," Matt shouted as she pulled out of the driveway.

Keith's directions were right on the money. Not that it would have been hard to find the house because it wasn't like the town was huge. Billie pulled her car into the side of the road and looked up toward the house. The front door opened and Stephanie stepped out followed by a man. He wrapped his arms around Stephanie and kissed her cheek. Billie smiled. Stephanie had raved about her husband the few times they'd had coffee. When the man started down the steps Billie's heart felt like it stopped.

*Mike.*

"Oh my God." Billie yanked her gearshift into drive and sped away from the side of the road. She didn't look back to see if they'd noticed, but she was sure they must have because her tires spun on the rocks. She didn't care.

"That fucking asshole said his name was Mike." Billie quickly made her way through the town and didn't ease her grip on the steering wheel until she was on the highway back to town.

The man she made out with and been fantasizing about was Stephanie's husband. The bastard cheated on Stephanie and lied about his name. Even his friends were in on it. They probably didn't give their real names either. He was good. He'd come to her rescue and told her everything a woman wanted to hear.

Billie had a dilemma now. Should she tell Stephanie what her husband did? Stephanie was a sweet person and the poor woman thought the sun shined out of his ass and he was downtown picking up women.

What was she going to do?

# *Chapter 5*

"Thanks so much for watching Olivia, Mike." Stephanie opened the front door and walked out.

"Hey, anytime I get to spend with my niece is a pleasure. Plus, I had the day off and what a better way to spend it than chasing a three-year-old around." Mike chuckled as he stepped out behind her.

"Still, I appreciate it." She wrapped her arms around his neck, and he kissed her cheek.

"I'm heading up to Ian's…" Mike stopped when he heard rocks flicking as a car sped up the road. "Fucking idiot."

"Don't worry about it. Teenagers are always speeding up and down Beach Street." Stephanie reached down and grabbed Olivia as she tried to run down over the front steps.

"Unca Mike." Olivia squealed as she squirmed to get away from her mother.

"Uncle Mike has to go to work." Stephanie rested the little girl on her hip, but Mike didn't know how his sister-in-law could comfortably hold her with her pregnant belly starting to show.

"I'll come back this weekend, and we'll go to the beach and get mommy some more rocks, Livy," Mike called her by the nickname his other nieces called her.

"Promise?" The little girl stuck out her lip and stared at him with the same green eyes her mom had.

"That kid is good." Mike chuckled. "Yes, baby. I'll see you in four sleeps."

"Four sleeps." She clapped her hands and squealed again.

Before he headed to Ian's place, Mike wanted to check out the work on his home. They'd only started the day before, but Keith said his guys were excellent and fast. Mike was excited to move into his own house.

Sure, it was big, but he didn't plan to move ever again. Besides if he wanted he could rent out the extra four rooms and make money on his investment. That wouldn't be what his mother wanted. She was so excited that she asked to meet the woman he was seeing. Mike felt a little guilty to tell her there was nobody special in his life. Not that he didn't want that. Over the last couple of months, he hadn't met anyone he even wanted to see a second time. Well, except Billie. The woman spoiled him for any other woman.

"You're a fucking idiot." Mike shook his head as he pulled into the driveway of his future house.

He walked up on the deck and scanned the length of it. There were a lot of boards broken and torn out, but there were piles of lumber stacked against the house. He figured it was to fix the broken and missing pieces. He stepped inside and stopped when he heard someone shouting.

"Hey, buddy. You can't go in there." The man stomped around from the back of the house holding a hammer and a yellow hard hat on his head.

"It's okay. This is my place." Mike hadn't met any of the workers yet.

"I don't care. You can't go into a construction site without a hard hat." He stepped in front of Mike to keep him from entering.

"Listen, this is my house." Mike narrowed his eyes, and the man did the same.

"Don't care. Regulations." He propped his shoulder against the door jamb and shoved the hammer back in his tool belt.

Mike stepped back and pulled out his phone. Grumbling as he punched Keith's number. He wanted to hit the guy but didn't think that would be a good option since the man looked like he could bench press a truck. Not that Mike couldn't hold his own in a fight but as his uncle always told them, talk if they will, walk if you can, run if you must. If all else fails, defend yourself but never use your fists in anger. It was one of the many things he'd learned when his uncle taught he and his brothers Karate.

"Yo," Keith answered the phone.

"Yeah, I'm trying to get a look at my house but this guy won't...." Mike heard the click and looked at his phone. Keith had hung up on him.

"What's wrong? Did your big brother hang up on you?" The asshole grinned.

"Service out here is not always great." Mike walked down to the bottom of the steps and punched Keith's number again.

When his brother didn't answer on the fifth ring, Mike started to head up the steps again. The jerk was still slouched in the doorway looking at his nails.

"Look, I just want..." Mike started, but he put his hand up.

"I want to be a millionaire but don't look like that's gonna happen." He shifted and leaned against the other side of the doorway.

"I've had about...." Mike was losing his patience and quickly.

"Asshat," When Mike turned, Keith jogged up the front steps.

"Hey, Keith." The jerk grinned.

"Hey, Matt." Keith turned to Mike and frowned.

"He won't let me inside," Mike complained.

"Yes, you aren't wearing a hat." Keith knocked on the top of Mike's head.

"I'm not going to work in there. I just want to see what they've done so far." Mike snapped.

"Doesn't matter. If you go in there and something happens, it costs my company. I love ya bro, but I'm not paying out a ton of money because you're an idiot." Keith tossed him a yellow hat similar to the one Matt was wearing.

"Now you can come in all you want." Matt stepped out of the way.

"By the way, this is Matt Carter." Keith slapped Matt on the back. "Matt this is the brother that owns this place, Mike but I guess you figured that out."

"I'd say it was a pleasure, but I don't think we got off on the right foot." Matt held out his hand. "Let's start over. I'm Matt, and I'm the foreman. You got any questions, and Keith's not around. Just ask."

For a moment Mike considered slapping the guy's hand away, but if this guy was going to be working on his house, he should keep a civil relationship.

"Glad to meet one of the guys who's going to put this place back together." Mike shook Matt's hand.

"Keith, hard hat." Matt tapped the top of his head before disappearing around the back of the house.

"That guy is a hard nose for the regulations." Keith chuckled as he placed a white hard hat on his head. "Come on I'll show you the plans and what we're doing inside."

A little less than an hour later Mike walked back out of his house. Keith's guys were good at what they did. It hadn't been more than a day, and they already had most of the place stripped down to the beams. It looked horrible, but Keith assured him that it would look a hell of a lot better in a few weeks.

"I'll leave this hat on the front step," Mike shouted to Matt.

"If you want to keep coming and checking up on us you should just keep it in your car." Matt chuckled, but something told Mike the guy wasn't joking.

"Great idea. Terrific job so far." Mike forced a smile as he made his way to his car.

Matt rubbed him the wrong way, but maybe they just got off on the wrong foot. Either way, he couldn't see ever having a beer with the guy. He certainly wasn't like the men who worked for Keith's security firm. Those guys were like brothers.

As he pulled into Ian's driveway, he heard a loud squeal coming from inside the house. Mike walked up the front steps and opened the door in time to see Sandy chasing a very naked Grace down into the kitchen.

"Gracie, you have to put your clothes back on." Sandy seemed to be at her wit's end.

"No, no, no." almost three-year-old Grace squealed as she ran away from Sandy. "Yes, yes, yes." Sandy stepped to the side and scooped Grace up in her arms.

"No, Mama." Gracie giggled when Sandy sat on the floor and pinned the little girl down to put on her clothes.

"Listen here, little girl. You may be making it to the potty most of the time, but I'm not taking any chances of you pooping on the floor." Sandy managed to get Grace half dressed before the little girl wiggled out of her mother's grasp and ran right into Mike.

"Gotcha," Mike caught her and tossed her in the air. "You're a little nudist, aren't you?"

"Mitey," For some reason, Grace had trouble saying Mike and had dubbed him 'Mitey.' He didn't care. It was cute and who could not be charmed by the blue-eyed baby doll.

"Gracie, are you giving mommy a hard time." He rested her on one arm as he tickled her belly.

Sandy wasn't Grace's biological mother, but she was the only one the little girl knew. Her mom died. Grace and her big sister Lily came to live with Ian when their mother died. It was such a tangle of betrayal and lies that it was a wonder Ian, Sandy, and the kids were dealing with it so well.

"Hey, good catch." Sandy took Grace out of Mike's arms and motioned him to follow her upstairs to her office.

"You've got your hands full with that one." Mike chuckled.

"Since we've been potty training her all she wants is to run around naked." Sandy laughed. "Now little girl it's nap time for you."

Mike walked into Sandy's office which was also the master bedroom. Baby Alex was kicking and babbling in his crib. Mike picked him up and held the baby over his head. Damn his brothers, and their wives made the cutest kids.

"How's the big man of the house." Mike twirled the baby around in a small circle.

"Don't shake him up he just…." Sandy didn't get a chance to finish when Alex spit up all over Mike's face and shirt. "Ate."

"Damn it." Mike eased Alex into the crib so Sandy could clean the baby.

"Don't you know not to hold a loaded baby over your head." Sandy laughed and tossed him a towel.

"I didn't know he was loaded." Mike pulled off his shirt and used the towel to wipe off his face. "This shit stinks. What the hell are you feeding the kid?"

"Breast milk." Sandy laughed hysterically, and Mike gagged. He wasn't as amused as his sister-in-law.

"Well for that I'm stealing one of Ian's T-shirts." Mike opened the drawer that Sandy pointed to because she was laughing so hard she couldn't speak.

"Why is my brother half naked in the bedroom with my wife?" Ian sauntered into the room. His question only made Sandy laugh harder.

"Cause your kid regurgitate breast milk all over me." Mike turned and entered the ensuite off the bedroom. He needed something to get the smell of the spit up cleaned off of him before he threw up himself.

When he felt somewhat clean, he walked back into the bedroom. Ian had Sandy in his arms kissing her like she was about to disappear. Mike cleared his throat as he yanked the shirt over his head.

"Sorry, I see this man and all I want to do is jump his bones." Sandy sighed.

"Well, it's nice to know even when you have a half-naked man in your room you still want me." Ian laughed as he swat her on the ass.

"How's the reno going?" Ian asked.

"They just started yesterday, but they got most of it down to the bare bones. How's working with dad?" Mike propped himself against the dresser.

"Better than I expected. I enjoy this nine to five thing. Working with dad and Robert is interesting." Ian sat at the foot of the bed.

Robert Connolly was his father's lifelong friend, and they'd opened the clinic in Hopedale over twenty years before. It was the only doctor's office in the town, and they had patients come from the neighboring communities as well. Mike's father and Robert were also the types of doctors that still did house calls. Especially for people who couldn't get to the office.

Ian joined their father's medical practice when he and Sandy got married. Sandy worked from home mostly for Keith as a computer analyst. It worked for them. Sandy was also a police officer with the Hopedale division of the Newfoundland Police department, but she was currently on maternity leave from the police force.

"Any luck on finding that girl Sandy was tracking for you?" So, Sandy did fill Ian in on Billie.

"Thanks for keeping that a secret, Sandy." Mike narrowed his eyes at her, and she shrugged her shoulders.

"In my defense, I was drunk when he asked, and I can't say no to him." She plopped down at her desk and started clicking on the keyboard.

"Why all the secrecy?" Ian asked, and it did seem stupid to keep it under wraps.

"You know the way mom and Aunt Cora get. I didn't want them making a big deal about her. Besides, it doesn't look like I'll ever find out how to get in touch with her." Mike crossed his arms over his chest.

"Maybe if you'd gotten, shall we say, a last name before sticking your tongue down her throat I might have more luck." Sandy motioned him to stand next to her.

"What's all this?" He looked at the screen, and all he saw was a bunch of letters and numbers.

"I searched for women between twenty-five and thirty in Newfoundland. Then I added some other parameters. You said she was a social worker and her name was Billie. That's a very unusual name, and it's probably a nickname. So, I checked what it could be short for and came up with Wilhelmina, Sybilla, but Belinda was the most obvious." Sandy explained as she continued to click on the keys.

"What did you find?" Mike crouched so he could see the screen better.

"Diddly-squat." Sandy sighed. "First off, I found a bunch of Belinda's and Wilhelmina's, but the ages didn't match. I found a couple of Billie's but one was in Stephenville, and the other is no longer a social worker. I could look through the motor vehicle database for their license pictures and see if that works." Sandy worked hard to find Billie.

"Don't worry about it. It's just one of those things." Mike stood up and headed for the door.

"Was there a reason you dropped by, to begin with?" Ian asked.

"Can't a guy just drop in and see his family?" Mike grinned.

"You want to stay for the night?" Ian laughed.

Was it so obvious that he didn't want to be in St. John's? He couldn't wait for his house to be ready but he couldn't keep crashing at his family's homes because he dreaded to go back to town

"Nah, I need to get back. I should probably start packing up things I'm not using and start shipping it out here. It would save all my brothers from having to carry to much stuff when I move." Mike grinned.

"You know I think I'm out of town that week." Ian laughed.

"I wouldn't put it past you to hide when it's time to do all the hard work." Mike laughed as he hugged Sandy and waved to his brother.

The drive back to St. John's was short and as he pulled into his parking spot his phone rang. He pulled it out and glanced down at the screen.

"Hey, Jason." Mike headed for the entrance of the building.

"Wanted to see if you were up for a chat." Jason Breton went to law school with Mike. They worked for the same firm and were good friends. Although, Jason was moving into criminal law.

Jason also played with the band Mike and his brothers put together a while back. Rockin' The Law was the name, and they weren't looking for fame or a record deal. They just played mostly for parties and charities. Only four of his seven brothers played even though all of them were musical but Keith, Ian, and James weren't into performing. John, Nick, Aaron, and Mike loved it. Along with Aaron's friend, Cory Fleming. A police officer who worked with John, James, Nick, and Aaron.

"Sure, I'm just heading into the apartment now. Did you want to drop by?" Mike made his way up the four flights of stairs to his floor.

"Sure, beer?" Jason asked.

"If you're buying, I'm drinking." Mike laughed and unlocked his door.

"Are the b'ys home?" Jason always used the Newfoundland slang for boys. Mainly he just wanted to know if Ernie and Bobby were home.

"Ernie's on duty for the next two days, and Bobby isn't off until midnight." Mike closed the door and tossed his keys on the table next to the entrance.

"See you in a few." Jason ended the call, and Mike shoved his phone in his pocket.

Mike had finished showering the last of the stink of Alex's puke when the buzzer rang. He didn't have to look to know it was Jason. He always gave the button four short pushes and then a long one. Mike hit the button to open the main door to the building and went back to his room to get dressed.

"Hey, you didn't have to get cleaned up for me." Jason teased when Mike walked back out of his room.

"Ian's baby puked on me, and the smell was horrid." Mike grabbed a beer out of the box and hopped up on the bar stool.

"Your brothers are popping them out like a Pez dispenser." Jason took a long gulp of his beer before he rested his elbows on the counter.

"I know." Mike laughed. "So, I know this isn't a social call because you never drop by in the middle of the week. What's up?"

"Your cousin." Jason stood up and plowed his hands through his shoulder-length hair.

"I have four, but I'm going to guess you're referring to Jess."

Jason and Jess had dated a few years before and were hot and heavy for a while. They seemed made for each other, and even Cora said it was a match, but something happened. Neither Jason or Jess would talk about it, and his cousin made sure she was never in the same room with Jason.

"Who else would I be talking about?" Jason plopped down on the stool next to Mike.

"Maybe if I knew what happened between you two, I'd be able to help." Mike turned to face his friend.

"I love her, but she's never going to forgive me." Jason rested his elbows on the table and pulled his hands down over his face.

"What the fuck did you do?" Jason was his friend, but Jess was his cousin, and if Jason did anything to hurt her Mike wouldn't hesitate to punch the man.

"I didn't want her to get hurt." Jason sighed and turned his head to look at Mike.

"What are you talking about?" Mike threw his hands in the air.

"Jess wanted to join the police academy." Jason turned, so he was looking Mike in the eye.

"I never knew that." He'd never heard Jess say she was interested in following her father's footsteps.

"I was the only one she told because she wanted to surprise her dad. I was a jerk and told her it was too dangerous." Jason rested his cheek on his fist. "We had a huge fight, and I told her to stick with her flower shop. It was what she was good at."

"And she didn't kick you in the nuts?" Mike laughed.

"Maybe she should have. She told me she'd do what she wanted and I opened my big mouth and told her if she did we were over." Jason sighed.

"So, you ended, and Jess didn't join the academy." Mike was a little pissed at his friend.

"No, she ended it and told me never to cross her path again." Jason took another gulp of his beer.

"But she didn't go to the academy." Jess still ran her flower shop.

"I know, but I've got no idea why she didn't. The day she threw me out of her place she was leaving to turn in her application." For the first time, Mike could see how much this was hurting his friend.

"What do you want me to do?" Mike wasn't sure why Jason was bringing all this up now.

"She's working at this bar in St. John's now. There's a guy that works with her, and he's bad news. I've heard he hits on anything with a pulse. I've got no idea why Jess isn't at her flower shop, and I don't like her at this bar." Jason pulled an envelope out of his pocket.

"I didn't know Jess was working at a bar." Mike opened the envelope and pulled out the papers.

"I'll get Keith to look into this, but I'm sure if this guy tries anything with Jess, she'll put the fear of God in him." Mike stuffed the papers back into the envelope.

"I'm sorry about all this." He said.

"I should kick your ass for hurting her, but since I know, she could and didn't then I'll let it go." Mike laughed.

"Maybe she should have used her black belt on me." Jason popped another beer and clinked it against Mike's bottle.

Mike glanced at his watch as he entered his office and cursed under his breath. He'd been at a tuxedo fitting for Keith's wedding and got held up. Now he was late for a meeting with a bitch who was fighting her husband for custody of their twelve-year-old daughter. Mike had been appointed by his firm to act on behalf of the little girl. He was the only children's lawyer the company had, and they used him frequently.

"Mrs. Bitchface is here." Stella shuffled into his office and set down a stack of folders on his desk.

"That's not nice, Stel." Mike chuckled.

His secretary Stella Bond said what was on her mind and if she didn't like someone, they knew it. Not that she would ever be rude to a client, but it wouldn't matter if she were because her husband Charles owned the firm. Stella didn't need to work, but her children were off to college, and she refused to become one of those charity wives.

"I didn't call her that to her face. Even when she told me I shouldn't be wearing red because it makes me look fat." Stella raised her eyebrow. "I just smiled and ushered her into the conference room. I still didn't say anything when she told me that I needed to run across the street and get her an expresso because the one we had in the office was not up to her standards."

"So, you're telling me Mrs. Duffy is her usual charming self." Mike laughed as he grabbed the file out of his briefcase.

"Ever so charming." Stella fluttered her eyelashes and then emulated sticking her finger down her throat.

"Is Mr. Duffy here as well?" Mike grabbed a notepad.

"Yes. To be honest, I feel for the man and poor little Whitney." Stella poured a cup of coffee and handed it to Mike.

"Whitney would be better off with her father. I think that woman only wants her for the child support." Mike headed out of his office.

"She's a gold digging bitch that's for sure." Stella followed as they walked to the conference room as if they were going to the gas chamber.

Mike couldn't believe that he was able to talk Mrs. Duffy into giving up custody of Whitney. Mr. Duffy paid a bundle, but the man seemed happy to pay his ex-wife. It also cost Mike much of his dignity since the woman kept gliding her foot up his leg under the table.

Whitney wasn't entirely clear from her mother because of the visitation, but something told Mike the young girl wouldn't have to worry about the visits. The grin on the woman's face when they showed her the seven-figure settlement said she'd grab the money and run.

Mike thanked God every day for a loving family because he'd never have survived being in the middle of some of the child custody cases he'd seen. He was so glad to get out of the office and back to Hopedale for the weekend. It was his first night in his house. They'd finished the master bedroom as well as the ensuite. Matt didn't look happy about Mike being there, but he didn't give a shit. Although, Keith told him to give the guy some slack because he had some personal problems.

He couldn't believe they'd been working on his house for over a month and from what Keith calculated Mike could be in the house in two weeks. A month before Keith's wedding. It was exciting and terrifying at the same time.

"Mike, I know you're excited about your new place, but that's an awfully big house for a single man." His mother set a plate in front of him at the table.

He'd dropped in for supper because the family was tying up last minute wedding plans. Several of his brothers covered their laughs with coughs, and he mentally rolled his eyes because he knew what was coming next.

"I'm sure Mikey's not gonna be alone dere long. Kathleen" Nanny Betty scurried out of the dining room.

"Yeah, he probably won't spend one night alone in that place." Nick chuckled.

"Probably should installed a revolving door." John nudged Mike.

"I'm sure that's not what Nan meant when she said he wouldn't be alone long." His mother chastised his brothers.

"Come on, Mom. You don't think your sweet mama's boy's a virgin, do you?" Aaron laughed.

"Aaron Jacob, I'll not have that type of conversation at the table, and there are children in the next room." His mother pointed her finger at his youngest brother.

"What's a virgin?" Mike coughed to cover the laughter when his nephew Danny asked the question.

"Sweet God in heaven." His mother sighed.

"A.J. I should make you explain that to my son," James growled.

"Honey, remember that book we read about where babies come from?" Marina crouched in front of the little boy and took his hands in hers. He nodded and glanced around the table. "Well before that happens that's what they call people who haven't done that."

"Uncle A.J. are you a virgin?" Danny asked.

Mike's mother had to slap his father on the back because he started to choke on his water. Aaron's face turned red, but Mike was sure it wasn't from embarrassment. He was obviously trying hard to hide his laughter.

"Yes, sweetie. Uncle A.J. is a special kind of virgin." Marina glared at Aaron. "Now go out with your brothers and cousins and finish your supper."

"I just wanted to get a napkin." Danny grabbed a handful of paper napkins off the buffet and scampered out of the room.

"A.J. a virgin." John laughed.

"The only thing virgin on him is his nose, and he fingered that once or twice." Keith sat back in his chair and rested his arm on the back of Emily's chair.

"As if all you O'Connor brothers were so innocent." Emily elbowed Keith.

"Okay, I don't want to hear any more of this talk. You bunch are going to be the death of me." His mother plopped down in the chair as Nanny Betty came back into the dining room and took her seat.

"Come on, Mom. I seem to remember walking in on some pretty racy conversations between you and dad." Nick pointed his fork at his mother.

"Well then maybe you shouldn't be walking in without knocking first." His father retorted.

That was what he loved about his family. They were real, and they wanted the best for each other. As he glanced around the table at the couples, he wondered if someday he'd have the same.

*Maybe you let her get away a few months ago.*

# *Chapter 6*

Abbie sat across the table from Billie babbling about a trip down south. Dana seemed to be equally excited about all of them taking a trip together, but Billie wasn't sure she was up for it.

Peggy had moved in with her and things were going great. Chloe was utterly enamored with Cougar, and the cat was equally charmed. Chloe asked for a pet, but Peggy wanted to wait until she was older. By the time the little girl was at the right age, Peggy was involved with Eugene, and she was afraid of what he would do to the animal. It broke Billie's heart.

It was Friday night, and Abbie convinced Billie to go out to dinner and a few drinks. Billie's parents had taken Chloe for the evening because Matt offered to take the little girl to the amusement park. Billie was surprised he'd suggested it, but for some reason, Peggy didn't seem to be. Billie noticed Matt spending a lot of time at her place lately, but appeared on edge. She'd asked about it, but he said it was nothing.

"So, what was Peggy's excuse for not coming with us tonight?" Abbie asked.

"She wanted to get a hot bath, have a glass of wine and binge on Netflix." Billie lifted her glass and sipped on her wine.

"You don't think she's allowing that bastard to come over when you're not there, do you?" Dana growled.

"Hell no, besides he's still under the restraining order. I think she's done it this time. I mean it's been two months since she moved in with me and I can see the change in her. She's happy and relaxed." Billie had even seen Peggy smile more than she had in a long while.

"Is she still looking for a job?" Abbie asked.

"Yes, the woman from the shelter is helping her." Billie sighed.

"Are you okay?" Abbie tapped her finger on top of Billie's hand.

"I'm fine." Billie shrugged.

"It's still bothering you that Stephanie's husband was the guy from the club, isn't it?" Dana wrapped her arm around Billie's shoulder.

"Yeah." Billie pushed her hair behind her ear. "I like Stephanie, and she was good to Pop. I can't believe what a jerk her husband is and I feel like someone should tell her."

"Do you really want to be the one to break up a marriage or cause trouble?" Abbie raised an eyebrow.

"She's pregnant, isn't she?" Dana was right.

"Yes."

"If it were me, I'd want to know, but that's just because if a man cheated on me, I'd beat them senseless, cut off his danglers and toss it in a blender." Abbie flicked her brown hair over her shoulder, and blue eyes sparkled with mischief.

"That's because you're a crazy bitch." Dana joked. "But Billie, I'd really think about it before you open that can of worms."

They were probably right, but her grandfather's party was coming up, and Stephanie would be coming with her husband. What was she supposed to do smile and pretend he didn't kiss the hell out of her that night?

The taxi dropped Billie at the end of her driveway, and she waved to Abbie and Dana as the car pulled away. She glanced at her phone as she walked up the path. There was a missed call from her mother, and Billie shook her head. Like clockwork, her mother called at eleven every night just to say goodnight. It was after midnight, so Billie sent her a text to let her know she was home safe.

Billie unlocked the front door, pushed it open and kicked off her sneakers. The house was dark, but the television blared from the living room. It was obvious Peggy couldn't hear because she had no idea how loud it was. Billie walked into the room and turned off the television. Peggy must have forgotten to turn it off when she went to bed. On her way into the kitchen, she stepped in something wet and cursed.

"Cougar if you choked up another hairball in the middle of the hallway again I'm going to make you clean it up," Billie grumbled as she flicked on the kitchen light.

She grabbed the doorjamb but pulled her hand away quickly when she felt the moisture. The room started to spin, and it was as if all the air whooshed out of her lungs. Dark red covered the walls and counter. In the middle of the kitchen floor was a large pool of the same deep red but Billie couldn't comprehend exactly what it was or she didn't want to believe what she saw. She tried to back out of the room, but she couldn't make her legs move, and there was a high-pitched scream that hurt her ears. It took her a few minutes to realize the sound came from her and the reason she couldn't move was that her best friend lay face down in the middle of her kitchen surrounded by blood.

Thank God for nosey neighbors because Billie didn't know how long she would have stood in her kitchen and stared at Peggy's bloody body before her brain started to work again. The police pulled her out of her house and sat her in the back of an ambulance. That's where she was with an oxygen mask over her face and wrapped in a blanket when her father and brothers appeared.

"Belinda, are you okay?" Her father pulled her into his arms.

"What the fuck happened? Where's Peggy?" Matt glanced back and forth between Billie and her house.

"Sh... sh... so much.... bl... blood." Billie sobbed.

"Did they bring her to the hospital?" Philip asked.

"No…" Billie turned her face into her father's shoulder and cried hysterically.

"I'm sorry to interrupt, are you Ms. Carter's family?" The police officer that had introduced himself as Sergeant Avery stepped next to Matt.

"That's her father, Bill. I'm Philip, and this is Matt. What's going on?" Her oldest brother was usually calm and collected, but at that moment he looked about ready to jump out of his skin.

"I'm Sergeant Rick Avery."

"Peggy's dead, isn't she?" Billie blurted out and started to sob again.

"I'm afraid so," Rick said softly.

"Wh…. What?" Matt staggered back against the open ambulance door.

"What happened?" Her father's voice cracked.

"Right now, we're investigating, but it appears someone got in through the back door," Rick explained.

"She had a restraining order against her ex-boyfriend," Philip told Rick.

"Ms. Carter told us, and we've got an all points bulletin out for him," Rick explained.

"That bastard killed her. I'll beat him to death." Matt shouted and started to stomp off, but before he got more than a couple of steps, Rick and Philip grabbed his arms.

"I know that's just the shock talking, but you can't say things like that nor can you go after him. We'll take care of this." Rick's firm voice appeared to stop Matt from going off half-cocked.

Billie stared at the front door of her house as police walked in and out. Yellow tape stretched across her driveway, and it seemed as if the entire neighborhood were on the side of the road watching. She tried to distract herself and stared at the ground, but panic started to take over when she noticed her socks soaked in blood.

"Take them off, take them off." Billie couldn't control her legs as she kicked her feet. It was stupid because she knew it wouldn't get them off.

"Honey, you've got to stop kicking. I'll pull them off." Her father cupped her face, and she pushed the oxygen mask over on her face again. The paramedic gave him a pair of gloves, a plastic bag, and towels. Her dad quickly pulled off the stained socks, dropped them in the bag and turned around.

"The police will probably want to keep these." Her father passed them to the paramedic and used the towels to clean the blood off her feet.

Matt paced back and forth between the ambulance and the back of his father's truck. Philip appeared about ready to pounce if Matt decided to take off and find Eugene himself. The only thing that kept her from freaking out completely was her father had her tightly wrapped in his arms.

"Ms. Carter, my supervisor would like to speak with you before we let you go. He's on his way here now." Rick handed her a bottle of water.

"Can I go to my parents after that?" She asked.

"I do think you should go to the hospital just to make sure you're okay. You did have quite a shock." He touched her shoulder.

"I'm fine. I just want to be around my family." Billie gasped. "Oh my God, Chloe."

"Who's Chloe?" Rick asked.

"She's Peggy's daughter." Her father answered.

"She's only eight years old. What's going to happen to her? Peggy has no family." Billie pulled out of her father's arms and yanked off the oxygen mask. "I need to go to her."

Philip was the one to grab her, and for a moment she struggled until Matt's firm voice stopped her.

"Chloe has a family. She has us, and that's where she'll stay." Matt's voice was more like a growl.

"Ms. Carter Staff Sergeant O'Connor is here." Rick nodded toward a black truck as it pulled up next to the ambulance.

"Umm, O'Connor. Not John O'Connor?" Billie stammered.

"Yes, he's my direct supervisor." Rick watched the truck.

Billie's heart felt like it was about to jump out of her chest. As if things weren't bad enough now she was about to come face to face with the one man she never wanted to see again.

"There's nobody else." Billie didn't want to be difficult, but with the way, she felt she'd probably punch the man, and that wouldn't be good.

"No, Ms. Carter. Trust me he's one of the best." Rick smiled and walked around the ambulance.

"Do you know this guy?" Philip asked.

"He's Stephanie's husband." That was all her family needed to know.

"That's good then." Her father rubbed her shoulder as he tucked her under his arm. Billie turned her head into him and closed her eyes.

"Ms. Carter this is John O'Connor." Billie heard Rick and took a deep breath before she turned and opened her eyes.

The man in front of her was not who she expected to see. It wasn't the same man she'd met at the club or the same man she saw with Stephanie. Maybe there was more than one John O'Connor.

"Sorry, we had to meet under these circumstances." John met her gaze.

"You're Stephanie's husband." Matt blurted out before Billie could speak.

"Stephanie's my wife. How do you know her?" He asked.

"Stephanie was my grandfather's therapist." Billie's voice trembled.

"I see." John glanced at Rick. "Has the scene been cleared yet?"

"Forensics is still in there," Rick replied.

John nodded and turned back to Billie. Stephanie didn't exaggerate about her husband's looks. He was incredibly handsome but if this was her husband who was Mike and why was he with Stephanie. Was she having an affair?

"It's getting a little cold out here. I think we'll get you to the hospital and I can talk to you there." John must have noticed her trembling, but it wasn't because she was cold. She only felt numb and completely confused.

"I don't want to go to the hospital," Billie whispered.

"I think you need to, Belinda." John wrapped a blanket around her shoulders. She hadn't noticed it fall off.

"He's right, Pumpkin." Her father turned her and helped her into the back of the ambulance.

"Sir, we found a cat in the back room, but it won't let us near it." The voice came from her doorway.

Cougar.

"That's my cat. His name is Cougar, and he doesn't like strangers." Billie tried to jump out of the ambulance, but her father stopped her.

"I'll get him." Matt stomped toward the house.

"I don't know if that's a good idea." John stepped in front of her brother.

"What are you gonna do? It's my sister's cat, and Chloe loves the fucking thing. So, I'm going to get the cat, and you can't stop me." Matt stepped around John but didn't get very far before John stopped him.

"I understand you're upset here, but we can't let you in there until it's cleared." John was taller than her brother, but they were about the same width. John whispered something to Matt that made him stop and back away. "I'll make sure the cat get's out safely and brought to Ms. Carter."

Matt didn't say anything, but for a moment he stared at Billie's house and then stomped off to her dad's truck. Philip spoke to John as well before he left. The last thing Billie saw before the doors of the ambulance closed was John holding his phone up to his ear.

Billie felt like she was in the middle of a nightmare as the ambulance bounced over a bump at the end of her road. Peggy was dead and poor Chloe had nobody. Billie didn't even know who Chloe's father was or how to get in touch with him. Peggy never wanted to talk about him, and there was no name on the birth certificate. Billie had seen it when Peggy had moved in with her. Peggy had asked her to put all the essential papers in the safe.

It was at that moment that Billie made a choice. She'd take care of Chloe and make sure the little girl got everything she needed. The only problem was how were they going to tell an eight-year-old that her mother was dead.

The tears streamed down her cheeks only mirrored the tears that she would have to see when Chloe found out she was never going to see her mother again. The thought made Billie sob uncontrollably as she clung to her father.

*Chloe I'll take care of you.*

# Chapter 7

It was the fourth of his brothers to tie the knot. This one had been quick, but Keith never looked happier, and Emily was glowing. Mike grabbed a beer from the bar and twisted off the top. From the way things were going, he'd be the last of the brothers to settle down.

It was almost comical how his family thought he was playing the field. He hadn't had sex for six months and not because he couldn't. He had a couple of women that called him on a regular basis for booty calls. Mike was sick of the meaningless sex. He wanted to spend time with someone in bed and out.

Maybe it was because he'd been watching his older brothers all settle down. They were all so sickeningly happy. Not that he wasn't glad for them, but it was difficult for him to be around them. Especially, when they'd give unsolicited advice on how he needed to settle down.

"Bro, we're a dying breed." Aaron nudged him.

"Hey, with the way this is going Mikey here is the next to sail off into the sunset." Nick laughed.

"Maybe I'll just be the cool single bachelor that your women call and complain to." Mike laughed. That was certainly not what he wanted.

"Bachelor maybe but definitely not cool." Isabelle poked him in the chest.

"That's right I'm the cool one." John draped his arm around Isabelle's shoulder.

"Dream on. Your cool factor dropped after you took the plunge, bro." Nick teased.

"Yeah but his sexiness skyrocketed." Stephanie tucked herself under John's other arm and kissed his cheek. She and John had found out they were about to have another baby and they were both over the moon.

"Please, don't use sexy in the same sentence with my cousin." Kristy gagged.

Mike started to feel smothered as everyone circled the bar. He stepped back and let out a breath.

"Hey, are you okay?" Stephanie touched his arm.

"Just been busy at work." Mike forced a smile.

"That makes what I'm about to ask really bad." Stephanie pointed to the door leading to the patio.

"What is it?" Mike didn't care how busy he was. When it came to family, he'd be there. Just like they always were for each other.

"John, I need to talk to Mike about that situation." Stephanie kissed John's cheek and linked her arm into Mike's elbow.

It was a beautiful night even though it was a little chilly for the end of August. Mike walked with Stephanie to one of the patio tables outside the country club. They sat down, and Stephanie smiled.

"I've got a friend who may need some advice on a situation." Stephanie folded her hands in front of her.

"Do I know this friend?" Mike asked.

"I don't think so. She's the grand-daughter of one of my clients." Stephanie explained. "She's trying to get custody of her friend's daughter."

"It's hard to get a judge to take a child away from their parents unless there's something dangerous." Mike had seen enough of it to know.

"Her friend was the girl murdered last month," Stephanie explained.

"Did her friend have a will or anything to give her custody?" This was a different situation altogether, and chances were child welfare would be the ones to deal with any arrangements for the child.

"No, but she always told Belinda that if anything happened to her, the little girl needed to be kept safe." Stephanie sighed.

"Then Belinda and her husband need to tell child welfare that,"

Mike said.

"See that's one of the problems. Belinda isn't married."

"That could make things harder."

"But the little girl is deaf, and Belinda knows sign language. She's also a social worker herself." Stephanie sighed. "She's desperate."

"If she's a social worker than she should know how this works," Mike said.

"She does, but John tells me you know sign language too."

"What difference does that make?" Mike didn't know how him knowing sign language could help her friend's situation.

"Belinda don't need a lawyer for herself. She needs one for the child." Stephanie took his hands. "They want to place the little girl with the man Belinda thinks killed her friend and the little girl is terrified of him."

"Well, that changes things." Mike sighed. "I'll see what I can do. Text me her information."

"I'll do that when I get home." Stephanie smiled. "You know I think you'll like Belinda."

"Jesus, don't tell me you're turning into another Aunt Cora." Mike chuckled.

"No, she's just a great girl." Stephanie kissed his cheek and headed inside.

Yeah, a great girl. Billie's beautiful face flashed in his mind. He couldn't believe that he'd let her slip through his fingers. If he hadn't been so stupid, he would have stopped her before she took off that night. The worst thing was he couldn't get her out of his mind and what was worse the past two weeks he'd been having dreams of her and not ones that were fun.

The dreams always started with her screaming and begging him to help her. When he'd reach for her, she'd disappear. It was fucking with his sleep. It was ironic that Stephanie's friend knew the murdered woman because when the dreams had started Mike had asked John about it. Mike was sure that the woman was Billie but had breathed a sigh of relief when he'd saw the young woman on the news. Not that it wasn't awful the woman was brutally killed, but it wasn't Billie.

"Uncle Mike." He turned around to see his niece Lily staring up at him. She looked like a little angel with her hair pulled up on top of her head and curls hanging around her face. To top it off she was wearing a white dress to match Emily's. She was one of the flower girls and his other niece Evie was the other.

"Hi, Lily." Mike crouched so she wouldn't have to look up.

"Mommy said we have to say goodnight to everyone. Poppy Stewart is taking us home." Lily pouted.

"You don't want to go with Poppy?" Mike chuckled.

"I was having fun, but Gracie is tired, and Alex is crying. So,

Mommy said it's time for us to go home." Lily wrapped her arm around his neck.

"I'm sure you're a little tired too." Mike lifted her into his arms.

"Yeah, but can you dance with me just once before we go?" She smiled.

"I would be honored to dance with one of the prettiest flower girls I've ever seen." Mike kissed her cheek and headed inside.

As pathetic as it was, he was the only one of his brothers on the dance floor that wasn't dancing with a woman his age, but Lily's smile made that all right. He didn't even mind the snide comments from Aaron about not being able to get a date. The truth was he could have gotten a date, but he didn't want to bring some random woman to his brother's wedding. He'd been there and done that. The next time he invited a woman to a family occasion it was going to be for more than a one-night date.

Billie flashed through his mind again, and he sighed. Maybe he should get Sandy to try and find her again. It was the only way he was going to get the woman out of his mind.

# Chapter 8

Billie couldn't believe the child protection worker was seriously considering allowing Eugene to have custody of Chloe. Just because he had an airtight alibi didn't mean that the asshole would take care of Chloe. Why Eugene was even trying to get custody of the child was beyond her. Peggy had told her more than once that Eugene ignored Chloe and he wasn't her father. It didn't make any sense why they would even consider him.

It was a wonder she hadn't worn a path into her parent's living room floor while she waited for Chloe's lawyer. It was a stroke of luck that Stephanie called her mother to get an idea of what to get Billie's grandfather for his upcoming birthday party. Her mother explained they were postponing the party until things with Chloe was cleared up. That was when Stephanie told her mother about a lawyer she knew.

Billie wanted custody of Chloe since the little girl didn't want to talk to anyone but Billie and her family. That didn't seem to matter to Felix Morris the CPS worker dealing with Chloe's case. He blamed his supervisor, but Billie knew of Felix from some of her co-workers in Labrador. She hadn't had any run-ins with him, but she'd heard he could be a colossal jerk.

"When is this lawyer going to be here?" Matt sat in the armchair next to the window.

"He was going to see Chloe at the foster home, and then coming here." Billie sighed and braced her back against the wall.

"If that pencil neck would get his head out of his ass he'd know Chloe belongs with us," Matt grumbled.

"He's just doing what he thinks is best for Chloe." Billie tried to sound as if she believed what she said, but the truth was Matt was right.

"I don't like him." Her grandfather lowered the newspaper and looked out over the top of his glasses. "Any man that can't complete a sentence without sniffing has been sniffing something up his nose."

"Pop that's not a nice thing to say. He could have allergies." Billie couldn't help but smile because Felix's constant sniffing got on her last nerve as well. She also didn't like how impatient he was with Chloe. He didn't know sign language and would ask Chloe questions as if she could hear him.

"Mark my words, that man don't have no allergies, and how he got that job is beyond me, he wouldn't know his arse from a hole in the ground." With that statement, her grandfather went back to his paper.

Billie rested her head back against the wall and closed her eyes.

Peggy's funeral had been two weeks before, and it was the worst thing she'd gone through since losing her grandmother. Then there was the fact that she couldn't sleep. Every time she'd close her eyes all she could see was Peggy's bloody body in the middle of the floor. If she finally got to sleep, she'd have nightmares of Peggy begging for help. She didn't tell anyone about the dreams because she was afraid it would make it difficult for her to get custody of Chloe.

The front door of her parent's house opened, and Chloe ran inside. The first thing she did was run right to Matt and jump into his arms. She loved Matt and as gruff as he was, he'd become a different person with the little girl.

"Chloe, how did you get here?" Billie signed when she could get the little girls attention.

"My new friend brought me." She signed back with a big smile.

"Who's your new friend?" Billie hoped that Chloe's new friend was an adult and didn't help her run away. Chloe pointed toward the door.

When Billie turned around, she gasped. It might have been five months since he'd held her and kissed the hell out of her, but she would know him from a mile away. A man like that was hard to forget, but then the scene that played out in front of her eyes in front of Stephanie's house flashed in her mind.

"What are you doing here?" Matt growled before Billie could

ask.

"I'm Chloe's lawyer." Mike didn't look at her brother. He kept his blue gaze locked with hers.

"We'll have to change that. You're the last fucking person I want to deal with." Matt snapped.

"Watch your mouth around the little girl." Mike broke their gaze and glared at Matt.

"She doesn't hear me." Matt snapped.

"She can read lips," Mike replied.

Billie glanced back and forth between her brother and the man that starred in her dreams before the nightmares started. She didn't know how they knew each other, but it was evident there was no love lost between them either.

"It's good to see you again, Billie." His smile returned as his eyes met hers. "Or should I call you Belinda?"

"Most people call me Billie." Her voice came out in a squeak.

"I like Billie." He took a step closer, and it was as if a magnet pulled her toward him until the flash of his arms around Stephanie brought her out of her trance.

"How did you get permission to bring Chloe here?" She stepped back and tried to compose herself.

"I received some details that changed the situation." Mike glanced over her shoulder at her brother. "Matt, could I speak to you in private for a moment?"

"Outside." Matt's voice came out like a snarl.

"What's wrong with you?" Billie grabbed his arm as he stomped past her.

"There's nothing wrong with me. Why don't you get Chloe settled?" Matt pointed toward the bags next to Mike's feet.

Matt pushed by Mike and disappeared through the front door. Mike didn't follow at first. He studied her face, and she wanted so much to go back to the night she met him.

"You look great, Billie." Mike smiled.

"I thought you wanted to talk to me." Matt's voice had Mike shaking his head.

"Excuse me." Mike nodded his head and followed Matt out through the front door.

Before Billie could follow, Chloe grabbed her hand. The little girl stared up at her with wide eyes. It was like looking at Peggy, and it broke Billie's heart that she would never see her friend again. The police still didn't know who killed Peggy or if they did they didn't say.

"Do I get to live here now?" Chloe signed when Billie crouched down.

"I hope so, but we won't worry about that now. Let's bring your things into the bedroom." Billie signed. The little girl wrapped her arms around Billie and hugged her tightly. When Billie looked up her grandfather smiled at her.

"Now all the family is under the same roof." He nodded and went back to reading.

Billie wondered just how long that would be.

# Chapter 9

Could things get any more fucked up?

How was it possible that Billie was the sister of Keith's employee and Stephanie's friend? She wasn't actually his client, but she was involved in the case. Mike stepped outside and scanned the front of the house for Matt. It seemed Billie's brother was hiding things from his family which was why he didn't tell Billie the reason he was able to bring Chloe home.

Matt was at the end of the driveway glaring at him with his hands fisted by his sides. Mike knew Matt didn't like him and Mike had to admit he was kind of anal about certain things. Not to be an ass but because the house was where he planned to spend the rest of his life and he wanted it to be perfect. When Mike found little things, he wanted changed Matt would get annoyed.

"Your family doesn't know, do they?" Mike kept his voice quiet as he approached Matt.

"I couldn't tell them until I knew for sure." Matt seemed to ease the tension in his body.

"You didn't know yourself?" Mike wondered how a man couldn't know he'd fathered a child.

"It's a long fucked up story." Matt closed his eyes and plowed his hands through his hair.

"I've got all day." Mike shoved his hands into his pants pockets.

"Do you think I'm going to tell you when I haven't even told my family about any of this?" Matt glared.

"They're going to ask because the only reason I was able to get Chloe placed in your home was that I received papers saying you were Chloe's father." Apparently, Matt trusted Keith with the secret.

"How the hell did I not realize you would be the lawyer Stephanie knew? You're the only lawyer, right?" Matt linked his hands behind his head and sighed.

"Nick did go to law school, but he changed careers." Mike could see the tension in Matt's face. "Look, I know you don't like me but I'm damn good at my job, and my priority is Chloe. Can we just bury the hatchet and get your daughter kept where she should be?"

For a few seconds, Matt stared over Mike's shoulder at the house. He seemed to have some internal struggle going on in his head, and Mike started to feel some guilt about giving the man such a hard time.

"I loved her," Matt whispered.

"Chloe's mother?" Mike asked.

"Nobody knew about the night we conceived Chloe. Peggy was Billie's best friend. That night I was home alone. Billie had gone away for the weekend with a couple of friends, but Peggy was still dealing with her mom's death." Matt blew out a puff of air. "You don't want to hear about this."

"I don't need to know, but it seems like you need to tell someone. Matt, I'm not a bad guy." Mike said.

"Wait, how did Billie know you?" Matt changed the subject.

"We met a few months ago downtown." That was all he was going to say.

"Keith told me about you and the other two. Keep your fucking hands off my sister." Matt growled.

"What happens or doesn't happen between your sister and me is none of your business. I want to know when you're going to tell your family about Chloe." Mike wasn't sure anything would happen with Billie. The way she stepped away from him seemed to say her attraction toward him had changed.

"My sister is my business. Don't think you're going to make her another notch on your bedpost. I know where you live." Matt glared.

"Matt, what's going on?" Mike stiffened as Billie walked up

behind him.

"It's just some stuff to do with his house." Matt lied.

"His house?" Billie glanced up at him and then quickly looked away.

"It's my house your brother is helping to renovate," Mike answered hoping she would look at him.

"That's an awfully big house for a single person." Billie glanced back at the house.

"Trust me he won't be alone there much," Matt interjected, and it made Mike want to punch the guy.

"I don't doubt that." Billie snapped and turned to face her brother.

"Chloe is looking for you." Billie turned to go back to the house.

"I need to talk to you as well, Billie." Mike touched her arm.

"What do you need to talk to her about?" Matt snapped.

"It's Billie who's petitioned for custody of Chloe." Mike raised an eyebrow at Matt. "Unless there's something that could change that."

Matt mumbled something under his breath and stomped back up to the house. Mike turned back to Billie, but she had her head down. He couldn't even pretend to understand what she'd been through. Nobody would unless they'd been there.

"I've been trying to find you for the last five months." Mike couldn't think of anything else to say.

"Why?" Billie tipped her face up and met his gaze.

"Because I haven't been able to get you out of my mind." Honesty was always best.

"I'm sure you found some help to take your mind off me." Billie rolled her eyes.

"If I'd known that the Belinda, Stephanie talked about was you, I would have been here the second I knew." Mike reached to take her hand, but she stepped back.

"I wasn't aware that you and Stephanie only talked." Mike couldn't understand the snarky tone of her voice.

"Did I do something to offend you?"

"I'm not offended." Billie crossed her arms across her chest, and it pushed her breasts up.

Mike felt his dick twitch, and he quickly averted his eyes before he grabbed her and reminded her just how hot it got that night with just a kiss.

"I'm guessing the friend you were running off to that night was Chloe's mother," Mike said.

Tears filled her eyes, and she swallowed hard. She looked down at the ground, but Mike put his finger under her chin and tipped it up, so she had to look at him.

"I found her," Billie whispered.

"I'm sorry." The pain in her eyes made his stomach clench, and his heart hurt.

"There was so much…." Billie covered her face with her hands and took a slow deep breath.

"You don't have to talk about it." Mike touched her cheek. "But if you do, I'm here to listen."

"Are you screwing around with Stephanie?" She'd said it so fast and soft that Mike wasn't sure he heard her correctly.

"I'm sorry, what?" Mike chuckled.

"I saw you." She finally looked up at him again. "A while ago. I was going to talk to Matt. That's how I knew how big your house was. Stephanie asked me to come by for coffee and when I pulled up in front of her house, you two looked pretty intimate."

Mike laughed and then stopped. When he saw the expression on her face, he quickly realized she was serious.

"Let me get one thing straight. I would never in a million years betray one of my brothers by having an affair with their wives. First, my brothers would take me out in the woods and beat me within an inch of my life. Secondly, my mother, grandmother, and father would skin me alive." Mike continued. "If it's the day I'm thinking of, I was there to babysit my niece because Stephanie had a last-minute appointment and I was the only one that could watch Olivia."

"Oh," Her cheeks turned a little darker. He guessed she was embarrassed.

"Billie, I love Stephanie but as a sister. Stephanie loves John with all her heart, and there isn't anyone that would come between them."

"I'm sorry." Billie sighed.

"You don't have to be sorry." He met her gaze, and it happened again. She took his breath away with that beautiful smile.

"You should know I thought you were John and assumed you were screwing around on Stephanie." Billie tucked a piece of her hair behind her ear.

"You did have me all wrong." Mike chuckled.

"From what my brother just said, maybe I didn't." Billie's smile faded.

"I'm not saying I'm a virgin because I'm far from it, but I haven't been with anyone since I met you," Mike whispered and took a step toward her.

"Belinda, don't be rude. Bring him in here so we can figure out what to do next." Mike heard a female voice from the house.

"I think we need to go inside." Billie walked around him but he grabbed her hand, and she turned. "Not now, okay."

Mike dropped her hand and followed her into the house. She was right. It wasn't the time or place to talk about how much he'd been thinking about her. How he'd fantasized about her and him together.

The older woman standing inside the door had Mike doing a double take. He remembered a picture of himself and Lyle with a woman that resembled the lady currently smiling at him.

"Mike, this is my mom, Marg Carter." Billie linked her arm into the woman's arm.

As soon as Billie said the name Mike knew precisely who the woman was.

"Mrs. Carter?" Mike couldn't believe it. "Are you the same Mrs. Carter that used to teach at Holy Cross Elementary?"

"Yes, that was a long time ago," Marg replied.

"I'm sure you don't remember me, but you taught me in grade one." Mike smiled.

"Wait, your last name is O'Connor." Marg stared at him for a moment. "Michael O'Connor, my goodness. I should have known those blue eyes."

Marg wrapped her arms around him and hugged him tightly. Mike met Billie's shocked expression behind her mother. When Marg stepped back, she cupped Mike's face in her hands.

"You were one of the sweetest boys I've ever taught. I still remember the day when young Lyle came to my classroom. You two took to each other so quickly." Marg smiled up at him.

"Lyle and I are still great friends." Mike chuckled.

"How is he?" Marg stepped back but linked her arm into his and guided him toward the kitchen.

Before Mike knew what happened, he was sat at the kitchen table with a cup of coffee telling Marg all about Lyle, Bobby, Ernie and himself. Billie had followed them, and Matt stood in the doorway of the kitchen he looked more than a little pissed.

"Oh, look at me taking up time that we should be figuring out how sweet little Chloe can stay with us permanently." Marg reached across the table and placed her hand over his.

"It's okay." Mike sat back in the chair and glanced up at Matt.

"Mom, I'm sure Mr. O'Connor has a hectic schedule." Matt was obviously trying to keep his anger hidden from his mother.

"I've got all day. I've cleared my schedule for this today because of the situation." Mike grinned at Matt.

"Chloe is staying here. It's where she belongs." Matt sat across the table from Mike and glared at him.

"Then I guess we need to get all the cards on the table." Mike rested his arms on the table and glared back.

Mike needed the man to come clean with his family. Matt was the little girl's father. He was the first choice for custody. Billie seemed determined to be Chloe's guardian. The last thing he wanted to do was hurt her.

# *Chapter 10*

Billie was sure her heart was about to jump out of her chest at any minute. Since the moment Mike walked through the door her heart pounded. Now he sat in her mother's kitchen looking even more delicious then he did the night she met him.

She couldn't help but be relieved that he wasn't with Stephanie. The only thing that bothered her was how Matt reacted to Mike. Her brother wasn't as captivated as she was or her mother for that matter.

The sad thing was she didn't have the time to deal with her overwhelming attraction for Mike. Chloe was the reason he was there, and she could have kissed him when he brought Chloe to the house. Kissed him, licked him and probably….

*Focus Billie.*

"Billie, are you okay?" She jumped at the sound of her name mainly since it was Mike asking.

"Yes. I'm fine." She hurried to the other side of the kitchen and poured herself a cup of coffee. She didn't usually drink it, but at that moment she needed to focus on something besides the way Mike's blue T-shirt fitted to his incredible body.

"Damn it," Billie grumbled.

"You seem jumpy, Belinda. I don't think you should be drinking coffee." Her mother took the cup from her hand. "Here, drink this." Her mother gave her a cup of herbal tea. "It's that new Chamomile tea that I picked up last week."

"Mom, I'm fine." Billie reached for the coffee again.

"Belinda Margaret, you're not doing Chloe any good if you're jumping at every little thing. Drink the tea." Her mother dumped the coffee down the sink and put the empty cup in the dishwasher.

"Now, Michael, what do we have to do to make sure Chloe stays with us?" Her mother sat next to Mike and gave him her full attention.

"Well, let me start off by saying you don't have to be concerned with Mr. Wilks getting custody of her." Mike pulled a folder from a briefcase. Billie hadn't even noticed him bring it in.

"Oh, thank heavens for that." Her mother pressed her hand against her chest and took a deep breath. So, did Billie and Matt.

"He's not her father, and since he wasn't married to Peggy, he's not her step-father either. Legally he has no chance." Mike continued. "Even if Chloe's father did come forward now he would first have to prove he was her father. He would also have to prove he

119

was capable of caring for her."

Matt began to tap his fingers on the table, but his mother reached across and covered his hand with hers. Billie had no idea what was going on with her brother lately, but he worried her.

"No more coffee for you either, Matthew." Her mother said.

Mike continued, but something in the way he stopped and glanced at Matt told her that there was something Mike held back. It was pretty obvious Matt knew what it was and she hoped it wasn't going to interfere with Chloe's well-being.

"That's a fine young man." Her grandfather declared at the supper table.

Mike had declined her mother's invitation to stay for supper but asked if Matt could walk him out. Billie felt a little hurt that he hadn't asked her, but then again why would he?

"I remember all those O'Connor boys were very well behaved. The whole family was incredibly close." Her mother smiled at her.

"I've met all the brothers now, and the younger ones are a little on the wild side," Matt grumbled as he caught Billie's gaze.

"Matthew, you've had your wild days too." Philip reminded her judgemental brother.

"The three younger ones have a reputation for being players." Matt held his fork up and pointed it at Billie. "I saw the way you looked at him. Trust me he's just looking for another roll in the hay."

"Matthew Walter Carter, you've got no right to say something like that about someone you don't know well. For all, you know he could be the man your sister ends up marrying."

Her mother's statement had Billie choking on the juice she'd just swallowed. Philip slapped her on the back until she was able to catch her breath. She jumped up from the table and grabbed a handful of paper towels to clean up the juice she'd spilled on the table.

"Trust me, Mom. That guy isn't looking for a wife. He's looking for a …." Matt stopped when her father slapped the back of his head.

"I wouldn't finish that sentence, young man." Her father warned. "Your sister is much smarter than you give her credit. I'm sure she wouldn't fall for a man that would treat her that way, and I'm not saying young Mr. O'Connor would."

It seemed Matt got the message, but Billie couldn't get the words her mother had spoken out of her head. She certainly wasn't ready to get married, but Mike was the first man in a very long time to set her pulse racing and her body humming.

"I still say he's a fine young man." Her grandfather said.

Billie wouldn't tell her grandfather she agreed because Mike O'Connor was definitely fine. Every single inch of him was more than fine.

The tug on her arm brought her out of her head. Chloe stared up at her as if she was about to burst into tears. Billie pulled her onto

121

her lap and kissed her cheek.

"Why is Matt so mean to my new friend?" Chloe signed.

Matt winced and closed his eyes because he seemed to realize when Mike said Chloe could read lips, he'd been right.

"Matt is just worried." Billie didn't want Chloe to be mad at Matt. He had become attached to the little girl, and Billie knew it would kill her brother if Chloe saw him as less than the hero he'd become in her eyes.

"Billie's right." Matt signed. "I didn't mean to make you think I didn't like him. He'll make sure you stay with us."

Billie prayed her brother was right because it seemed if Felix had his way Chloe would remain in foster care. A flutter of hope sprang to life when she pictured Mike standing up to Felix. Like Chloe's knight in shining armor. Possibly even hers.

# Chapter 11

Mike stared at Keith as if he had two heads. Mike asked his brother to come over to talk about the conversation with Jason, but Keith's response had him shaking his head.

"Uncle Kurt will kick your fucking ass." Mike chuckled.

"No, he won't. Jess doesn't want him to know, and you're going to keep it to yourself as well. I just wish I knew where Jason got his information."

"So, when did Jess start working for you?" Mike grabbed two beers out of the fridge and handed one to Keith.

"Crash and Trunk have been training her for a while, but she didn't want anyone to know." Keith leaned against the counter and sipped his beer.

"Jess is a black belt in Karate, and she'd been trained by Uncle Kurt since she was able to walk." Kurt had taught them all, but the only ones in the family that stuck with it were Jess, Ian, and Keith.

"Yes, which was the only reason I agreed to this. Crash and

Trunk have been teaching her. She hasn't had a lot of experience with firearms, and they've been helping with that." Keith explained, but Mike still knew their uncle would be pissed if he knew one of his daughters were in danger.

"That still doesn't explain why she's watching this guy and how Jason knew." Mike couldn't figure out that little tidbit.

"That's Jess's doing and believe me I'll have a chat with her about that," Keith grumbled. "She's keeping on eye on that asshole because Matt asked me to check on him. He beat the hell out of Chloe's mom, and Matt's convinced he had something to do with her death."

"From what I've seen on that file Jason gave me, the guy is a woman beating asshole with a record a mile long." Mike motioned toward the papers he showed Keith.

"I didn't want Jess doing this in the first place, but the sneaky little thing had Emily, Crash, and Trunk gang up on me," Keith grumbled.

"Emily knows about this?" Mike was surprised.

"Trust me I can't keep anything from that woman." Keith smiled. "She has ways of finding out." When Keith waggled his eyebrows, Mike knew exactly how Emily got her information.

"Must be nice." Mike felt that twinge of jealousy he always got when he saw the glowing happiness his brothers showed when they talked about their wives.

"Maybe you should stop running around and find someone to help you fill this house with more than an echo." Keith twirled the top of the bottle in a circle.

If he only knew how much Mike wanted that very thing and when he thought about it a certain beautiful brown-eyed beauty came to mind. He smiled when the memory of the night they met came to mind.

"Already have someone in mind, bro?" Keith grinned.

"Did you know Matt's mom is Mrs. Carter from Holy Cross?" Mike changed the subject.

"No, I didn't. If I remember correctly, she was the same teacher that told mom I should be in the gifted program." Keith smiled.

"So, until Jess gets something on this guy she's going to keep working at the bar with him. What happens to her flower shop?"

Jess owned a small flower shop in St. John's. It was the reason he and his brothers had dubbed her the flower child. Albeit, one that could probably kill someone with one hand. He still didn't know why she'd never turned in her application for the academy.

"She hired a couple of girls, and she works herself there on Saturday." Keith tossed the beer bottle in the recycling and turned back to Mike.

"Why didn't she follow her dream of being a cop?" If Keith knew about everything else, he had to know why Jess changed her mind.

"Bro, that's something you'd have to ask our little cousin. I didn't know until you told me." Keith moved toward the front door.

"I need you to talk to Matt about telling his family about Chloe's true paternity." Mike opened the door of his house. "That C.P.S asshole knows now. Although, I've got to admit I liked pulling the rug out from in under him."

Felix's expression was priceless when Mike tossed the paternity results in front of him and his snooty supervisor. The way they shuffled through their files and stammered over their words was incredibly satisfying.

"He called me tonight and told me what you did. He's thankful, but I don't think he likes the way you were eyeing his sister." Keith chuckled. "I'll talk to him about it though. He doesn't seem to like those workers either."

"I met his sister about a month ago at a club. We hit it off, and it was nice to see her again. That's all." Mike shrugged his shoulders.

"Is this the same girl Sandy's been searching for?" Keith raised an eyebrow.

"Fuck, did she tell everyone?" Mike sighed.

"The only reason I know was because I saw the printouts she had. It's a shame you didn't know that Matt's sister was no longer a social worker because she was the first name Sandy found." Keith chuckled as he jogged down over the steps.

"Thanks, a fucking lot. Asshole." Mike shouted.

"You don't go through all that trouble for a one-night stand, bro. Just make sure to smooth things over with her brother before you go making any moves and if you're just in it for a wham bam thank you, mam, leave her alone." Keith disappeared down the path toward his property.

Mike closed the door. He scanned the foyer of his house and sighed. Everything was almost finished. The only thing's left was his home office and the landscaping, but he still didn't feel content. He bought the house hoping he wouldn't feel as detached but the truth was, without someone to share it with, it was just another place for him to feel alone.

The only time he didn't feel that way was when he thought about Billie. Now that he'd finally found her, the feeling was stronger, and he knew without a doubt, he needed her in his life. The buzzing of his phone had him jogging back to the kitchen to snatch it off the counter. He didn't recognize the number, but he answered it anyway.

"Mike O'Connor." He put the phone to his ear.

"Mike, it's Billie." Her voice echoed through him.

"Hi," well could he sound any more idiotic.

"The police are here to take Matt. They want to question him about Peggy's death. One of my neighbors said they saw him at my house that night." Mike grabbed his keys and was out the front door before she finished the sentence.

"Billie, find out where they're taking him and text it to me. Tell

Matt not to say a word until I get there." Mike was already turning onto the highway toward St. John's.

"I didn't know who else to call." Her voice came through as a whisper.

"I'm glad you called. I'm not a criminal lawyer, but right now he just needs someone there. Hopefully, this is nothing." Mike could hear the voices in the background.

"Mom's upset and so is my dad. Chloe's crying and I'm scared to death. Please call me when you know what's going on." The crack in her voice went straight to his heart.

"I promise. I've got your number now, Billie." Her chuckle made him ease off on the gas since she got his attempt at humor. "Text me with where they're taking Matt, and I'll meet him there."

"I will. Thank you, Mike." Billie said, and the call ended.

Mike pulled into the St. John's division of the Newfoundland Police Department. Since he knew most of the officers, he had no problem finding someone to direct him to where Matt was not so patiently waiting.

"Mike, he's like a caged animal in there." John met Mike at the entrance of the interrogation room.

"He didn't do this, John." No matter how much he disliked Matt, he knew there was no way he'd hurt Peggy. He didn't know how he knew that, but he was a good judge of people.

"Off the record, I don't think so either, but when I'm told to bring him in because a neighbor saw him leaving at around ten, I've got to follow orders," John said.

"I know, bro. I'll let you know when we're ready." Mike opened the door and walked into the room. Matt paced back and forth with his hands shoved into his front pockets.

"What the hell is wrong with your family?" Matt threw his hands up in the air.

"John's just doing his job." Mike motioned for Matt to sit.

"Why didn't they just call? I would've come down, and none of my family would be upset. For Christ's sake, Billie had to pull Chloe off my leg." Matt flopped down in the chair.

"Matt, that's not how it works, but for what it's worth, I don't think you could ever hurt Peggy." Mike needed Matt to know that. "Now, let's talk about that night."

"Thanks for believing in me. Considering how I've treated you, I'm surprised you even want to help me." Matt rested his arms on the table and looked Mike straight in the eyes. "Peggy texted me to tell me Billie was gone out. Chloe was baking cookies with mom, and I told my mother I had to run out and pick up some things for work. That was a lie. I was going over to see Peggy."

"Were you dating her?" Mike asked.

"I wouldn't call it dating because nobody knew. It was so stupid to keep it quiet, but I wasn't sure how my family was going to react to it because Peggy basically grew up with us. Billie thinks of her as a sister. Anyway, we were going to talk about telling everyone about Chloe and everything. I loved her. I think if I'd been honest with myself I fell in love with Peggy a long time ago but it just seemed wrong to pursue it. Stupid huh." Matt pulled his hands down over his face.

"Not really, sometimes you find love in the places you don't expect." Mike had seen it enough to know it was true.

"We decided to tell everyone and deal with the aftermath. We were going to do it the following weekend but then…." Matt swallowed hard, and his eyes glistened with tears he held back.

"What time did you leave?" Mike knew from his brother that the coroner placed the time of death between ten and midnight.

"I was back at my parents by nine. Mom had just tucked Chloe in bed, and Jeopardy was just over. Pop watches it every night, and it comes on at eight thirty." Matt seemed pretty sure of the time.

"So, John's going to be the one coming in and asking questions. If I hear something I don't like; I'll make sure you don't answer." Mike opened the door and waved to his brother. John was further down the hall looking at his phone.

For the next hour, John grilled Matt on every detail of that night. It pissed Mike off, but Matt seemed to be calm. Mike was glad he didn't fly off the handle because that wouldn't look good.

"One last question and you can go," John stood up. "Would

you be willing to take a DNA test?"

"Why would he have to do that?" Mike placed his hand on Matt's shoulder.

"Peggy had sex before she was killed and she also had some skin under her nails. The samples are both different, and we want to see if Matt matches either of them." John wrote something on the pad in his hand.

"She was…. Raped." Matt stammered.

"It doesn't look like she was raped. No tearing or bruising but whoever she had sex with wasn't the same person she scratched." John met Mike's gaze.

"We made love that night." Matt's voice trembled. "It was the first time since we admitted our feelings to each other."

"And you sure of your timeline?" John tucked the pad into his jacket pocket.

"One hundred percent. You can check with my family." Matt didn't flinch when John hummed.

"I'll talk with them. You're free to go but don't leave town." John opened the door to the room. "Just in case I've got more questions."

"The only place I go is work and home." Matt stood up.

"Good. Thanks for being so co-operative." John reached out to shake Matt's hand. "I'm sorry for your loss. I can't imagine losing the love of my life."

Mike knew John was completely genuine and it seemed Matt sensed that too. He relaxed as they walked out to the reception area.

"I need to call someone to pick me up." Matt pulled out his phone, and Mike stopped him.

"I'll take you home." Mike wasn't going to tell Matt that he'd planned to see Billie anyway. At the moment, Matt was civil toward him. Mike didn't want to mess that up by pissing him off.

Matt remained quiet for most of the drive home. The only sound was the soft music from the radio. Mike felt bad for the guy. He was about to get his happily ever after and some sick fuck took it away from him. That realization hit him like a punch in the gut. He didn't want to be that guy that looked back with regrets and wonder what if.

"Matt, I need you to know something." Mike turned the radio off.

"What's that?" Matt turned in his seat.

"The stories you heard about my younger brothers and me are mostly true." Mike couldn't start with a lie.

"Mostly?" Matt narrowed his eyes.

"The truth is it got old, and I'm not looking for a roll in the hay. I'm looking for someone to share my life with." Mike pulled into the driveway and turned to face Matt.

"You understand I'm straight, right?" Matt chuckled.

"Funny guy here." Mike shook his head.

"You're talking about my sister." It wasn't a question coming from Matt.

"I don't know how to explain it. I haven't been able to get her out of my mind since the night I met her. Not for the reasons you think because nothing happened between us." Mike plowed his hands through his hair. "I've got no idea why I'm discussing this with you since we aren't exactly best pals."

"I'm coming to see that you aren't as bad as I made you out to be," Matt said. "But if you hurt my sister I'll kick your ass."

Matt reached out, and Mike grabbed his hand. There was a little test of strength in their handshake, but there was also a truce. One that gave Mike the opening to see if something was there with Billie.

# *Chapter 12*

Billie sat on the sofa with Chloe curled up beside her. The little girl cried herself to sleep when Matt left with the police. It broke Billie's heart not only for Chloe but her mother. There was just one thing that stuck in her mind. Why was Matt at her house the night Peggy died?

She rested her head back against the sofa and prayed Mike could help her brother. Billie didn't believe for one minute he could ever hurt Peggy or anyone for that matter. Although, he seemed ready to beat Eugene that night, but Peggy's slimy ex didn't do it. Apparently, he had an airtight alibi, and there was a video of him at work. That didn't mean he didn't arrange it.

"What if they arrest him?" Her mother's voice floated out from the kitchen. Billie heard the rumble of her father's soothing voice, but she couldn't understand what he was saying. Probably something about how it was all a mistake.

Billie heard him call her name, but it was off in the distance.

He smiled at her, and she smiled back. He called her name again, and she felt his hand touch hers.

"Maybe we should just leave her alone." That was him again.

"If what you said to me in the car is what you want. Don't let it slip through your fingers. Just remember I'll kick your ass if you hurt her." That was Matt.

Billie's eyes flew open, and she jumped to her feet. Chloe was no longer on the couch next to her, and her grandfather was not in his usual place watching television.

"What's going on?" She scanned the room.

"You fell asleep." Matt chuckled. "Mike here wants to talk to you."

"Matt, is everything okay?" She grabbed his arm, and he pulled her into a hug.

"I'll tell you all about it later but first, don't let time slip away from you." Matt kissed her cheek and left her alone with Mike.

"They didn't charge him with anything?" Billie turned to look up into Mike's blue eyes.

"No, and I'm pretty sure they won't." Mike smiled and reached for Billie's hand.

"How can I ever thank you?" Billie squeezed his hand, and a tear rolled down her cheek.

"Take your brother's advice." Mike winked.

"Huh?" What was he talking about?

"I let you slip through my fingers once. I felt something that night, and I know things are complicated with you right now, but I don't want to waste any more time. If there's one thing I learned from your friend's death is, we aren't promised tomorrow." Mike grasped her other hand in his.

"We don't know each other," Billie took a step toward him.

"I'd like to fix that situation." Mike smiled.

"I don't know, Mike. Things are so…." Billie dropped her head and stared where their hands joined.

"Life is short, sis." Billie looked up to see Matt propped against the doorjamb. "Plus, I've already warned him I'll kick his ass if he hurts you."

"Matt, is there something you're not telling me?" The first thought to cross her mind that Matt might be sick.

"I'm about to rectify that. Can you come into the kitchen with everyone?" Matt glanced at Mike. "I'd appreciate the backup."

Mike dropped her hands and motioned for her to go ahead of him. Billie's heart raced. Between worrying about what Matt had to say and the woodsy scent of Mike's cologne swirling around her, she felt dizzy.

"Matthew, please don't tell us you did this." Her mother sat at the table wringing her hands with her father's arm wrapped tightly around her.

"Mom, I didn't hurt Peggy." Matt sat across the table from her mother and reached out to her. She grabbed his hands as if he'd disappear.

Billie sat next to him and unconsciously grabbed Mike's hand when he sat next to her. Who was she kidding? She grabbed his hand because she needed to touch him. How was it possible to feel the need to be close to someone she hardly knew?

"Let's start with Chloe," Matt took a deep breath that he blew out slowly.

"What about her?" Philip asked. Billie hadn't even realized he was still in the house.

"I'm her biological father," Matt said.

The room was so quiet that Billie could hear the soft hum of the dishwasher. She hadn't realized she squeezed Mike's hand until he covered her hand with his other one. When she glanced at him, he didn't seem to be the least bit surprised with Matt's confession.

"I'm sorry, you're what?" Philip rested his fists on the table and bent down, so he was eye level with Matt.

"Chloe's my daughter," Matt admitted.

"What? How? Never mind, I know how but what?" Philip shook his head. "Peggy was like our sister for Christ's sake."

Billie still couldn't comprehend what Matt said. Sure, she

understood what he said but Peggy and Matt? A couple? Was it just a one-night stand? Did her brother take advantage of her friend? That didn't seem like something Matt would do but what else could it be? Matt was five years older than she was and she was eighteen when she got pregnant.

"Chloe's our granddaughter?" Her mother gasped.

"Yes, Mom." Matt turned to Billie.

"You haven't said anything, Sis." Matt stared into her eyes.

"I …. What can I say?" Billie swallowed. "Why didn't you tell me? Why didn't she?"

"I didn't know until a few months before Peggy…." Matt stopped, and Billie could see the pain in his eyes. "It was one night. We were both feeling lost and alone, and it just happened. I guess I was always attracted to Peggy, but because she was so much younger I would never act on it but that night…." Matt looked at his mother. "I did love her, Mom. I fought it for so long after that night, and when I found out she was pregnant, she swore the baby wasn't mine."

"Why would she lie to you?" Philip finally sat down.

"Because that night I told her it couldn't happen again and she didn't want me to feel trapped." Matt lowered his head. "I've kicked myself for saying that since I found out."

"So why were you there that night?" Billie asked.

"We finally admitted our feelings for each other. We were

going to tell everyone that weekend but…" Matt stopped and covered his face with his hands. Billie let go of Mike's hand and wrapped her arms around her brother.

It was almost midnight when Billie walked Mike to his car. She felt terrible for him to be in the middle of all the drama of her family. Not that she wasn't thrilled he stayed but not exactly the best way to impress someone.

"I'm sorry about all that." Billie stood next to his car.

"Don't be sorry." Mike sat back on the side of his vehicle and grasped her hands. "At least now he has his little girl, and I'm going to make sure it stays that way."

"I guess that means he'll get custody of Chloe." Billie realized.

"I was going to push for that. Since her mom is deceased, her father would be the next of kin." Mike pulled her closer. "I really want to kiss you right now, but since I remember what happened the first time I kissed you, vividly, I think we should probably start with a first date."

"I'd like that." Billie gazed into his eyes.

"I've got a hectic week with some cases, but I'm not waiting until Friday. Tomorrow's Tuesday, and that seems like a great day for a date." He squeezed her hands.

"That sounds great." Billie stepped back.

"I'm guessing you've been staying with your parents." Mike

didn't release her hands when he stood up to his full height.

"Until I find another place. I can't go back there." Billie dropped her head.

"You know I've got a big house with lots of rooms." Billie's head snapped up to look at him. He had a huge grin on his face that made her remember the night she'd met him.

"Are you asking me to move in with you, Mr. Lawyer Man?" Billie laughed.

"At least then you won't disappear on me again." Mike released her hand and cupped her cheek. "But if you do need a place to stay until you find something, my offer stands. No strings."

"Thanks for the offer." Billie cupped her hand over his. "Right now, I'm okay staying with my family."

"I'll see you tomorrow around seven. Nothing fancy. Dinner at Roadhouse." Mike ran his finger down her cheek and for a moment she thought he'd kiss her, but he stepped back and sighed. "Yep, I gotta go."

"See you later, Mike." Billie walked back up the driveway.

"You definitely will, Beautiful." Mike winked and then he was gone.

She watched his car disappear at the end of her road and turned to go back to her house. Rita walked outside with a garbage bag and brought it to the bin on the front of the house.

"Hi, Rita." Billie waved.

"Oh, hi Belinda." Rita closed the bin and walked toward Billie.

"How's your mom doing?" Billie leaned on the rail at the top of the steps.

"She gets frustrated really easy but who can blame her." Rita sighed. "I haven't gotten a chance to tell you how sorry I was to hear about Peggy."

"Thanks,"

"I always liked her." Rita smiled. "We used to have a lot of fun when we were kids."

"Yes, you know when everything settles down, you should come out one night with Abbie, Dana and I." Billie pulled out her phone. "Give me your number."

"I don't know about going out. I can't leave mom but you three can certainly come over to the house for a bottle of wine. I'm sure mom would love to see the girls." Rita punched her number into Billie's phone.

"That's an even better idea." Billie texted the number so Rita would have hers as well.

"I've seen Matt and Philip coming in and out, but I haven't gotten a chance to say hi." Rita blushed a little, and Billie wondered if the woman had a little crush on one of her brothers.

"Well next time you see them just say hi." Billie smiled.

"I will. I better get back in. Mom usually wakes up at six." Rita said. "I'll see you soon."

When Billie walked inside the house, it was quiet. Everyone but her mother had gone to bed. Billie figured her mom was still in shock with Matt's confession. Billie found her mom sitting at the table with a cup between her hands staring at it.

"It's getting late, Mom." Billie sat across from her.

"Life's funny, you know." Her mother lifted her head and smiled.

"Why do you say that?" Billie rested her chin on her fist.

"Matthew and Peggy finally admit their feelings for each other, and then some crazy man takes all that away in the blink of an eye." Her mother reached across the table and took Billie's hand.

"Peggy never gave me any clue she was in love with Matt." Billie felt a little slighted because she thought they told each other everything.

"I knew there was an attraction. It had been there for a long time, but for some reason, your brother kept his distance. I think it's why he never dated seriously." Her mother smiled. "But you little girl. I knew your fate a long time ago."

"Huh?" What was her mother talking about?

"When I taught at Holy Cross, there was a Christmas concert. Your dad stayed home with Matt and Philip, but you screamed to go with me. You were three. So, I didn't see anything wrong with taking you." Her mother chuckled. "It was the year I taught Michael. Of course, his entire family was there for the concert, and you sat in the front row next to one of the other teachers. You managed to escape and run down the center of the auditorium, but a young woman caught you before you got too far."

"I was just too cute." Billie giggled.

"You were, and you charmed the woman. It turns out she was Michael's aunt Cora, and she said something to me that night after the concert. She told me she could see you as an adult and that Michael was your future." Her mother laughed probably because Billie's mouth fell open.

"I laughed at the time and thought the woman was a little quirky. I found out a few years later that the people in her family called her Cora the Cupid. She seems to know when a couple is meant to be together and as far-fetched as that seemed to me at the time, I'm starting to believe maybe she was right. I saw the way you looked at him and the way he looked at you. The way he sat next to you while Matthew told us everything. He's protective but not overbearing. Billie, don't let him get away." Her mother wiped a tear from her cheek.

"Mom," Billie swallowed the lump in her throat

"Look at me being all weepy." Her mother wasn't the type of woman who cried at every little thing, so this was odd to see her cry.

"I don't know if Mike's aunt is right, but just so you know, we are going out tomorrow night. I only met him once, but there is something about him, Mom." Billie sighed.

"He was always such a sweet boy. Very protective of the people he cared about." Her mother smiled.

"I don't know what's going to happen, but I'm going to see where it goes. I don't want to have any regrets." Billie stood up and stretched. "I'm going to call it a night. I promised Abbie I'd be at the office early since I've missed so much time."

"I'm sure Abbie understands." Her mother followed her upstairs.

"She does, and I honestly think Abbie's just working to avoid dealing with her grief over Peggy." Billie hugged her mother before she entered her bedroom.

"Goodnight, baby girl." Her mother closed the bedroom door behind her and Billie entered her room.

So many things ran through her mind. Shutting off her brain and sleep would be hard. Billie found it hard to get her mind around the fact that her best friend in the world had kept such a huge secret from her. Two huge secrets. Did she not trust Billie or did Peggy think Billie would be upset? That was something she would never know now.

Then there was Mike. The story her mother told her earlier was too far-fetched to believe. She really didn't know Mike, but there was some unknown force that pulled her toward him. She felt it the first night they met, and it was still there when he appeared earlier. She was a firm believer that things happened for a reason but what was the reason for Peggy's death? Billie didn't know, but Mike and her mom were right. Life was too short, and she was about to grab it with both hands and see where it took her.

# *Chapter 13*

"So, this girl thought Stephanie was cheating on John with you?" Sandy laughed so hard Mike couldn't help but shake his head.

"Why's that so funny?" Ian stared at his wife, and Mike wondered the same thing.

"Anyone who's met Stephanie knows she's head over heels in love with John." Sandy looked at Mike and tilted her head. "I mean Mike you're kinda sexy, but you'd never turn her head." Sandy burst into a fit of laughter again. "Stephanie and Mike, John would rip Mike's arm off and beat him to death with it."

"You know your wife has a sick sense of humor." Mike looked at Ian.

"It's part of my charm." Sandy tossed her hair over her shoulder and gave Ian a wink.

"So why exactly are you here if you're supposed to be going on a date with this girl?" Ian asked.

"I'm not picking her up until seven." Mike couldn't look his brother in the eye.

"And waiting home alone watching the time tick by made you nervous." Ian chuckled. "Wow, this must be a special one. Never thought I'd see you nervous over a date."

"Oh, our little Mikey's growing up." Sandy pinched Mike's cheek.

"How do you live with this woman?" Mike pushed her hand away.

"I give a great blow…." Mike put his hand over her mouth before she finished the statement.

"I don't need to know that." Mike stood up and glanced at the time on his phone. It was a little after six. "I'm going to head out before your wife starts telling me what other things she does."

"Oh, I do this thing…."

"La, la,la … I'm gone." Mike plugged his ears as he hurried out of the house. When he got next to his car, he heard Sandy yell from the doorway.

"I'll give Billie a call and tell her about that thing." Sandy wiggled her fingers when he glared at her.

Mike pulled into the driveway of the Carters. He did his best not to be too early but it was six thirty, and he honestly couldn't wait to see Billie. So, with a red rose on the front seat of his car he glanced toward the house. Billie was in the window, and she took his breath away.

He'd been so mesmerized by her that he left the flower in the car. Before he had a chance to knock Matt pulled open the door. His face was unreadable, and for a moment Mike thought something was wrong.

"Remember what I told you," Matt growled and if Mike hadn't seen the slight quirk of his lips he'd have thought Matt had changed his opinion.

"You do know my uncle is a third-degree black belt and has taught all of us Karate. I also have four brothers and the same uncle that are police officers?" Mike rested his shoulder against the door jamb.

"No, I didn't know that, but you hurt my sister, and I won't care." Matt chuckled as he moved so Mike could enter the house. He slapped Mike on the back and led him into the living room.

"It's so good to see you, Michael," her mom wrapped Mike up in a hug.

"Nice to see you too, Mrs. Carter." Mike wasn't the least bit uncomfortable with Mrs. Carter's hug.

"Hi, Mike." Billie smiled and as if by magic everything else faded into the background. Mike barely registered Marg kissing his cheek. All he knew was the most beautiful woman in the world stood in front of him.

"What a welcome. A threat from your brother and a hug from

your mom." Mike chuckled and moved slowly toward her. "But just a hi from you."

"This is the first date; you don't expect anything else, do you?" Billie laughed.

"I'm not going to answer that. Are you ready to go?" He didn't expect anything, but he did want more with her. A lot more.

"Yes." She smiled and allowed him to lead her out to the car.

Billie didn't seem the least bit surprised when Mike opened the door for her or that there was a rose waiting on the seat for her. At least she didn't show it.

On the drive to the restaurant, they made small talk. Billie told him they'd be telling Chloe over the weekend that Matt was her father. They also wanted to get his name added to the little girl's birth certificate. Mike quickly offered to help them with it.

The restaurant was quiet. Probably because it was a Tuesday evening. The waitress sat them at a table in the corner with the view of St. John's harbor, but that probably had more to do with Mike's call earlier that day.

"I've never been here before," Billie said as he helped her off with her jacket. He almost swallowed his tongue when he saw what she was wearing under it.

The white sleeveless blouse stood out against her caramel skin. She wore jeans that hugged her hips and ass and accentuated her tiny waist. His cock hardened instantly as he pulled out her chair.

"You're a real gentleman, aren't you?" Billie smiled as he sat across from her.

"I try to be, but that outfit is making it difficult to remember that." Mike took her hand and kissed her palm.

"What's wrong with my outfit?" She met his gaze, and his stomach did a flip-flop.

"Not a damn thing. You're stunning." Mike didn't notice the young waitress next to the table until she cleared her throat. Billie hypnotized him.

"I'm sorry to interrupt but would you like something to drink before you order?" Mike tore his gaze away from Billie to look up.

"I'll just have a beer. What would you like, sweetheart?" Mike glanced at Billie and didn't miss the little shiver when he used the endearment.

"I'll have the same." She gave the waitress a sweet smile and then brought her eyes back to him.

Mike heard the waitress say something, but he was already under Billie's spell again. He could just sit there and stare into her eyes all night, but when her eyes flicked down to his lips, his dick jerked. Kissing would be a better way to spend the night or touching or …

He needed to stop where that train of thought was going before the zipper on his jeans made a permanent imprint on his member.

"You take my breath away." Mike kissed her wrist and felt the goosebumps rise on her skin.

"How many girls have fallen for that little line." Billie giggled.

"I don't use lines, Sweetheart. I'm honest and straightforward, and when I say you take my breath away, I mean it." Mike was practically leaning across the table when the waitress returned with their beer.

"Are you ready to order?" She asked.

"We haven't looked at the menu yet. Can you give us a few minutes?" Mike pulled back but kept Billie's hand in his. The waitress disappeared again, and Mike sighed.

"I think we better order." Billie picked up her menu and pulled her hand from his.

Mike wasn't surprised when Billie ordered a steak and house salad. The night they met she'd told him she wasn't one of those women who ate like a bird. It was sexy as hell to him. He liked that she felt comfortable enough with him to eat like normal people. Most women would order a small salad and eat half of it. It always bothered him when women would do that and then reach over and grab fries off his plate.

When their plates had been cleared away, and they'd declined dessert. The waitress brought them both coffee. They talked about their families and growing up. She'd admitted that she always wanted to live someplace outside the city and he knew exactly why. He might have been born and raised in Hopedale, but he spent more than ten years in the city. Between Toronto and St. John's, he'd had his fill of city living. For the life of him, he couldn't remember why he'd ever wanted to leave Hopedale in the first place.

"Maybe this weekend you can come to my place, and I'll show you around Hopedale. Then impress you with my cooking skills." Mike winked.

"I'd love to check out the kind of skills you have." Billie returned his wink, and his cock came to full attention. The woman was going to be the death of him.

"That statement can be taken two ways." Mike squeezed her hand.

"Take it however you want to." She rested her elbow on the table and cradled her chin in her free hand. "What's wrong? Feeling a little speechless?"

"Trying to get my brain back where it should be." Mike couldn't keep his gaze from dropping to her plump lips. When she licked them, he shifted in his seat uncomfortably. He never wanted anyone more than he wanted Billie at that moment.

"Do you want to get out of here?" Billie asked him.

"Oh yeah." Mike jumped to his feet.

"I think we need to pay the bill first." Billie giggled.

"You're driving me crazy," Mike whispered in her ear as he helped her on with her jacket. His reward was a quick intake of her breath and a small shiver.

Mike tracked down the waitress and quickly paid the bill. Billie, of course, tried to pay for her portion but he put a stop to that. He didn't know where they were going, but at that moment he needed to be alone with her. He still had his key to his old apartment and had left his old bed there in case he needed to crash there at some point. Bobby and Ernie had made sure he knew he was always welcome there but he was sure it wasn't an invitation to take a woman back there.

Mike opened her door, and she slid into the passenger seat. As he rounded the car, he caught something move out of the corner of his eye. He turned around but didn't see anything. The hair on the back of his neck stood up, and he slowly turned around in a circle. Nothing.

"Did you forget how to get into the car?" Billie teased when he finally got in and closed his door.

"Kinda, my brain has taken a trip down south." Mike turned in his seat and reached across to cup her cheek.

She leaned into his touch, and Mike slowly moved closer as he studied every inch of her beautiful face. When he met her eyes, and he got lost in the dark brown pools. He'd always been partial to lighter eyes, but Billie's were the most beautiful he'd ever seen.

"Are you just going to stare or are you going to kiss me?" Billie ran her finger down his cheek, and he shuddered.

"Kissing you isn't the problem. It's trying to keep it at just a kiss." Mike slid his hand around to the back of her neck.

Mike swept his lips lightly over hers and inhaled. A second time he lingered against her mouth a little longer. When she sighed, there was no stopping. Mike covered her mouth with his, and she opened to him. The first flick of her tongue had him pull her closer, and he moaned into her mouth. The taste of coffee and her had him painfully hard, but who cared. Kissing her was like a drug, and he couldn't get enough.

Billie met his kiss with just as much passion and heat. Mike knew they needed to stop since they were still in the parking lot of the restaurant. For some reason, he had trouble doing that when she threaded her fingers through his hair, tipped her head and gave him better access to her mouth.

He was sure the zipper of his jeans was going to burst open because he was hard as a rock and felt like he was about to come just from kissing her. Mike somehow managed to pull his lips from hers and pressed his forehead against hers while he tried to catch his breath.

"What's going on in there?" Mike jumped when someone pounded on the side of his car, but since steam covered the windows, he couldn't see who it was.

"Oops," Billie giggled and moved back to the other side of the car.

"Fuck," Mike grumbled as he lowered his window.

Mike rolled his eyes at the grinning face that stared back at him. Aaron rested his arms on the open window as he flashed his biggest smile. The one his little brother used on way too many women.

"What's going on big brother?" Aaron winked at Billie.

"None of your fucking business, asshole." Mike pushed Aaron's arms off the window.

"I'm on duty, and since you're in a public parking lot, I had to make sure you weren't breaking the law." Aaron hadn't taken his eyes off Billie.

"Yeah, because you'd never do anything like that," Mike grumbled.

"Well if I had a beauty like this lovely lady, I can't say I wouldn't be tempted." Aaron reached his hand across the car. "I'm A.J., Mike's younger and much better-looking brother."

"And much more annoying too," Mike laughed.

Billie reached out to shake Aaron's hand, but his sly brother pulled her forward and placed a kiss on the top of her hand.

"I'm Billie and Matt wasn't joking about your younger brothers, was he?" Billie pulled her hand back but placed it on Mike's knee.

"Matt?" It seemed his baby brother hadn't met Billie's brother.

"Billie's very protective big brother. He works for Keith and warned about you and Nick." Mike laughed.

"I'm sure I've no idea what you're talking about. I'm the only angel in the family." Aaron stuck out his bottom lip. "You don't believe any of that, do you, Billie?"

"Oh, of course not. I can see you're as pure as the driven snow." Billie laughed.

"Are you done?" Mike sighed.

"For now, but I hope I get to see more of you, Billie. Maybe you can put a smile on Mr. Grumpy here." Aaron hitched his thumb toward Mike and moved back from the car.

"Goodbye, A.J." Mike started the car.

"Never say goodbye, Mikey. Remember, Nan, says goodbye is forever." Aaron shouted as Mike's window closed way to slowly.

"I think I should probably get you home." Mike put the car into drive and reached out to grab Billie's hand as they pulled out of the parking lot.

"Yeah, it's getting late." Billie linked her fingers into his, and he felt that flip in his chest again. He was falling and falling fast.

"It's probably a good thing A.J. showed up." Mike lifted her hand and pressed his lips against it. "I'm not sure how much more restraint I had in me."

"I know the feeling." Billie sighed.

It was a little after eleven when he pulled into her driveway. He held her hand as he walked her to the front door. When they were next to the entrance, she turned and slid her arms around his neck. He wrapped his arms around her and pulled her closer.

"I had a wonderful time." Billie circled her fingers around the hair at the nape of his neck. It gave him goosebumps.

"Me too." Again, she entranced him with her eyes.

"Is your offer for the tour and supper still open?" Billie pulled him slowly down to her.

"Most definitely." Mike ran his tongue across her bottom lip and gently bit it.

"Is it possible not to be interrupted by your brother?" She said against his mouth.

"I'll deadbolt all the doors, but I'm afraid Keith has a key." Mike chuckled when she groaned.

"I don't normally sleep with someone on a second date." Billie pulled back and gazed into his eyes. "But with you, it seems like I've known you all my life."

"I never thought that of you, Billie but I want you to know that I've never wanted anyone the way I do you. I'm no angel but the one thing I am is honest, and I wouldn't tell you that if it wasn't true."

"I should let you go. You've got a bit of a drive." Billie smiled, but she didn't move.

"It only takes fifteen minutes." Mike brushed his lips against hers.

"Text me to let me know you got home safe." She kissed him

again.

"I will." Mike kissed her once more and reluctantly stepped back and let his arms drop.

"Goodnight, Mike." Billie opened the door, stepped inside and waved as she slowly closed the door.

"Yep, I'm hooked," Mike mumbled to himself as he jogged back to his car.

# *Chapter 14*

"Earth to Billie." Abbie waved her hand in front of Billie's face.

*Damn.*

She'd been daydreaming again and missed most of what Abbie had said. It was something about a house being sold or was it a condo.

"Girl, you really got it bad." Abbie chuckled as she hopped up on her desk and crossed her legs.

"I'm sorry, I've just got a ton of things on my mind." That wasn't technically a lie but the only thing on her mind at that moment was a certain blue-eyed lawyer that was picking her up at lunch.

"Honey, that smile on your face tells me you are only thinking about Hottie McHottersen." Abbie teased.

"It's just all so fast. We only had one date but we've talked every night this week, and he keeps sending me these cute little texts." Billie held up her phone to show Abbie the last text she'd received.

"I'm counting the minutes until I see you today. It's one hundred and ninety-five in case you wanted to know." Abbie read it and fanned herself. "Well, that's just the most romantic thing I've ever read."

"I know, and every time my phone beeps my heart beats a mile a minute when I see his name." Billie covered her face because no man had ever had this effect on her and it scared her a little.

"Billie, with everything that's happened over the last couple of months, be thankful that something good came out of it. I'm not saying Mike's your forever and I'm not saying he's not. Just grab onto this happiness and roll with it."

To hear Abbie speak with such passion was surprising. She didn't typically, but it seemed Peggy's death had their whole circle realizing how someone can be ripped from the world so quickly.

"I wish the police knew who killed Peggy." Billie gazed out through the large picture window at the front of the office.

"Me too," Abbie whispered.

An hour later her phone buzzed again, but this time it was a text from her landlord. Billie hadn't been inside the house since the night she found Peggy. Mr. Wells wanted her to pay to have the house cleaned entirely before she handed over the keys. He'd been texting her every day, and she was sure he was starting to get pissed.

Before she had a chance to open the text, the front door of the office opened and in walked Byron Wells. Billie didn't want to deal with him at that moment, but she at least owed him a proposed date of when she would have her things cleared out, and the keys turned back over.

"Mr. Wells, I was just about to text you back." Billie stood up and walked around her desk.

"Belinda, I realize that it's a traumatic time, but I need that house available so that I can get another tenant in there." His voice raised with a heavy rasp from obvious years of smoking. He rubbed his hand over his thinning hair as his eyes dropped to her breasts. Billie rolled her eyes because the man never looked at her face.

"I've paid the rent up to the end of next month, so that means I've got a little over a month and a half to vacate." It always pissed Billie off when he'd ogle her.

"But I want my house back." He still hadn't raised his eyes from her chest.

"If you're willing to refund one month's rent with my damage deposit, I'll make sure you have the keys by the end of this month." That statement got his attention because his eyes looked like they were about to pop out of his head as they snapped up to meet hers.

"You don't expect me to pay you back the damage deposit?" He shouted.

"Of course, I do, there isn't any damage to the house." Billie kept her voice calm.

"Someone was murdered in my house." He continued to yell.

"Yes, my best friend but the house wasn't damaged. So, you need to make that choice. As I said, give me back the rent for next month and my damage deposit, and I'll give you back the keys the end of this month." Billie crossed her arms across her chest mostly to hide her breasts from his gawking.

"Fine, but I want my keys by the end of next month." He snapped. "But don't expect me to give you a good reference."

He stomped out through the door, and Billie let out a huge breath. As much as she loved the house she'd rented from him, the man gave her the major creeps. Not that he'd ever done anything.

"I've got a feeling he's going to give you a fight when you demand your damage deposit." Abbie stood behind her as they watched Byron stomp across the street and get into his car.

"At this point, I want to tell him to keep it and never go inside again." Billie walked to the small table where they kept the coffee pot.

"You need to get your things, Billie. Plus, I'm sure there's some stuff there Chloe would like to have that belonged to Peggy." Abbie stood next to her and pulled her into a huge hug. "If you need someone to go inside with you, I'm sure Dana and I can help."

"I'm not going to worry about it until next week." Billie sighed as she hugged her friend back.

"That man gives me the creeps but look on the bright side, seventy-three minutes until Hottie McHottersen." Abbie pulled back and wiggled her eyebrows. Leave it to Abbie to make her laugh.

Matt had come and picked up her car so she wouldn't have to leave it in the parking lot. Her brother still seemed like he had the weight of the world on his shoulders. The bags under his eyes and the tension in his posture filled her with concern.

"Now, if you need me to pick you up, call me." Matt pulled her into a huge hug.

"Mike said he'd bring me home." Billie rolled her eyes.

"I know, but you never know. His car could break down, or you may have to kick him in the nuts for getting too handsy." Matt let her go and stepped back.

"Thanks for the vote of confidence, Matt." Mike's chuckle had Billie moving to look around her brother,

"Just making sure my little sister knows she won't be stuck if you get out of line." Matt pointed his finger at Mike.

"Just so you know, I'd never do anything to hurt your sister or make her feel uncomfortable. I don't understand why you think otherwise." Mike and Matt stared at each other.

"Oh, for the love of God. Let me check and see if I've got a ruler in my office so you two can take them out and see who's bigger." Abbie grumbled from behind Billie.

"No need for that. Matt and I've got an understanding." Mike reached out his hand to Matt, and for a moment Billie thought Matt was going to slap it away.

"As long as you understand she gets hurt. You get hurt." Matt took Mike's hand and shook it.

"Matt, you can go now." Billie shoved her brother toward the exit.

"By the way, Matt. You'll have the revised birth certificate for Chloe by next week." Mike's words brought both Billie and Matt to a halt.

"Really?" For the first time since the whole situation happened Billie saw the emotion in his eyes.

"Yes," Mike smiled at him.

"Thanks, Mike." Matt nodded and then hurried outside.

"I think you just gained some points with my brother." Billie walked toward Mike.

"I didn't do it to get points." Mike rested his hands on her hips and pulled her close to him.

"I know Matt appreciates it." Billie linked her arms around his neck and pulled his head down to meet hers.

Billie brushed her lips against his and sighed because she'd craved the touch of his lips all day. He placed quick kisses on her lips, and every time she'd try to deepen one of them he'd pull back and grin.

"Mike," Billie growled when he pulled back again.

"What?" He gave her a quick kiss again on her lips.

"I want a kiss." She narrowed her eyes and tried to tug him closer.

"I just gave you like a dozen." He chuckled.

"They weren't kisses; they were pecks." Billie groaned.

The next thing she knew he dipped her and covered her mouth with his. He devoured her mouth sliding his tongue into her mouth and swirling it against hers. The kiss wasn't rough but demanding. Almost as if it was a promise as to what was to come.

"Is that what you call a kiss?" Mike pulled his lips from hers and stood her back up straight.

"Ummm, wow." Billie sighed

"Now that was one hell of a kiss. I think I need a cold shower." Abbie fanned herself.

They stopped at a couple of places before they headed out of town to Hopedale. Since neither of them had lunch, Mike picked up a couple of sandwiches, and they ate them on the way. They talked most of the way, but Billie took in the beautiful scenery while they drove. She didn't get to enjoy it when she drove there a few months before and certainly not when she zoomed out of the town.

"It's so pretty out this way," Billie spoke softly almost with reverence.

"Yes, it is, but when you grow up here, you don't notice it until you leave and have to deal with the craziness of the big city." Mike pulled off the highway, and Billie saw the huge sign that said, 'Welcome to the town of Hopedale.'

"I don't know how you wouldn't notice being almost surrounded by the ocean." Billie motioned with her hand.

"Because people who live here see it every day." Mike pulled into the driveway of his property and parked the car.

"I don't know how anyone could get tired to this." Billie sighed.

"I'll never get tired of the beauty." Mike grasped her hand and kissed it.

"I was talking about Hopedale." She smiled.

"And I was talking about you." Mike leaned into her and brushed his lips across hers.

"You're smooth, aren't you?" Billie jumped at the sound of the strange voice.

Mike glanced over Billie's shoulder and groaned. It made Billie turn her head and come face to face with a beautiful auburn-haired woman.

"Hi, Emily." Mike pulled back and got out of the car. Was this woman one of Mike's former lovers or possibly current one? He'd sworn that he hadn't been with anyone in a long time.

"I was just on my way back to the salon." Emily smiled at Billie as Mike opened the door.

"Home to have a quickie for lunch." Mike laughed.

"Oh, Mike, Keith and I don't do quickies. We have marathons." Emily winked and held out her hand. "I'm Keith's wife, Emily. You must be Billie."

"It's nice to meet you." Billie tried to keep her relief hidden.

"Emily and Keith live just beyond that path." Mike pointed to an opening in the trees. "It seems Emily has started using it as a shortcut."

"Hey, I've started walking back and forth to work because it's summer." Emily slapped his arm. "And I wanted to make sure that things are still going ahead tomorrow."

"Yep, if everyone is still up to it." Mike pulled Billie into his side.

"Okay, we'll see you tomorrow then." Emily waved as she hurried down the driveway. "It was nice to meet you, Billie. Hopefully, we can have a longer chat tomorrow."

Billie didn't say anything as Mike led her to the front door of his home. She'd seen it the day she came to see Matt, but she never got to get a closer look. The ranch-style house's deck circled the entire thing. The front door was a dark oak with a large window with what looked like a sailboat etched into it.

"That door is beautiful." Billie smoothed her hands over the boat as Mike led her inside.

"My grandfather was a fisherman, and I wanted something of him in my house." Mike closed the door and grasped her hand.

"That's sweet."

The front foyer was not overly large but to the left was a closet, and on the right, a table stood against the wall underneath a large oval mirror. As they moved further into the house, it opened into a large open area that was obviously the living area.

"Mike, this is incredible." Billie turned around.

"Your brother did a great job." Mike shrugged out of his suit jacket and hung it over a chair.

"Matt did this?" Billie never realized her brother was so talented.

"He's the one who designed the layout. According to Keith he walked in and had a rough drawing done within fifteen minutes." Mike explained. "He really should have been an architect."

"He always liked to draw growing up." The memory of Matt's room when they were kids flooded her thoughts. He would draw things and pin them up on the wall, but she never realized he still used that talent. With everything she'd found out about him over the last few days, she was beginning to believe she didn't know her brother at all.

Mike gave Billie the grand tour including all four bedrooms, although only two had furniture in them. He explained that he was still deciding what to do with the other two rooms. The view from the master bedroom was incredible. Trees surrounded the large backyard.

"I love this view. I can see the ocean from here but then again no matter where you are in Hopedale, you can see that." Mike wrapped his arm around her, and she turned to face him.

"It's a beautiful place." Billie pressed her hands against his chest and gazed up into his face.

"It feels more beautiful with you here." She could feel his heart thudding against his chest.

"Is this crazy?" Billie met his intense stare.

"What?" He pushed her hair behind her ear and ran his finger down to her neck.

"This. You. Me." Billie sighed when he lowered his head and lightly brushed his lips against her ear.

"I don't know if it's crazy but I know I've never wanted anything or anyone more." His hot breath feathered across her neck causing goosebumps and setting her on fire at the same time.

"I want you too." Billie didn't know when she'd started to unbutton his shirt but her hands pressed against his warm skin and his pectoral muscles flexed as her fingers explored his body.

"Billie," His voice sounded strained as his mouth covered hers and he pulled her flush against his hard body.

He devoured her mouth and plunged his tongue between her lips. Billie slipped his shirt off his shoulders and slid her hands across his shoulders until they met at the back of his neck. They were getting carried away, but she didn't care. His hand slid down to cup her ass and pull her tighter against the proof of his arousal. His other hand slid slowly under her shirt, and the heat of his touch was like a brand against her skin that made her gasp with need.

"Billie," Mike groaned against her lips as she pushed him back toward his bed.

When the back of his legs touched the bed, he lifted her, spun around and eased her back on the bed. She felt the loss as soon as he released her to rip off the rest of his shirt. She gazed at the perfection of his torso and the tattoo wrapped around his left side under his chest. She wasn't sure what it was, but it was sexy as hell. There was another on his shoulder that looked like some sort of tribal thing. It was hard to concentrate, especially when he unbuckled his belt, opened his dress pants and let them drop to the floor. Once he'd rid himself of his shoes and socks, he eased himself onto the bed and hovered above her. Her body vibrated with need, and there was still more clothing between them then she wanted, but when she grabbed the bottom of her shirt to remove it, he stopped her.

"Beautiful, that's my job." He grinned as he knelt between her legs. Slowly his hands slid under her shirt, and he eased it up her body at the same time he placed soft kisses across her stomach as he exposed her bare skin inch by inch.

"Mike, you're driving me crazy." Billie squirmed under him when he finally pushed her shirt over her head and tossed it to the floor.

"I'm only getting started." He winked, and she didn't know whether to kiss him or kill him.

The appreciation in his intense blue eyes told her he wasn't as in control as he tried to make her believe. He shook when she snaked her arms around him and lightly dragged her nails down his back. She could feel his arousal pressed against her leg and it only made the ache between her thighs grow.

"Now who's driving who crazy?" Mike groaned as she rubbed her leg against his hard cock.

Billie pulled him down and his mouth covered hers as they wiggled and squirmed to remove the rest of the clothing that prevented his bare skin from touching hers. She knew Mike had been around the block a lot and frankly she was no white virgin herself but something inside her screamed that what was about to happen between them was so much more than just two people giving in to their desire.

*Could it be, more?*

# Chapter 15

Mike hadn't planned to go this far when he showed Billie around the house but when she looked up at him with those brown eyes something struck him right in the chest. He didn't want to admit it, but he knew without a doubt what it was. He'd heard his brothers talk about it when they first knew.

The urge to be close to Billie overwhelmed him, and he wasn't sure he liked the loss of control. Who was he kidding? He loved it. His cock was painfully hard, and it took everything he had not to explode before he was inside her.

"How are you so perfectly sexy?" Billie nibbled on his earlobe.

Mike squeezed his eyes shut and bit his lip to keep control of his urge to ejaculate every time she did that. He pulled back with a shudder when her tongue swirled around the outer edge of his ear.

"Billie, have you looked in the mirror lately because you're like a wet dream come true." Mike's gaze traveled down the length of Billie's naked body. Her breasts were round and firm with dark nipples that called out for him to suck. Mike didn't want to disappoint and lowered his head to suck one into his mouth.

Billie arched off the bed. He loved that her breasts were so responsive because he was a boob man. When he moved to the other, she moaned his name, and it was the first time he'd ever loved hearing his name.

"Fucking, beautiful." Mike groaned when she grabbed the back of his head and tugged on his hair.

"I need more." Billie gasped.

"Tell me, Beautiful." Mike licked one nipple then the other.

"I want you inside me." She pleaded.

Mike covered her mouth with his and pulled her body tightly against his. He wanted inside her more than he wanted to breathe. His heart raced, and part of it was because of his arousal, but part of it was because he was terrified. Yes, Mike O'Connor was terrified because he knew when he entered her his life would never be the same.

"Billie," He groaned when his hand slipped between her legs slid his finger through her wetness.

"Mike," She gasped as his finger slid easily inside her heat.

"You're so wet, baby. It makes me so fucking hot." Mike pushed a second finger inside her and pressed his thumb against her clitoris.

"Yes, right…. ahh…there." Billie's back arched off the bed,

and Mike watched her face as he brought her to orgasm. "Oh…my…. yes."

"So fucking gorgeous." Mike was in awe as he watched her come apart.

"I want to feel you inside me, Mike." Billie panted.

Mike pulled his hand from between her legs and licked the moisture from his fingers. They were both beyond the point where he could dive between her thighs, but he needed to taste her. He reached into the nightstand to grab the unopened box of condoms and tore the box open with his teeth. His hands shook as he pulled out a strip because he wanted her so bad.

"Let me put it on." Billie pushed herself up on her elbows and reached for the strip he held.

"Not now. If I let you touch me now, I'll lose it." Mike tore the condom open and rolled it on.

He knelt between her legs and cupped his hands under her knees and yanked her toward him. His cock was next to the entrance of her sex, and he moved forward just enough that the tip slid between her folds and her eyes closed.

"Billie, open your eyes. I want to look into them when I slide inside." Mike hovered over her as her eyes fluttered open.

Slowly he slid inside her and kept his eyes locked with hers. When she ran her nails down the length of his back, it made it hard to keep his own eyes open, especially when he felt her clench around him.

"Ahh... Mike don't stop." Billie moaned as she arched up against him.

"That's it, Beautiful." Mike groaned.

He slowly pumped in and out, but he wasn't sure exactly how long he would be able to hold on. Billie's heat surrounded his cock, and her soft moans had him ready to explode. He slid one hand between them and pressed his finger against her sensitive nub. Within thirty seconds she dug her nails into his ass and screamed his name as her sex tightened around him and that was it. Mike shook as he exploded inside her.

"Fuck. Yes. Billie." Mike moaned.

He dropped his head into the crook of her neck as he rode out the last of his orgasm. For a minute, he thought it wouldn't stop but when her body relaxed under him, and her hands fell to her sides he slowly pushed himself up.

"That was intense." Billie sighed and ran a finger across his lower lip.

Mike hooked his arm under her waist and rolled over, so she was on top of him. She pressed her lips against his chest, and he tucked his hands under his head. He studied the first woman in his life to ever take his heart.

"I don't know if I'm going to be able to move anymore." Mike smiled because the muscles in his body still twitched.

"Well, you did promise me food, so you better move at some point." Billie folded her hands across his chest and rested her chin on them.

"I'll order pizza if I got to." Mike couldn't tear his eyes away from hers.

"Right now, I could eat the leg off of the lamb of God." Billie laughed.

"Hey, Mike." A deep voice echoed from the front of the house.

Billie rolled off him with a gasp and jumped off the bed. He was on his feet but wasn't quite as frantic as Billie was because he knew the voice. He grabbed a pair of jeans and a T-shirt from his dresser and turned just in time to see Billie spinning in the middle of his room with her clothes held tightly to the front of her body.

"I can't find my underwear," Billie whispered.

"Mike, you have about two minutes before Nan gets here. You better get that ass covered." James shouted.

"Your grandmother's coming here?" Billie looked about ready to jump out the window and run.

"Get dressed. Don't worry my brother will stall her if we aren't out in time." Mike yanked on his shirt.

"That's great because my panties have vanished." Billie tossed the blankets off the bed.

Mike scanned the floor and the bed for her missing undies, but he didn't find them anywhere. Billie mumbled something under her breath, but Mike caught the tail end of it and burst into laughter.

"Yes, Mike's grandmother I do make a habit of losing my underwear." Billie frantically fastened her bra and pulled her shirt on but she was still naked from the waist down, and Mike couldn't help himself. He grabbed her by the hips and spun her around.

"Calm down," Mike whispered.

"I can't find my freaking underwear, and your brother is down the hall, and if my calculations are correct, your grandmother will be here in less than a minute." Billie bounced back and forth from one foot to another.

"She just pulled in the driveway, Mikey boy," James shouted.

"Fuck," Billie groaned and then bit her lip.

Mike took one more look around his room and finally located the missing undies. In their frenzy of undressing her panties had landed on top of his bedpost. Mike turned her around and pointed toward them.

"Well, if we tried to do that it would never work." Billie laughed and jumped on top of the bed. It looked sexy as hell to see her naked ass scurry across his bed.

"I'll head Nan off and tell her you're in the bathroom. Although, I've got no idea what she's doing here today." Billie disappeared into the ensuite as he closed the bedroom door.

James stood in the foyer with his hands tucked into his front pockets and a huge grin on his face. Something told Mike Nanny Betty wasn't as close as James said.

"It's a good thing Keith stalled her." James chuckled.

"Why the fuck is she coming today?" Mike turned into the kitchen.

"The fence building tomorrow. Nan's bringing over some of the food today." James said it as if Mike should have realized it and the truth, he should have.

"Does she know I have company?" Mike glanced out the front window to check for Nanny Betty's arrival.

"Why do you think I'm here?" James chuckled. "You weren't answering your phone, so Keith and I put two and two together."

"Thanks, bro." Mike was so glad he had brothers that had his back.

"So, are you hiding her?" James motioned toward Mike's room.

"No, she had to…" Mike stopped when Billie appeared.

"Make myself presentable." Billie smiled.

"James this is Billie Carter. Billie this is one of my older brothers, James."

"Very pleased to meet you." James held out his hand.

"It's great to meet you since you just saved me from a huge embarrassment." Billie shook his hand, and James laughed.

"Hey, we've all learned to protect each other from Nan's surprise visits." James laughed.

"I tried stalling her but…" Keith burst in through the door and stopped. "Oh, okay. So no more stalling necessary."

Mike and James laughed, and Billie smiled because Keith looked like he'd ran the entire way from his parent's place. He yanked open the fridge and pulled out a bottle of water and gulped it down in about ten seconds.

"Looks like you're getting a little out of shape there, big brother." Mike teased.

"I'm in perfectly fine shape, but you try running from mom and dad's place with biker boots, jeans, and a leather jacket. Asshole, we could've just let nan show up and surprise you." Keith pointed the empty bottle at Mike.

"I think we owe you a huge thank you, Keith." Billie rested her hands on the counter in front of her.

"You're welcome, honey." Keith smiled at her. "You not so much." Keith tossed the stopper of the bottle at Mike and dropped the bottle in the recycling bucket next to the fridge.

Before Mike could respond, the front door flew open and Tom walked in with a huge box. James was the first to relieve him of what looked like a cumbersome box.

"Thanks, James." Tom sighed. "Your grandmother said to get outside and bring in the rest of the boxes and bags."

"On it." Mike jogged out through the door followed by Keith.

He prayed Billie didn't get spooked by Nanny Betty because the truth was, he loved his grandmother, but sometimes she could be a little too blunt. The last thing he wanted was Billie to feel insulted by her.

*Grandda help me.*

# Chapter 16

James placed the box on the counter and followed Mike outside. Billie started for the door, but the older man stopped her.

"My dear, don't let Betty see you try to lug in those boxes with the boys around." The man smiled at her and held out his hand. "I'm Tom Roberts."

"Billie Carter," Billie shook the man's hand, and he held it for a moment as he cupped his other hand over hers and smiled.

"It's a pleasure to meet you." He tapped her hand and then released it. "It's good to see Mike finally settling down."

"Oh, no we just started… I mean… we don't know…." Billie sighed when the man chuckled.

"I understand." Tom nodded toward the door.

A small gray-haired woman scurried into the kitchen holding a black purse in one hand and supermarket bag in the other. Billie quickly relieved her of the bag and was shocked at how heavy it was. For such a tiny woman, she didn't lack strength.

"Tank you, ducky." The woman dropped her purse on the counter next to where Billie placed the bag. "Now let me get a look at ya."

Before Billie could move the little woman she assumed was Mike's grandmother cupped Billie's face in her hands. She stared into Billie's eyes for a moment, then nodded, and smiled.

"Our Mikey's a good lad. He'll take good care a' ya." She turned around, and that was it. She started to pull things out of the bag and store it on the counter next to the stove.

"Ummm… Do you need any help, Mrs. O'Connor?" Billie glanced back and forth between Nanny Betty and Tom.

"First ting ya need ta know is, Mrs. O'Connor was me mudder in law, and she was a witch. Me girls call me Nan or Nanny Betty." With that statement, Nanny Betty went back to her unpacking.

Billie turned when she heard Mike's voice. He returned with Keith and James as well as another man who was obviously another brother. What the hell did they have in the water in Hopedale because the men were all hot as hell?

"How the hell did you find a woman like that?" The man winked at her.

"Nicky, shut yar yap and bring over dat box." Nanny Betty tossed the empty bag toward Tom and pointed to the counter in front of her.

Billie couldn't help but laugh when the man pressed his lips together and obeyed his grandmother. Nanny Betty reminded her a lot of her late grandmother, and she had to blink to keep tears from forming in her eyes.

"Billie, this is Betty O'Connor." Mike wrapped his arm around his grandmother

"We kind of met already but it's really nice to meet you…. Ummmm…. Nan." Billie wasn't making the same mistake twice.

"Looks like nan already gave her the speech." James laughed.

"I'm the better-looking brother, but you can call me Nick." He was as cocky as the brother she'd met the week before.

"Or at least the more conceited brother." Mike moved next to Billie and wrapped his arm around her shoulder. She didn't miss the possessive move, but she also didn't dislike it.

"It's nice to meet you, Nick, but you should know I think you're all quite handsome." Billie laughed when Mike growled in her ear.

"How many of us have you met?" Keith asked.

"Mike, of course. You, Nick, James, and A.J." Billie stopped for a minute and then held up her finger. "Oh, and I met John when…"

"I'm sorry about your friend." Nick's cocky attitude disappeared, and genuine compassion replaced it.

"Thank you." Billie swallowed the lump that formed in her throat. The same one that showed up every time she thought about

Peggy.

"Doncha worry, ducky. Between Johnny and da rest of me b'ys, dey'll find dat sleeven dat hurt yar friend." Sleeven was a term she'd heard many times growing up in Newfoundland. It was a nice way of saying asshole. Nanny Betty scurried over to Billie and took her hands. "Yar one a us now."

Something about the way the woman looked at her had a tear slip from Billie's eye because it was the first time in a long time she felt like just maybe they'd find out who killed her friend.

"Until den, we're all here fer yar family and you." Nanny Betty gave her a gentle hug and stepped back. "Now, tell yar mudder and fadder dere more den welcome ta join us here tamara'"

"What exactly is going on here tomorrow?" Billie cleared her throat glad Nanny Betty had changed the subject.

"It's kind of a housewarming as well as a fence building party." Mike laughed. "I was going to ask you today but I got ... distracted."

Billie felt the heat rise in her cheeks and turned away from the grinning faces of Mike's brothers. They obviously knew what kind of distraction Mike meant.

"Basically, Mike gets free fence building labor and Nan, Mom and my aunts feed us all. Then when the work gets done, we'll pull out the instruments and have a little party." Nick explained.

"Pull out the instruments?" Billie glanced back and forth

between Mike and Nick.

"Mike didn't tell you about our band?" Nick laughed.

"Yeah, okay." Billie rolled her eyes because Nick had to be pulling her leg.

"I'm serious." Nick almost seemed offended that she didn't believe him.

"Billie, we do sing in a band." Mike chuckled. "It's one we put together about ten years ago. We play at functions to raise money for charities."

"You and your brothers have a band?" Billie stared at Mike.

"Not all my brothers. It's John, Nick, A.J. and myself along with a couple of friends." She must have had a weird expression because Mike laughed.

"Not dat all my b'ys can't sing. Keithy here used ta sing solo at church when he was a youngster." Nanny Betty pat her hand against Keith's massive arm.

"Nan, I'm sure Billie doesn't want to hear about us singing at church." The big burly Keith actually blushed.

"Ya should bring da little one too and yar brudders." Nanny Betty grabbed her purse and turned to Tom who quietly stood in the background.

"Are you ready, Love?" He looked at Nanny Betty with such love and affection that Billie felt a little guilty standing there witnessing it.

"Now, Mikey, doncha touch any a dat stuff. Me and yar mudder'll be here in da mornin' to start cookin'" Nanny Betty turned toward her grandsons. Each one of them kissed her on the cheek. "I'll see ya tamara." Then she was gone as quickly as she came.

"Well, we should get outta here. The guys were here this morning to set the posts so we should be able to start putting up the rails in the morning." Keith said.

"Between your guys and us, we should get it done in a few hours," James said to Keith.

"Are we painting it too?" Nick asked.

"No, it's composite," Keith said.

"What the hell is that?" Mike asked.

"You said you wanted a fence that was maintenance free. Composite is like plastic, but it looks like wood." Keith sighed. "Just trust me it's going to look good."

While Mike walked his brothers out, Billie made her way to the back of the house and looked around. The yard was huge, and she could see where the posts stood. She wondered why a single man would want such a huge yard, but part of her hoped it was for the same reason she would want one.

She'd always dreamed of having a huge family, but she was twenty-nine. Not that she was hearing the clang of her biological clock, but she would at least like to have a child before she got too old.

There was just one thing that kept her from being completely happy. Someone had murdered her friend and took her brother's chance at happiness. She prayed Nanny Betty was right and her grandsons could find the bastard that killed Peggy.

"Can you picture it?" Billie jumped when Mike wrapped his arms around her from behind.

"Your fence?" Billie leaned back against his hard body and relaxed.

"Kids running around." Billie turned her head so fast that she actually felt a click in her neck. Did she just hear him right?

"Kids?"

"Yeah, I've got a lot of nieces and nephews. I want a place to keep them contained when they come to visit." Mike chuckled.

"You're a good uncle." Billie forced a smile.

"I try to be." Mike turned her around and pulled her into his arms. "I'd like to be a father someday too."

"You would?" Billie gazed up into his eyes.

"I never thought I would. Until I met you." Mike whispered.

"How can we be talking about things like this? We hardly know each other." Billie reached up and cupped his cheek.

"I know everything I need to know. I know I've never felt like this before." Mike pressed his forehead against hers, and she could hardly breathe as he spoke. It was as if he read her thoughts.

"Me either."

"It seems crazy, doesn't it?" Mike kissed her cheek.

"Yes." Billie linked her fingers behind his neck.

"I don't care how crazy it is. I just know I'm head over heels in love with you." Mike pulled back and gazed into her eyes.

"It's crazy, but I love you too." Billie pulled him down so she could brush her lips against his.

Mike took over from there and covered her mouth with his. His kiss was tender and told her his words were from his heart. For the first time in her life, Billie felt as if all her hopes and dreams would come true. Mike picked her up in his arms, and she wrapped her legs around his waist as she pulled back from his kiss.

"I know I promised you supper, but right now, I need to make love to you." Mike walked back into the house and closed the sliding door.

"We can eat anytime." Billie gasped when he kissed his way up the side of her neck and sucked her earlobe into his mouth.

When Mike eased her back on the bed, the only thing she could think about was making love to the man she loved.

# *Chapter 17*

Mike stood in his kitchen and stared through the patio door. The sun appeared over the horizon, and the sight was hypnotizing. Although, he knew if anyone saw him they'd think he lost his mind because he couldn't wipe the huge smile off his face. Billie did that.

When he'd reluctantly drove her home the previous night, he couldn't stop touching her. He held her hand the entire way, and she'd laughed when he continued to ask her if he'd told her how much he loved her. It was a wonder she didn't run from the car considering how he was acting but she smiled and said she liked to hear it.

It was a little after six in the morning, and he had a full day of work, family, and craziness ahead of him. He could have sworn Sunday's were supposed to be a day of rest.

He poured another coffee and brought it to his room to get ready for the day. It seemed stupid to shower since he was going to be doing manual labor most of the morning, so he just pulled on an old pair of jeans and T-shirt.

He just walked out of his room when his front door opened and Keith and Emily walked in. She had a huge grin on her face, and Keith looked like the cat who ate the canary.

"You two do realize that it's like seven am?" Mike chuckled.

"Yeah, we were a little excited this morning." Emily looked about ready to bust.

"I can see that." Mike poured two more cups of coffee and started another pot. Keith grabbed one, but Emily declined.

"I'm trying to cut down on the caffeine." She hopped up on the stool next to the counter and gave Keith a wink.

Mike glanced back and forth between the couple. They were still newlyweds, but this was strange even for them. Then it hit him.

"You're pregnant." Mike pointed a finger and grinned.

"How did you know?" Emily gasped and covered her belly with her hands. "I'm not showing."

"Princess, the glowing smile, no coffee and up before ten on a Sunday. Mike's not stupid." Keith wrapped his arm around her shoulders and kissed the top of her head.

"I wanted to surprise everyone after supper." Emily slouched and pouted.

"I won't say a word, but you've got bad poker face." Mike laughed as he kissed her cheek. "Congrats to both of you."

The O'Connors were multiplying quickly. Nobody knew how

much Mike wanted a family of his own. He always teased his brothers about being tied down, but the truth was they were lucky bastards.

Billie flashed in his mind, and he couldn't help but smile. He finally understood what it felt like to love someone so much you wanted to be with them every minute.

"Speaking of glowing smiles." Emily put her elbows on the counter and rested her chin in her fists. "How's Billie?"

"She's amazing, beautiful and will be here in a few hours." Mike sipped his coffee.

"Ah ha." Emily turned in the seat and pointed at Keith. "I told you."

"Fine, I'll clean the cat's litter box." Keith rolled his eyes.

"You've got to do that anyway now. I'm pregnant." Emily poked Keith in the ribs. "I'll think of a payment later."

"What are you two talking about?" Mike shook his head in confusion.

"I told your brother last week you got bit by the love bug." Emily grinned.

"I swear, Aunt Cora is rubbing off on all the women of this family." Keith laughed.

"Oh, hush. I'm happy for you Mike. It is good to see you settling down. Maybe it will rub off on Nick and A.J." Emily rolled her eyes.

"I wouldn't hold my breath on A.J., but I think Nick might have his eye on someone." Keith put his cup in Mike's sink.

"Oh?" Emily wiggled on the stool. "Tell me."

"Jesus, woman. I said might." Keith sighed. "So, I told the guys to be here by eight."

Keith knew something about Nick he wasn't about to share. It was strange Nick hadn't talked to Mike about it, but then again Mike had been a little distracted.

An hour later his brothers and the guys that weren't on jobs from Keith's security firm showed up ready to work. The truck with the supplies for the fence pulled into the driveway around the same time, and everyone went to work unloading it.

A short time later his house filled with the rest of his family. The older kids played in the front of the house, and the younger ones were on the front deck with his brother's wives. His mother, grandmother, and aunts had taken up residence in the kitchen to prepare way too much food, and his father and uncles were helping with the fence.

Mike stepped back from where he'd just nailed up another panel and scanned the yard. It was impressive to see that they were more than halfway done. As he was about to pick up another board, his phone buzzed in his pocket. He smiled when he read the text from Billie.

*We're almost there. Are you sure it's okay for all of us to come?*

*Do you want my grandmother to answer that?*

*Umm... no. We're just turning off the highway.*

*I'll be out front, Beautiful.*

Mike slid his hammer into his tool belt and jogged up to the house. He had almost made it inside when he heard a shout from the far end of his yard.

"Hey, slacker. Bring out some more drinks." Aaron shook an empty water bottle.

"Billie's almost here. I'm meeting her out front. Come get it yourself lazy ass." Mike didn't wait for Aaron's answer as he closed the patio door.

"I can't wait to meet her, Mike." Cora stopped Mike before he got to the front door.

"You've already met her, Cora." His mother grinned.

"She has?" Mike stopped.

"Yes. It's Marg Carter's daughter." His mother raised an eyebrow at Cora and Mike was confused as to the little exchange.

"Right again," Cora stated and went back to making sandwiches.

Mike didn't have time to question his mother and aunt because he just wanted to get out front to see Billie. It hadn't been twenty-four hours, but he missed her.

He groaned when he got outside, and Stephanie and Sandy had already greeted Billie as she arrived. A crowbar would be needed to pry those two away from his woman.

"Don't worry; I'm sure they'll let you kiss her hello." Mike turned around. James wife Marina sat on a chair bouncing Sandy's little boy on her knee.

"Watch that kid. He likes to spit up on people." Mike laughed

"That's why he's faced away from me." Marina winked.

Billie looked up and met his gaze as he jogged toward the car. She smiled and squeezed through Stephanie and Sandy who'd started to chat with Billie's grandfather. Mike pulled her into him as soon as he was next to her.

"I hope you don't mind the audience, but I want to kiss you now." Mike cupped her cheek in one hand.

"I don't think anyone will care." Billie smiled and stood up on her toes.

Mike brushed his lips against hers entirely meaning to keep it rated PG, but as soon as his lips touched hers, he pulled her closer and covered her mouth with his. Billie moaned into his mouth as he slid his hand behind her head and tilted it so he could have better access.

"Hey, you two, kids watching," Sandy shouted.

Billie pulled away first and pressed her head against his chin.

Mike looked over her head at his sister-in-law. She laughed and linked her arm into Stephanie.

"We'll finish that later," Mike whispered as he turned around and waved at her parents. They both smiled and followed Stephanie toward the house. Sandy pushed Frank's chair towards the steps. Mike kissed Billie's cheek just before he ran up to help Philip and Matt carry it up over the steps.

Chloe walked next to Marg and stared back at Mike's nieces and nephews in the front yard. Mike crouched in front of Chloe.

"Do you want to go play with them?" Mike signed.

Chloe shrugged and looked up at Billie as she moved next to the little girl.

"It's okay. I'll introduce you." Mike wanted her to feel comfortable.

"They can't talk to me." Chloe signed back and lowered her head.

Before Mike could answer Lily ran up the steps next to Mike. His niece turned around and glanced back at Sandy.

"Go ahead, honey." Sandy smiled.

"My name is Lily." His niece signed slowly but correctly.

"She heard about the little girl and asked if she could learn how to talk to her." Sandy smoothed back the little girl's strawberry blonde curls.

"That's wonderful, Lily." Billie crouched and took his niece's hand.

"I only started yesterday, but I'm gonna practice every day." Lily smiled at Chloe as Mike signed what she said.

"You learned sign language so you could talk to me." Chloe looked completely surprised.

"You're our family." Lily signed

"She picked it up fast." Billie's eyes went wide with surprise.

"She tends to do that. Lily has an eidetic memory." Sandy explained.

"That's incredible," Matt said from behind Mike.

"Keith has it too." Mike glanced over his shoulder at Billie's brother.

"Great, everyone needs a boss who doesn't forget anything." Matt groaned.

Chloe hesitantly followed Lily down the steps but relaxed as Lily introduced her to the rest of the kids. His nieces and nephews amazed him. They sat in the grass and Lily helped them spell each of their names for Chloe.

"That child is an angel." Marg linked into Mike's arm and smiled. "I think she's a lot like her uncle, Mike."

"I don't know about that." Mike laughed.

"I do. I remember you being the same way when Lyle came into our class." Marg gave his arm a little squeeze and turned when his mother called out to her. "You've always had a heart of gold young man." Then she was gone.

Mike didn't know if what Marg said was true, but he was glad that Chloe was at ease. When he turned around to head back into the house his brother's wives, his cousins, and Billie stared at him with huge grins.

"What?" Mike eyed them suspiciously. If there was one thing, he knew when all those women were together there was trouble.

"Billie was just saying how sexy she finds a man in a tool belt." Stephanie raised an eyebrow.

"Yeah, it makes you wonder how they use those tools." Emily plopped her elbows on her knees and rested her chin on her fists.

"I'll show you how I use my tools later, Princess," Keith growled from behind Mike.

"I love how you use those tools, baby." Emily winked at her husband.

"Oh, for the love of God. I don't want to hear this shit." Jess gagged.

"I mean I love my cousins but Emily T. M. I." Pam laughed and pushed Emily's shoulder.

"I don't know about the toolbelt, but I've got a really naughty doctor." Sandy wiggled her eyebrows.

"Yep, I'm out of here." Isabelle plugged her ears and disappeared inside the house.

"Yeah, I think we should probably go back to work before we get jumped." Keith backed slowly down over the steps.

"Are you okay with this bunch?" Mike smiled at Billie.

"Oh, go away, she'll be fine. We'll have her corrupted in about an hour." Sandy laughed.

"Great," Mike groaned and stalked toward Billie. "Don't let them scare you too much." He kissed her lips softly as a chorus of oohs and aahs echoed behind him, and he rolled his eyes.

"I'll leave you to be corrupted." He kissed her quickly and followed Keith behind the house.

"I think they've accepted her into the club." Keith chuckled when Mike caught up to him.

Mike didn't know there was a club, but he was glad that Billie was comfortable around the women of his family. He started to wonder if he'd completely lost his mind because all he could think about at that moment was Billie becoming part of the family.

*Married? Are you really ready for that?*

# Chapter 18

Mike's family was fantastic. Especially his brother's wives. Since the men had finished the fence, the kids and the girls had all moved to the back of the house. Billie had to admit the males in Mike's family had movie star good looks and bodies to go with it. It was obvious where their looks came from when Billie looked at Mike's dad, Sean, and Uncle Kurt. For men in their early fifties, they could probably still turn heads.

She sat back and watched as Sean and Kurt walked around the edge of the yard with some tool that found any nails they'd dropped during the building process. The rest of the men were clearing away the unused materials, and Billie made sure she got a good view every time Mike bent over to pick up a bundle.

"Wearing jeans like that should be illegal." Marina sighed, as she ogled her husband.

"I'm still trying to figure out what they put in the water out here." Billie laughed. "Are there any men in Hopedale that aren't hot."

"I would say my cousins, but from the drool on the deck I'd say none of you women would agree." Kristy plopped on the bench next to Sandy.

"I bet you haven't missed chrome dome bending over." Sandy motioned to the very large, bald, shirtless, wall of muscle currently hoisting a bundle of panels over the fence to someone on the other side.

"Will you stop calling him that?" Kristy groaned.

"Why? It doesn't bother Bull." Sandy laughed.

"That's because Dean doesn't pay attention to you, but it doesn't bother me either." Kristy huffed and crossed her arms across her chest.

"I'm sorry, Bull or Dean. Who are we talking about?" Billie couldn't keep up with all the names.

"You'll learn, honey. All the guys that work for Newfoundland Security Services never call each other by their given names. There's Bull, Crash, Trunk, Smash, Hulk and who am I forgetting?" Emily counted off on her fingers.

"Shadow, Rex, and Cannon. Oh, and how could you forget Rusty." Sandy poked her.

"I never forget Rusty." Emily poked Sandy back.

Billie looked at the two women like they were insane. Not all of Keith's security guys were there, but Marina pointed to the ones that were and told her the nickname and their actual name.

"Let me guess, Rusty is Keith, right?" Billie laughed.

"Yep," Sandy leaned toward her. "But the only people who get away with calling him that is the guys and me when he pisses me off."

"Sandy's the employee that Keith would love to fire but can't because she's too good at what she does." Stephanie rubbed her hand over her swollen belly.

"What exactly do you do?" Billie figured most of the reason Keith wouldn't fire Sandy was that she was his sister-in-law.

"I'm a computer analyst." Sandy shrugged her shoulders.

"Oh, come on, she's modest. She's one of the best in the country." Stephanie rolled her eyes.

"Maybe but I don't wanna brag." Sandy flicked her hair over her shoulder.

Billie's attention was distracted when her phone buzzed in her pocket. She pulled it out and glanced at the screen. It was a text from Mike.

*Say you have to use the bathroom and meet me in my room.*

*Are you crazy? You have a house full of people.*

*Please!*

*I can't!*

*Pretty please!*

She couldn't resist anymore and made her excuse. She hurried through the house and down the hall to Mike's room. Constantly checking behind her to make sure nobody followed. Before she could turn the knob, the door opened, and she got yanked into the room. Mike pinned her against the door and covered her mouth with his as he pressed his body against hers.

Billie melted into the kiss and slid her arms around him as his arms snaked around her waist. He smelled freshly showered and hadn't put on a shirt so she could feel his warm skin against her arms. His tongue plunged into her mouth, and Billie moaned. She could feel his erection pressed against her belly and knew they were about to get too carried away. Reluctantly she pushed him back and dragged her lips from his.

"I've wanted to do that all fucking day." Mike's hand tucked her hair behind her ear.

"Me too but you still have a full house." Billie couldn't control her hands as they caressed his bare chest.

"We've got a few minutes. Not enough time to do exactly what I want but I can do this." Mike crouched and trailed his tongue across the top of her shirt and slid it between her breasts. "And this," he pulled her shirt down to expose her left breast and sucked her nipple into his hot mouth.

"Mike. Oh. My." Billie threw her head back against the door.

"You like that?" His tongue swirled around her hardened

nipple, and she nodded.

"We shouldn't be doing this." Billie gasped when he moved to the other breast and exposed it.

"I can't help it. I want you so bad." Mike groaned and sucked the other nipple into his mouth.

"Mike, your family is…" Billie inhaled when his teeth scraped over the tip.

"I love the sounds you make." Mike covered her breasts again and brushed his lips against hers.

"That's why we can't do anything right now." Billie could be very vocal during sex.

"As soon as the last person is out through the door, I'm taking you back here and making you scream," Mike whispered into her ear.

"Can you kick them out now?" Billie groaned when Mike stepped back and adjusted his very obvious hard-on.

"I'd love to, but they wouldn't leave." Mike chuckled and tugged a t-shirt on over his head.

Before they snuck back out of the room, Mike gave her another panty melting kiss, and then they joined everyone in the yard.

Nick was right about the instruments. Aaron and John were strumming on guitars in the middle of the yard while Nick and another police officer named Cory set up drums.

"Won't people complain about the noise?" Billie tucked herself under Mike's arm.

"Not really. The only other house close to here is Keith's, and I'm pretty sure he won't complain." Mike kissed the top of her head as they joined the rest.

Billie was impressed with the talent she witnessed. She'd found out the name of the band was Rockin' The Law which made sense because the members were either police or lawyers. She did notice Keith, James and Ian weren't part of it and when she asked Marina explained they weren't interested in being in the limelight but according to Marina they could also sing.

Billie had been pulled up to dance by just about every member of Mike's family. Even her dad yanked her up for an old-fashioned waltz. He had two left feet, but she loved it. Mike took every chance he could get to hand his guitar over to someone and pull her into his arms. Billie was in heaven.

As the sun began to set the older couples corralled the kids and brought them inside. Chloe stuck to Lily's side the whole day, and Matt seemed relieved she was comfortable with the other children. He told her as much when he sat next to her.

"You look happy, Billie." Matt wrapped his arm around her shoulder.

"I'm having fun." She rested her head on his shoulder.

"Not what I mean. That pretty boy over there grinning like a fool at you is making you happy." Matt sounded sad.

"He's a great guy." Billie turned so she could look at her brother.

"I know he is. That whole family's incredible." Matt didn't look at her probably because he didn't want her to see the tears in his eyes.

"I miss her too, Matt," Billie whispered.

"I was such an idiot to wait so long." Matt took a deep breath.

"You still have Chloe, and you'll find love again." Billie wrapped her arm around Matt's back, and side hugged him.

"I'm not even thinking about that. My life is Chloe now and finding the bastard that killed her mom." The last part came out in a low growl, and for the first time in her life, Billie was scared of what her brother would do if he got his hands on Peggy's killer.

"Matt, come dance with me. Kurt dragged John out on a call." Stephanie held out her hand and winked at Billie. She must have seen the somber mood on Matt's face.

"You can't find any other man around here to dance with?" Matt chuckled.

"Sure, I can, but I have to lure you away so Mike can dance with his girl." Stephanie laughed when Mike plopped down next to her on the other side.

Matt shook his head and gave Billie a quick kiss on the head. Stephanie grabbed his hand, and she waved over her shoulder as they moved to the middle of the yard to dance to some quick step Aaron was belting out.

"Is he okay?" Mike asked.

"I think he's just a little overwhelmed by all your family." Billie laughed.

"Fuck, I get overwhelmed by them." Mike pulled her to her feet and wrapped his arms around her.

"They're all great." Billie snuggled into his embrace.

For a few minutes, they swayed together, and she watched everyone dancing around. Even Philip acted like a fool as he spun Isabelle around the yard. It was as if the whole world was at peace. Her phone buzzed in her pocket, and she glanced up at Mike.

"I'm tossing that phone in the woods." Mike chuckled when he released her to answer it.

Billie glanced at the screen and smiled. She hadn't talked to Dana in a while and walked closer to the house so she could hear.

"Hey Dana," Billie put the phone to her ear.

"Billie, it's bad." Dana sobbed, and her voice sounded weird.

"What? What's bad?" Billie ran up the steps and into the house.

"Abbie, she's in the hospital and … your house…. Everything's gone. Fire." Billie could hardly understand Dana's babbling. It was as if she was mumbling everything.

"Dana, calm down. What fire? What happened to Abbie?" Billie hadn't realized she was shouting until she looked up to see Kathleen staring at her.

"Someone... tried... to... kill... us..." Dana sobbed each word.

"Where are you?" Billie ran outside and searched for Mike.

"The Health Science Center. Abbie's hurt." Dana was hysterical.

"I'll be there in twenty minutes. Stay calm Dana; I'm coming" Billie ended the call.

"What's wrong?" Mike's face was full of concern.

"I'm not sure, but if I understood Dana right, Abbie got hurt in a fire at my house." Billie couldn't understand why Dana and Abbie would be at her house in the first place or how the fire started.

"Let me tell James what's going on, and I'll take you." Mike didn't wait for her to answer as he ran to his brother.

Billie hugged herself as she waited for Mike to return. She watched him talk, and James nodded. Mike was back at her side, and they were in his car on the highway minutes later.

What the hell was going on?

# *Chapter 19*

Mike pulled into the hospital parking lot and took the first space he could find. Billie hadn't spoken a word the entire drive, but she clung to his hand. He prayed Abbie wasn't hurt badly because Billie had already lost one friend.

Mike explained the situation to James before they left. His brother promised to let everyone know what happened. Mike had a sinking feeling that this was all related to Peggy's murder, but he was not going to voice that to Billie.

Mike scanned the usual crowed waiting room in the emergency department for Dana. Billie tugged him toward the reception desk, and they waited for one of the nurses to notice them. Mike wrapped his arm around Billie's trembling shoulders.

"Mike, what are you doing here?" Bobby tapped Mike on the shoulder.

"Billie's friend's here," Mike explained.

"Fuck, I knew she was familiar." Bobby slapped his forehead.

"Her friend is Dana Sampson, right?"

"Yes, and Abbie Martin's here too." Billie stepped between Mike and Bobby.

"Where are they, Bobby?" Mike assumed his friend brought them in.

"Come with me." He motioned toward trauma center entry.

Billie clung to Mike as they hurried down the hallway behind Bobby. He wasn't sure what they would find when they got to the girls, but Mike prepared himself for the worst.

"Dana's in here with Abbie." Bobby pointed to a room to the left.

"How bad is it?" Billie was obviously trying to keep herself together, but her voice trembled.

"Abbie sustained a knock on the head and Dana had some smoke inhalation, but they'll both be fine. I think they're going to be kept overnight for observation, but you should probably check with the doctor." Bobby explained. "We gave Dana something to calm her down because she was scared out of her wits. She might be a little loopy."

Mike motioned for Billie to go on ahead and she hurried into the room. Mike closed the door so Billie could have some privacy with her friends.

"What happened?" Mike asked Bobby.

"Not sure, we got a call to the address. Flames had the whole house engulfed. Dana was locked in a closet. Someone jammed the door so she couldn't get out. Ernie was there and said she was lucky the neighbors heard her screaming. They told the fire department nobody lived there, but when they heard someone screaming they called." Bobby braced his back against the wall.

"What about Abbie?" Mike stood next to him.

"They found her unconscious next to her car. She said she was putting a box in the car and someone clocked her on the head. She doesn't remember anything after that." Bobby nodded his head down the hall.

Mike looked in the direction. John and Rick Avery headed toward them, and John looked pissed.

"What are you doing here?" John asked.

Mike told John about Billie's phone call and how her friends were the ones hurt. John and Rick exchanged confused looks.

"Her friends were stealing from her," Rick stated.

"What? No. What are you talking about?" Mike didn't know what was going on now.

"The neighbor said the two women broke into the house and were robbing the place." John read from the notepad he held. "He said he was pretty sure there was a guy too, but the guy took off when the fire got out of hand."

"Bro, I don't believe Abbie and Dana would do that to Billie. They're her best friends. There has to be some other explanation." Mike pushed open the door.

Dana was in one bed and Abbie in the other. Billie sat between them holding their hands and all three were crying.

"You guys could have been killed." Billie turned when Mike walked in followed by John and Rick.

"I got to get back to work. Give me a call later." Bobby waved at Mike and closed the door when he left.

"John? What are you doing here?" Billie stood up and poured a glass of water. She handed it to Dana.

"We've got some questions for Ms. Sampson and Ms. Martin." John turned to Mike as if asking him to get Billie out of the room.

"Billie, why don't we wait outside?" Mike held out his hand.

"I'm not going anywhere." Billie shook her head.

"I'm afraid we've got to ask you to step outside, Billie." John pushed.

"No." Billie crossed her arms over her chest. "I'm staying with my friends."

John glanced back at Mike. What did his brother expect him to do? Pick Billie up and carry her out of the room?

"Fine but please don't interrupt," John warned.

"I won't." Billie stepped to the far side of the room, and Mike joined her.

"Let's start with you, Ms. Martin." John stood next to Abbie's bed. "Can you tell us what happened?"

"Billie's landlord was being a dick and nagging Billie about getting her things out of the house. Dana and I knew she was having a hard time going in there since…" Abbie stopped and glanced at Billie then turned back to John. "Anyway, I was talking to Dana, and since we've got keys to the house, we figured we'd help by packing up as much as we could fit in our cars. We'd pretty much cleared out Billie's room. We were going to start Chloe's room, but I carried a box out to my car and then next thing I know I'm in an ambulance on the way here."

"Abbie, you guys didn't have to…." Billie stopped when John glared at her and Mike pulled her into his side.

"Ms. Sampson, what do you remember?" John glanced toward Dana.

"I went back inside, and I was in Chloe's room. I heard someone walk in behind me and I assumed it was Abbie. The next thing I know I'm grabbed from behind and shoved into a closet. I kicked the door and shouted, but nobody answered me. Then I smelled gas…" Tears streamed out of Dana's eyes, and she took a deep breath. "I screamed and screamed."

"Who was the man with you?" Rick asked.

"There was only Dana and me." Abbie glanced back and forth between Rick and John.

"So, you didn't break in and ..." John got cut off by a very pissed off Abbie.

"Are you fucking kidding me? You think Dana and I were there to steal from Billie?" Abbie jolted up in the bed and then flopped back.

"We would never do that." Dana choked out.

"I know you wouldn't." Billie stepped between the beds. "Why would you think that John?"

"A neighbor said you both broke into the house." John was professional, but Mike could tell he was pissed someone would give him false information.

"The older man across the street?" Billie asked.

"No, this guy was younger." Rick glanced down at his book. "Byron Wells."

"That's my landlord, and he doesn't live anywhere near me." Billie narrowed her eyes. "What the hell was he doing there?"

"I don't know, but I'm about to go have another chat with Mr. Wells." Rick turned and left the room.

"I'm sorry about this Billie," John said.

"It's not your fault but can you do me a favor," Abbie said.

"If I can." John smiled.

"Kick that asshole in the jewels and tell him it's from Billie and her friends." Abbie held her head.

"I can't do that, but I'll get to the bottom of this." John chuckled and nodded at the women as he motioned for Mike to join him outside the room.

Mike closed the door behind him and followed John down the hallway. John was lead on Peggy's murder case, and something told Mike that all this was connected. It was just too big of a coincidence.

"There's something those girls don't know." John pulled out his phone and held it up.

On the screen was the picture of a white sheet covering what looked like a body. The surroundings didn't look familiar either.

"Is that what I think it is?" Mike met his brother's eyes.

"It's the body of Eugene Wilks." John shoved his phone back into his pocket.

"That's Peggy's ex." Billie had told him about the asshole.

"Yeah, and I know Keith told you about Jess keeping tabs on him. Well, two days ago he didn't show up for work at the bar. Jess said the guy was a dick, but he never missed a shift. We know there was no way he killed Peggy because he was working, but we thought he might have hired someone." John stopped. "I shouldn't be telling you this, but I need you to be careful."

"Careful? What's wrong?"

"All this leads to one person." John looked up toward the room where Billie and the girls were.

"Spit it out," Mike growled.

"Billie." John sighed.

"You think Billie did all this?" Mike guffawed. "Are you fucking with me?"

"No, Mike. We think someone is doing this to get to Billie." John explained.

"Like a stalker?" The hair on Mike's arms stood up.

"Or someone out to get her." John shrugged. "All I know is all of this leads back to her."

"Where did you find Wilks?" Mike knew the answer before he asked the question.

"In Billie's backyard," John whispered. "Rick has a theory. He thinks whoever killed Wilks got interrupted by the girls and he was planning to burn the house down with Eugene inside."

"What do you think?" Mike knew his brother had his own theory.

"I think whoever it was expected Billie to show up and when she didn't, he got angry and tried to hurt her by killing her friends and having us believe it was Wilks."

"Is her family in danger?" He couldn't let anything happen to Billie but if someone was willing to hurt her friends what would stop them from destroying her family.

"We're on it. Uncle Kurt's talking to Keith about putting some of his guys on them. We don't have enough staff to have someone there round the clock." John rolled his eyes. "Fucking cutbacks."

"Keith's guys are going to have to get paid." Mike knew Keith wouldn't care about protecting his own family for free, but this was Billie's family.

"They will." John smiled but didn't say anything else. "I got to get back. Keep her with you. Trunk will be here any minute to stay with Abbie and Dana."

"You think they're still in danger?" Mike didn't like this at all.

"Can't be too safe." John waved, and Mike turned to go back to the room.

Billie stood in the doorway staring at him. He didn't know how much she'd heard, but he wasn't keeping any of this from her or the girls. They needed to know to watch their backs. He wasn't about to lose the love of his life.

"Mike, what's going on?" Billie's eyes were full of worry, and he hated to see it.

"Come back in the room, and I'll explain what I know." Mike wrapped his arm around her shoulder and kissed the top of her head.

He repeated everything John had told him to Billie, Abbie, and Dana. Billie clung to him tighter with every word he spoke. Neither of the girls interrupted him, but Abbie seemed about ready to bust.

"So, everyone will be safe. Keith's guys are good." Mike hugged Billie into his side.

"So, some sicko is possibly obsessed with Billie and to get her attention he's killing or attempting to kill people she cares about or loves. Is that what you're saying?" Abbie narrowed her eyes.

"That's the theory, but John doesn't want to take chances." Mike didn't like the look of rage in Abbie's eyes. "Chances are the fire destroyed any evidence, but you never know."

"But you're saying until they find out, we'll have someone following us around." Abbie didn't seem to like the idea of having a bodyguard.

"Abbie, it's for our safety." Dana's voice was soft and hoarse. Probably from the smoke of the fire.

"I don't want some goon following me around." Abbie snapped.

Before anyone could speak the door eased open, and Trunk stepped inside. Abbie and Dana couldn't see him because of the curtain.

"Hi." He nodded at Mike.

"Don't be afraid, Trunk." Mike grinned. "I'm sure Abbie won't bite."

When Trunk stepped forward into view of the girls, it was comical to see their eyes bulge out and mouths fall open. Billie's body shook with laughter.

"Abbie and Dana, this is Ben Murphy, but everyone calls him Trunk." Mike motioned to the man. "Trunk, on the left is Abbie and Dana's on the right."

"Nice to meet you both." Trunk stood with his hands folded in front of him.

"Holy, mother of Jesus. It's a real live Adonis." Abbie's eyes started from the top of Trunks head and slowly moved down.

"Not quite, but thanks for the ego boost." Trunk laughed.

"How in God's name do you need an ego boost? Do you have a mirror at home?" Dana seemed to wake up pretty quickly.

"Yes, I do." Trunk seemed amused by the girls.

"Okay, the name Trunk is it because your arms are the size of tree trunks?" Abbie gawked at the man and Mike didn't know how Trunk didn't feel like a piece of meat

"Not even close." Trunk chuckled.

"Oh, is something else as big as a tree trunk." Abbie wiggled her eyebrows.

"You're going to be trouble, aren't you?" Trunk shook his head.

"Yes, she is," Billie interjected.

"I'll be good if you tell me why they call you Trunk." Abbie grinned.

"I doubt you'll ever be good, but Trunk came from locking myself in one when I was trying to win a bet with my brother. I told him I could get out of our grandmother's travel trunk and told him to lock me in. Neither of us knew the thing wasn't locked before because the key was missing." Trunk didn't look the least bit embarrassed over his act of stupidity.

"Well, I'm just going to imagine my own story about why you're called Trunk." Abbie sighed.

"I'll be outside your room. Nobody gets in here without my say so." Trunk chuckled as he headed out of the room. "Good evening ladies. Mike."

"I think I'm going to be alright with being shadowed." Abbie smiled.

"As long as you remember to do what he says." Mike turned serious. "He's good at his job."

"I will."

# Chapter 20

Billie was exhausted by the time she left the hospital. Mike had spoken with his father, and her parents agreed to spend the night with Mike's parents. Matt and Philip were at Keith's, and Chloe was excited to have her first sleepover with Lily and Evie. The fact that it was a holiday weekend meant she got to spend the night with Mike. They stopped by her place to grab a change of clothes and toiletries.

Billie took a few minutes to talk with Rita and give her the short version of what had happened. She didn't want to scare the woman since it was just her and her mom. Billie did ask her to call her if she saw anybody strange around the house.

"I'll keep you all in my prayers and give the girls a hug for me." Rita hugged Billie.

"Make sure you keep your doors locked and call me if you see anyone around my parent's house." Billie hugged Rita again as she ran back to where Mike waited next to his car.

She was almost asleep when Mike pulled into his driveway. It wasn't late, but she guessed the adrenalin rush disappeared and she was about to crash. Mike opened her door and held out his hand.

"I can carry you into the house if you're too tired to walk." Mike crouched.

"I'm not that far gone. I can walk in but thanks for the offer." Billie gave him a soft kiss, and he stood up as she stepped out of the car.

"I'll grab her things out of the car." Mike spun around at the sound of the male voice behind him, and Billie almost jumped into his arms.

"Fuck, Lane. Why don't you just shoot me instead of trying to give me a heart attack." Mike blew out a breath.

"Sorry, I thought Keith told you I'd be here." Lane chuckled.

"Billie this is Lane West. They call him Shadow, and he just proved why. He's also Sandy's older brother." Mike pulled Billie from behind him.

"Yeah, you need to wear a bell." Billie held out her hand. "Nice to meet you."

"I'm sorry I never got to meet you earlier. I just got back from a job." Lane held out his hand. "Looks like another O'Connor gets the lady."

"Is that why you tried to scare me to death?" Mike laughed.

"No, but it's good to see one of you man whore's finally

settling down." Lane smiled as he pulled Billie's bag out of the back seat.

"Fuck you, Lane," Mike grumbled as he grasped Billie's hand and headed into the house.

"I'll pass on that, but I'll take a cup of coffee." Lane followed them inside.

"Would you like arsenic with that?" Mike flicked on the light in the kitchen which she fully expected to see in a complete mess from the party, but the place was as if nobody had been there all day.

"Your mother and aunts made sure the place was spotless before they hustled everyone out. Bull said your grandmother ordered everyone else to clean up outside." Lane plopped down on the stool.

Billie's eyes were so heavy that she was sure she'd fall asleep standing up, but she didn't want to be rude to Lane. The man was using his time to be a human shield to some sicko that was possibly angry with her.

"Sweetheart, why don't you go take a hot bath and go to bed. I won't be long behind you." Mike kissed her cheek.

"Lane, thanks for being here." Billie touched the man's shoulder, and he smiled.

"It's my job to protect pretty ladies." He winked.

"Goodnight." Billie headed to the bedroom.

She felt guilty about bringing trouble into Mike's family. She didn't want anybody to be in danger because of her. Hell, she didn't even know if someone was out to get her. Mike said it was just a theory. Billie couldn't think of anyone cruel enough to kill her. The police could be wrong but what if they weren't?

Billie was barely able to stay awake in the bath. She shuffled into Mike's room, pulled her nightshirt from her bag and crawled under the heavy duvet. When her eyes closed, a deep sigh escaped. She felt like she'd been awake for days.

It seems like seconds later she sat upright in the bed. Mike 's arm draped over her waist, and he mumbled something when she sat up, but he turned over on his side without waking. She didn't remember falling asleep, but now she was wide awake. She glanced down at Mike and smiled as he mumbled again.

Billie eased herself out of the bed because one, she was bursting to use the bathroom and two, she needed something to drink. She relieved herself and tiptoed out of the bedroom to make sure she didn't wake Mike. In the kitchen, Billie pulled down a glass from the cupboard but stopped when she noticed Mike's back deck lit up like a Christmas tree. She filled the glass, drank down the water and placed the glass in the dish tray before making her way to the sliding doors.

Billie moved to the patio door and searched for the switch to turn off the outside lights but couldn't find it. When she glanced out through the glass, her heart pounded in her chest. Someone lay facedown in the middle of the yard, but she couldn't tell who it was. Billie tried to open the door, but it wouldn't budge. She shouted out to

Mike but he didn't answer, and as she turned to run back to get him, a dark figure stood behind her holding a knife. The thick drops of blood hit the floor with dull thuds, and her whole body shook with cold. She screamed and tried to run, but her legs wouldn't move.

"Billie," Mike's voice was loud, but she couldn't see him, and as the figure moved closer, she tried to raise her arms, but it was as if paralysis taken over her body.

"Billie, honey," Mike shouted again.

The figure squeezed her arms, and she closed her eyes. She was about to die just like Peggy. No, she wasn't about to let this man take away her life.

"Billie, you need to wake up," Mike shouted.

Billie's eyes popped open, and her arms flailed over her. She didn't know how she ended up on her back, but he wasn't going to kill her easily.

"Billie, it's me. You were dreaming." Mike grabbed her hands, as she finally focused in on his worried face.

"Someone was laying in your yard." Billie shook her head. "I tried to go tell you but …"

"It was a nightmare, Beautiful." Mike pulled her into his arms and kissed the top of her head. "You're safe."

"It was so real." Billie pressed her cheek against his bare chest. "Did I wake you?"

"It's okay," Mike lay back with her tightly against his side. "You're safe."

Billie clung to him as she tried to calm her racing heart and erase the dream from her thoughts. She knew what triggered it. Someone tried to kill her friends and was more than likely the same person that murdered Peggy. They knew for sure it wasn't Eugene because he was dead too. Billie couldn't even feel a little sad about his death. He put Peggy through hell, and if it hadn't been for him, Peggy and Matt probably would have gotten together a long time ago. Maybe Peggy would still be alive.

Billie closed her eyes to hold back the tears that blurred her vision and blew out a shaky breath. Mike hugged her tighter, and her muscles slowly relaxed.

"It's okay, Billie. I got you. I always got you." Mike whispered and kissed the top of her head.

"What's your favorite song you sing?" Billie whispered.

"I'd have to think about that one." Mike's voice vibrated through his chest.

"Could you sing something for me?" Billie tipped her head back so she could look at him.

"Have you ever heard the song Angels Brought Me Here?" Mike smiled. Billie shook her head. "It reminds me of you."

"Why?" Billie pushed up on her elbow.

"Basically, the lyrics say that the singer's dreams come true when he finds the love of his life." Mike turned to face her. "It's the way I feel about you."

"Why did Lane call you a man whore?" She might have been tired but she'd heard the comment, and she didn't like it.

Mike dropped his head for a moment, and when he lifted it, he met her gaze. She didn't care what kind of life he had before her. Well, maybe a little.

"Honestly, I've had my share of one-night stands and never dated anyone long term. I guess I was searching for that special woman who'd make my heart race and make me feel like I could do anything." Mike ran his finger down her cheek. "You made me feel that way from the moment we met."

"Most women would think that was a line to get them into bed, but since I'm already in your bed, I can't doubt you." Billie kissed the top of his finger as it glided across her lips. "You scare me."

"Why?" Mike eyebrows furrowed.

"I've never felt like this. The overpowering pull I feel with you. Like there's a magnet drawing me closer." Billie dropped her head because it sounded so stupid when she said it out loud.

"It's scary but a good scared." Mike lifted her chin, so she had to look at him.

"It's just so fast." Billie sighed.

"Do you know Keith fell in love with Emily the first time he saw her. He didn't know at the time, but he knows now. John pulled Stephanie over during a traffic stop and couldn't stop thinking about her from that day on. The first time James met Marina, he'd just lost his first wife a few months before, but he knew. The first time Ian saw Sandy, he almost broke his neck on a set of steps. What I'm trying to say is I've learned by watching all of them when you meet the right person, you just know." Mike brushed his lips against hers.

"But this crazy person's out there, and we still don't know who he or it could be a she. It could be two people. Who knows? " Billie pressed her forehead against his.

"We'll figure it out," Mike whispered.

"Can you sing that song and hold me?"

Mike lay back on the bed and wrapped his strong arms around her. His voice was soft and beautiful. Billie tried to listen to the words, but between the vibration in his chest and his beautiful voice, she couldn't keep her eyes open. The last thing she heard was the words 'Angels brought me here'.

*Buzz Buzz.*

Billie turned over on her stomach and sighed.

*Buzz Buzz.*

She had to be dreaming. There was no way someone was calling her at the ass crack of dawn.

*Buzz Buzz.*

Billie popped up on her elbows and looked around. Her phone vibrated across the nightstand, and she wanted to pick it up and toss it out the window. When she snatched it off the stand, she was shocked to see it was almost noon.

"Holy crap." Billie sat up. She tried to wake up enough to remember how exactly to answer her phone. She slept way too long.

*Buzz Buzz.*

"Hello." She shouted not meaning too.

"What's wrong?" Abbie shouted back.

"Sorry, nothing I just woke up." Billie flopped back on the bed. "What's up?"

"Let's see. Dana and I are now roommates at my house, and being held hostage by two hot Greek gods with asses you could crack walnuts on." Abbie sighed.

"So, Trunk's still with you guys?" Billie yawned.

"Nope, he's night shift. Today we have Hulk, who by the way is a hunk and we have Rex who has the sexiest damn accent I've ever heard." Abbie needed to get a boyfriend.

"I've met Hulk but not Rex." There were so many men at Mike's house the day before she probably could have met Rex and didn't remember.

"I clicked a picture. Let me send it." Abbie laughed.

Billie shook her head. Only Abbie would make having bodyguards, fun. Her phone beeped, and she looked at the screen. Rex didn't look familiar because she would have remembered him.

"Did you get it?" Abbie laughed.

"Yes, he's hot." Billie stretched. "But he's there for a job not to be ogled by you."

"Hey, if he's gonna hold me, hostage, then I'm gonna ogle."

"How are you and Dana doing?" Billie hated that her friends were hurt.

"I've got a bit of a headache, but I'll be okay. Dana's throat is sore but they told her to expect that, but there's no permanent damage."

"Thanks for trying to clean out my house." What else could she say?

"Your crap is still in my car." Abbie chuckled.

"I'll get Matt or Philip to get it and bring it home."

"My question is, how are you doing?"

Billie didn't know how to answer that question. She didn't know how she felt about someone wanting to hurt her if that was in fact what was going on. The only thing she was sure of was the only place she felt at ease was in Mike's arms.

"I'm okay."

"Is Hottie McHotterson taking care of you?" Abbie was forever going to call Mike that name.

"Yes, he is. He's amazing." Billie couldn't help but sigh.

"That good huh? Lucky bitch." Abbie laughed.

"It's not just that but yeah that good. Mike's so sweet, protective and …" Abbie cut her off.

"You're arse over kettle in love with him." Abbie's excitement was palpable.

"Yes." Billie laughed.

"Good for you, honey. You deserve it but he better be damn good to you, or he'll be dealing with me. Not letting you go through that shit Peg went through." Abbie's jovial tone was gone. "None of us will go through that."

"I've got to get up and see if Mike's found out anything about the fire." Billie rolled to the side of the bed and sat up.

"Let me know, and I'll call if I hear anything."

"Okay, love you girl." Billie didn't say those words to her friends enough.

"Love you always," Abbie said just before the call ended.

After a quick shower, Billie dressed and headed out of the room. Philip was in the kitchen with Mike shoveling food into his mouth, but he wasn't alone. Mike was eating like it was his last meal.

"Hungry?" Mike asked.

"A little." Before Billie had a chance, Mike jumped up and filled a plate and placed it next to him on the counter.

"I'm going to marry your grandmother." Philip sighed as he dropped the fork on his plate.

"I think Tom might have a problem with that." Mike laughed.

"Maybe she'll adopt me." Philip stood up and brought his plate to the dishwasher.

"I'll be sure to let mom know you're running away from home." Matt appeared in the doorway. "Hey, sis. Sleep well?"

"Yeah. Are you guys okay?" Billie worried her brothers didn't like the whole situation.

"I had the best sleep I've had in years. Probably because your man here tried to work me to death yesterday." Philip chuckled.

"Ignore him, Mike. Damn pencil pushers don't know what a hard day's work is." Matt rolled his eyes and then laughed. "I just realized you don't exactly do manual labor at your job either."

"Trust me; I get my share of manual labor." Mike might be a lawyer, but when it came to helping out, he did just as much as the next guy.

"Any word this morning?" When all three men's faces fell, she knew the answer.

"Sweetheart, it's been less than a day. They'll figure it out."

Mike pulled her into a hug and kissed the top of her head.

She knew Mike meant well, but it had been a lot longer than a day since Peggy died and they still didn't have any leads on that. How was she supposed to go day to day without answers?

"Mike's right, Billie." Matt was the last person she expected to say that but if he had hope why couldn't she.

For the next two weeks, Billie felt as if she was on a tight leash. She went to work, tried to keep a somewhat normal life, but it wasn't normal to have huge muscled men in the office every day. It wasn't normal to have them at her parent's house. Not that they were in the way because most of the time they stayed out of the way.

Her grandfather did enjoy the company, and they were kind to him. Hulk, whose real name was Bruce Steel liked to play cards, and that made her Pop smile. Billie made sure to ask Keith if he could make Hulk a regular at her house. At least it made her grandfather happy, and nothing else had happened.

Billie started to spend most nights at Mike's house. She'd been there so often that her father wondered if she'd moved in but was afraid to tell them. Billie had assured him she would tell them before she made that move.

Chloe spent a lot of time with Mike's nieces on the weekends. Lily picked up sign language and was almost better at it than she was. Mike's other niece Evie learned as well. His nephews didn't seem as interested, but they didn't leave Chloe out when all the kids played.

Matt had even thought about moving to Hopedale with Chloe so she could be close to Lily and Evie. Billie didn't ever remember the little girl so excited over friends since she'd started school. Peggy always worried about Chloe fitting in with the hearing world.

"Mike said he's on the way." Trunk informed her just before five.

"Thanks, Ben." Billie couldn't get used to calling the guys by their nicknames.

"Trunk, are you with Dana and I tonight?" Abbie pulled on her jacket.

"Yes, Abs." Trunk laughed.

"Are you finally going to give in and play strip poker?" Abbie wiggled her eyebrows.

"Not on your life." Trunk shook his head.

"He's such a wimp." Abbie hitched her thumb over her shoulder and winked at Billie.

"Who's picking up Dana at the hospital?"

"Rex," Trunk glanced down at his phone, but a loud screech outside the huge picture window, made him spin around.

"What the hell …." Abbie moved to look outside.

"Get down." Trunk shouted and dove toward her and Abbie.

Seconds later the window in the door shattered and the picture window seemed to explode as what looked like balls of fire came through. Billie didn't have a chance to see anything else because Trunk covered both her and Abbie with his body. She did hear a car door slam, and then tires squealed again.

"Stay down." Trunk growled as the weight of his body disappeared.

It wasn't more than a second later he cursed, and Billie felt a hand wrap around her arm. She stood up and looked at Abbie, but the horror on her friend's face had her spinning around to look at the front of the store.

Flames were licking up the wall and across the waiting area. Billie stepped back and grabbed the edge of her desk. Trunk pushed them back toward Abbie's office and had his phone to his ear. Billie couldn't hear what he said because she couldn't focus enough on anything but the fire.

"Come on. We'll get out through the back exit." Trunk pushed them into Abbie's office and slammed the door.

The emergency exit was off Abbie's office, and Trunk ran to open it, but it wouldn't budge. He cursed and slammed his body up against it a couple of times. It still didn't move. Abbie squeaked when he picked up her office chair and threw it at the window behind her desk. It shattered, and he cleared away the jagged edges with the chair.

"Come on." Trunk reached his hand out.

Abbie ran toward him, and he lifted her out through the

window. Abbie's agency was in a small one-story building and as it turned out it had been a smart move. Billie started to cough from the smoke seeping under the door of the office and ran toward the window.

"Billie, come on." Trunk shouted.

He lifted her out through the broken window, and she noticed him flinch for a moment, but as soon as her feet were on the ground, he jumped through himself. He wrapped his arms around her and Abbie and hustled them out of the alley behind the building.

At the front of the building, Billie got a good look at what they escaped. The whole thing lit up with red and orange flames. Trunk had both of them wrapped in the circle of his arms as the sirens grew deafening. All Billie could do was stare as her friend's business burned.

"Billie," Mike's voice echoed through the noise, and she turned around.

He ran full force toward her, and she wiggled out of Trunk's hold and went to him. He had her tightly in his arms seconds later. She wasn't sure if it was her trembling or if it was him.

"Are you okay?" He pressed his lips against her temple.

"Yes, thanks to Ben."

They walked back to where paramedics checked Trunk and Abbie. Mike's friend Bobby checked Abbie out while another guy checked Trunk. He didn't look the least bit happy about being poked.

"Trunk's hurt." Billie noticed the cut on the side of the man's face and his arm had blood running down the length of it.

"If that tattoo is damaged I'm going to beat whoever did this to death." Trunk growled.

"I think it'll be all right, big guy." Bobby chuckled.

"Ben, thank you for saving us." Billie reached out and touched the man's hand.

"Sweetheart, that's my job." He smiled and then flinched. She did the same thing when she saw the piece of glass Bobby had pulled from Trunk's arm.

"When I find out who the hell is doing this shit, I'm going to want ten minutes alone with him, so I can pound the piss out of him," Abbie growled.

Billie turned into Mike's arms and glanced back to where the firefighters were now spraying the building with hoses. She'd like to have five minutes alone with whoever it was too. She'd never wanted to hurt someone physically, but this guy tried to destroy everyone and everything she loved.

*Oh, God.*

"You've got to stay away from me." Billie pushed Mike and stepped back from him.

"What? Are you kidding me?" Mike reached for her, but she shook her head and stepped out of his grasp.

"This guy is going after everyone I love." Billie stepped further back.

"I'll be fine, Beautiful." Mike stepped toward her, and she held up her hand.

"No, you don't know that." Billie looked away from him. "Mike, go home."

"I'm not leaving you." Mike grasped her arms and spun her toward him.

"Please, I can't bare if you get hurt." Billie held back the tears that threatened to fall.

"I'll be okay, and you're not pushing me away. I'm not letting you do that." Mike pulled her against his chest, and she was helpless to pull away.

"I'll be furious if you get hurt because you didn't listen to me." Billie buried her face in his shirt.

"I can handle you mad at me but not pushing me away." Mike had his arms tightly around her, and maybe she should be more forceful to keep him away but she just couldn't. Not at that moment. Possibly not ever.

# *Chapter 21*

"How's Trunk doing?" Mike asked Keith when he finally got Billie to go to sleep.

"Pissed that he had to get stitches and he threatened the doctor." Keith laughed.

"Let me guess, he better not fuck up the tattoo." Mike handed Keith a bottle of beer.

"I don't think it would bother him with any other one but that one he got for his brother." Keith popped the cap off the bottle.

"John said they're looking through the video footage from the security cams." Mike plopped down on the couch next to Keith.

"Yeah, Abbie was smart not to have it on site." Keith put the bottle to his lips. "I've had her checked out by the way. Her and the other girl."

"Why?" Mike stared at his brother.

"After what happened with Sandy and Emily. I'm not taking

chances with nobody I know or don't know." Keith tipped the bottle and swallowed.

Mike understood. They'd all been shocked when Sandy's half-sister had been the one trying to hurt Ian's wife. Then there was an old friend of Emily's family that kidnapped her. It was mind-boggling how people looked sane and ended up being crazy.

Mike stared at the muted television not really watching the ball game that was on. His mind ran a mile a minute. John asked Billie to make a list of people she knew. That only meant one thing. He was about to look into everyone Billie ever met.

"They were clear by the way." Keith nudged him with his elbow.

"Huh?" Mike had forgotten what they were discussing.

"Abbie and Dana." Keith shook his head.

"I never thought you'd find any different." Mike leaned back and closed his eyes.

"You know it's getting a little old." Keith sighed.

"What?"

"Every time one of us finds a woman, someone is trying to hurt or kill them." Keith was right.

"So, what you're saying is when Nick and A.J. get serious we should all be prepared." Mike chuckled.

"Fuck, those two are never gonna settle down."

"Didn't you think that about me not too long ago?" Mike pushed Keith's shoulder.

"Good point." Keith stood up and scuffed to the kitchen. Mike heard the clink of the bottle dropped into the recycling bin and Keith returned.

"Trunk has been ordered to relax for a few days. I've got Bull and Crunch with the girls and Hulk is with Billie's family."

"Lane still here?" Mike saw the man on the front porch when he walked in, but he wasn't sure if he was going to be there all night.

"Yep," Mike walked Keith to the front door, and he slapped him on the back.

"Thanks, bro." Mike knew it wasn't necessary to thank Keith.

"We protect family and that girl in there is family." Keith nodded toward the bedroom. "It looks good on you, bro."

"It feels pretty damn good too." Mike smiled.

He watched Keith disappear up the path toward his house and glanced at the bench to see Lane reading. He looked up nodded and went back to his book. Mike closed the door and headed toward the bedroom.

He crawled into the bed being careful so he wouldn't wake Billie, but as if she sensed him she opened her eyes and smiled. He couldn't resist those beautiful lips and leaned in to place a quick kiss on them.

"I want a kiss." She whispered.

"I just kissed you." He chuckled.

"That wasn't a kiss, that was a peck." She moved closer and slid her hand around his waist.

Mike cupped Billie's cheek and leaned in again. He brushed his lips across her cheek until he reached her lips then flicked his tongue across her lower lip and she sighed. He pulled her body closer and covered her mouth with his. Her tongue plunged into his mouth and swirled around his.

His cock jerked and hardened instantly as her hands slid down his back and inside his boxer briefs where she cupped his ass and pulled him closer. Mike slipped his hand under her nightshirt and found she was naked underneath.

"Baby, you had a rough day. Are you sure?" He kissed his way to her ear and whispered.

She grabbed his hand and moved it between her legs. She was wet and gasped when his finger slid between her folds.

"Does that answer your question?" Billie moaned and bit her lower lip when he slid his finger against her wet clit.

"Definitely,"

"I want you to make me forget for a little while." She sighed.

Billie wiggled out of her shirt as Mike kissed his way down her warm body. He stopped over one breast and flicked his tongue against the pebbled nipple. She made that purr that drove him crazy, and when he sucked it into his mouth, he slid his finger inside her.

"Oh, God. Mike." Billie's hips thrust upward.

His cock ached to be inside her, but he wanted to take his time with her body. He wanted to taste her and have her explode in his mouth. He made his way to her other breast and repeated what he did with the first, but this time he slipped a second finger inside her and pressed his thumb against her swollen clit.

"Yes… oh… yes." Billie moaned, and Mike grinned as he sucked her nipple into his mouth again.

Somehow her hand had grasped onto his throbbing dick, and it was everything he could do to keep from coming in her hand. He lifted his head and managed to push her hand away.

"You can have that in a bit. First I want to taste that sweet pussy." Mike kissed his way down her body as he slowly thrust his fingers in and out of her body. "I can smell how turned on you are, baby." Her arousal was driving him insane.

"Mike…" Billie gasped when his lips clamped over her swollen clit, and his tongue flicked against it quickly.

His fingers curled and pressed against that fleshy area inside that made her squeal. Her body stiffened, and she tangled her fingers into his hair and tugged. He never thought having his hair pulled could be so damn hot.

"Ahh… Ohh… Yes." Billie's body shuddered, and her wetness

drenched his hand. Slowly he withdrew his fingers and covered her soaking pussy with his mouth. He slid his tongue inside and moaned as her flavor slid over his tongue.

"Fucking, delicious," Mike whispered and continued to flick his tongue in and out until she screamed his name and shook from another orgasm.

"Inside, I want…. Ahhh…. I want you inside." Billie panted as she reached for the nightstand. He hadn't bothered to put the condoms back in the drawer since she'd been spending most nights in his bed. It took too much time to grab them.

Mike rolled over on his back to grab it but was surprised when she snatched it out of his hand and crawled between his legs. She tossed it on the bed and grabbed the waistband of his underwear.

"Oh no, you don't. I've been trying to get a taste of you, and you keep holding out on me." Billie tossed his boxers to the side and slid her hands up the length of his legs.

"I don't hold out. I just can't wait to feel you around me, and you tricked me." Mike liked blowjobs but hadn't found them as exciting as burying his cock inside a woman.

"You're about to find out what my mouth is like around you." Billie's hand grasped his engorged cock, and he shivered.

Mike tucked his hand under his head and watched as Billie proceeded to show him how much she wanted to taste him

Her tongue slowly swirled around the head, and he had trouble keeping his eyes open from the sensation. She pulled her hand back to the base of his dick and squeezed gently as her mouth slid down over the head then popped off again. She did that a couple of times, and when he didn't expect it, she took him completely into her mouth in one swift motion.

"Fuck," Mike groaned.

"Like that, huh?" Billie popped off his cock again and repeated the same motion.

"Baby, that feels so fucking good." Mike gasped when she began to slide her mouth up and down his length. He cupped the back of her head with one hand and fisted the sheets with the other. His hips thrust up in time with her and he felt that tingle that told him he was about to come but the way she had the bottom of his cock tightly in her hand it was as if he couldn't.

"I can taste you dripping on my tongue." Billie moaned and took him into her mouth again.

"If you keep that up I'll be doing more than dripping." Mike gasped as she sucked him harder.

Billie pulled back and gave his cock one more quick lick before she reached for the condom. He never thought he'd be sorry a blowjob stopped.

Billie slid the condom onto his cock as she positioned her wetness above it. Slowly she lowered herself onto him, and he grasped her hips as he pushed deep inside. He held her there for a bit to keep from losing it right then and there. Her pussy was hot, and she clenched around him.

"Billie…. Give me a second." Mike closed his eyes and took several deep breaths. "I've never wanted to come so bad in my life."

"That's what I'm trying to do." Billie started to grind against him.

"I know, but I want this to last longer than ten seconds." Mike chuckled and held her still.

When the pressure eased, he released her, and she ground her heat against his erection. Her breasts bounced as she rode him and he gently pinched her nipples. Billie groaned as she slid her hand between her legs. She started to circle her clit, and Mike almost lost it.

"Fuck, yes." Mike groaned as he felt her tighten around him. When she began to shake and call out his name, he pushed deep and exploded.

For a minute, all he saw was stars as his cock jerked inside her. His body tightened and shook, and for a moment he didn't think he was going to stop.

"Fuck, yes." Mike roared as his cock finally released the last drop and allowed his body to relax slowly.

Billie flopped down on his chest, and the only sound in the room was their heavy panting. Mike wrapped his arms around her and kissed the top of her head as he basked in the afterglow. Sex was always fun for him, but with Billie, it was on a whole different level. It was probably what Ian meant when he said sex with the right woman was like an out of body experience.

"Now, I can sleep." Billie kissed his chest as she lifted her head.

"Me too."

Billie rolled off him, and he hurried to the bathroom to take care of the condom. When he came back, she was still naked and curled up with her hand under her cheek.

"Do you want your nightshirt?" Mike noticed she didn't seem to like sleeping naked.

"I want to sleep as close to you tonight as I can." She pulled back the covers, and he climbed in next to her.

"Whatever you want, Beautiful." Mike didn't mind one bit.

"I love you, Mike." Billie snuggled into his side and rested her hand on his chest.

"I love you too, Billie. So much." Mike held her tightly and closed his eyes.

His last thought before he drifted off to sleep was when he found the bastard who tried to hurt Billie he was going to take him apart. Piece by piece.

Mike stood in his kitchen and waited for John to answer his phone. Billie was still asleep, and he wanted to talk with his brother before Billie got up. It was a little after seven, so he knew there was no way John was still sleeping.

"What the hell, Mike?" John growled into his ear.

"I need to talk to you." Mike didn't let his brother's tone distract him.

"It's my day off, and Olivia stayed with Steph's parents last night." John groaned and then Mike heard Stephanie giggle.

"Oops, did I interrupt something?" Mike laughed.

"Yes," John growled again.

"Well, when you're done drop over to the house. It's important." Mike ended the call before he heard more than a brother should.

An hour later his door opened, and John sauntered in with a smile.

"Isn't your wife pregnant?" Mike laughed when John helped himself to the coffee pot.

"Oh yeah, hormones are off the charts." John wiggled his eyebrows.

"Enjoying it while you can, huh?" Mike shook his head.

"Fucking right." John plopped down on the stool. "I'm assuming you want to know if we've got anything on the fire at the real estate office."

"Yes."

John pulled out his phone, and Mike wondered what the hell he was doing. When Mike tried to ask, John held up his finger.

"I'm waiting for an email from the Fire chief. We know someone threw something through the windows and we're assuming it was some sort of Molotov cocktail. Trunk said he got a strong smell of gas." John scrolled through his emails. "He also said he couldn't get the emergency door to open, but that was because someone had it jammed shut."

"So, someone tried to trap them?" Mike plowed his fingers through his hair and sighed.

"Has Billie started to work on that list for me?" John closed his phone apparently he hadn't gotten the report.

"No, she was ready to drop when we got back here."

"She needs to get me that list. This ass could be someone she knows." John cupped his hand around the mug.

"Did Keith tell you he checked out Abbie and Dana?" Mike asked.

"Keith did what?" Mike spun around at the sound of her voice.

"We can't rule anyone out until we're sure." John picked up his cup.

"I've known Dana and Abbie since kindergarten. They're like my sisters." Billie was pissed.

"No offense but Did you know Sandy's half-sister tried to kill her?" John raised an eyebrow, but the statement made Billie's mouth drop open.

"No, I didn't, but I know those girls would never do anything to hurt me." Billie crossed her arms over her chest and narrowed her eyes at John.

"Now we know too." Mike stood up and moved next to her. "It's just a precaution, nothing personal against your friends."

"I know, I'm just frustrated with this whole thing. Everything left in my house is gone. Abbie doesn't have an office anymore. My friends and family are followed around by bodyguards. We don't know who we have to worry about and it just sucks." Billie rested her head against his chest, and he pulled her tightly against him.

"It does suck, but you're tough and so are your friends and family." Mike kissed the top of her head.

Mike's phone rang, and he tried to reach into his pocket and grab it while still holding Billie. She stepped back so he could answer it.

He glanced at the screen and cursed when he saw it was his office.

"Hey, Stella." Mike wrapped his arm around Billie.

"I know you asked for a few days off, but we got a strange envelope here for you this morning. It says urgent in big bold letters." His secretary wasn't one to overreact about anything, so this envelope must have caught her attention.

"Can you open it for me?" Mike didn't know of anything he was expecting that would be considered urgent.

"Oh, dear lord." Stella gasped.

"What is it, Stel."

"I think you need to see this." For the first time since he met Stella, she seemed shaken.

"Can you fax it to me?"

"Mike, these are photos of ... oh my ... they're horrible." Stella's reaction was unnerving.

"I'll be there in twenty minutes." Mike ended the call and turned to John. "I need to go into the office, but something tells me you should probably come with me."

"What's up?" John was on his feet and following Mike and Billie out of the house.

"That was my secretary Stella, she said there was an enveloped marked urgent and when she opened it there was photos inside. She didn't say what they were, but she's a pretty tough woman, and whatever was in these photos upset her. She said they were horrible." Mike opened the door for Billie and John jumped in the backseat.

They arrived at Mike's office building, and Mike shouldn't have been surprised to see Nick waiting outside. John must have messaged him while they were on the way. Nick jogged over to the entrance to meet them.

"Hey," Nick slapped Mike on the back.

"Hey," Mike pulled open the door and motioned for Billie to go ahead of him. She hadn't said anything the entire way, and it was evident on her face that she was worried. "This may be nothing but Stella's reaction tells me I'm not wrong."

When they walked in Stella was pacing back and forth in front of Mike's closed office door. She saw him and let out a huge breath.

"I see you brought the right people." Stella followed into Mike's office and shut the door. "I haven't shown these to anyone, and as soon as I looked at the first one, I dropped it."

Mike walked around the desk and glanced down. The first thing he saw was someone laying on a floor surrounded by blood. He didn't know who it was because the bastard covered the head. What shook him to his core was Billie's face photoshopped on the picture. Mike held up his hand to keep the photo hidden from Billie.

"What is it?" Billie asked.

"You don't need to see this," Mike motioned for his brothers to come closer.

"Oh, my," Stella covered her mouth when she looked at Billie. It was obvious she recognized Billie's face.

Nick slid a glove from his back pocket and slipped his hand into it. He moved the top picture to the side to see the next one. It was another body, and again Billie's face was covering the person's real face. The third one was a body in the middle of what looked like a room that was on fire.

"What the fuck?" John motioned for Nick to check the next photo.

The last one had Mike shaking with rage. Again, Billie's face but the person didn't appear dead. The woman was tied to a pole as a faceless man appeared to whip her.

"What is it, Mike?" Billie hadn't come closer, but it was probably because Stella had wrapped her arm around Billie's shoulder. Probably Stella's way of keeping Billie from going closer to the desk.

"It's several crime scene pictures," John told her.

"Why do you all look so freaked?" Billie wasn't naive by any means.

"You don't want to know?" Nick growled.

"Yes, I do." Billie took a step forward, but Stella held her back.

"Your face has replaced the face of the victims." John sounded cold.

"My…. Face…" Billie's face lost every bit of color, and Mike wanted to kick his brother's ass for doing that. He hurried around the desk and helped Billie sit down on one of the armchairs.

"It's just someone's idea of a sick joke." Stella tried to reassure Billie, but his secretary didn't know what had happened.

"There's something else here." Nick held up a postcard with writing on the back.

"What is it?" Mike wasn't sure he wanted to know.

"You can't protect her forever." Nick read the note aloud.

"I've had enough of this." Billie was in tears, but Mike had a feeling it was anger, not fear.

"I got someone coming from the lab to get this. If there are any fingerprints, they'll find them." John put the phone up to his ear and walked out of the office.

"I don't know who's trying to torture me, but I'm not letting this guy play with my life or the ones I love." Billie stomped over to the desk, and when Nick stepped in front of her she glared at him

"Billie, I don't think you should…" Nick should know better than to step in front of a pissed off woman.

"Nick, I appreciate you're trying to protect me, but I'm not hiding from this idiot anymore." Billie moved around him.

Mike held himself back because he could see she needed to take her life back. It killed him as she closed her eyes and took a deep breath before she glanced down at the desk. Her initial reaction had him moving toward her but she held up her hand, and he stopped. "John said these were crime scene photos." Billie's voice was soft.

"Yes," Nick answered.

"The first one is Peggy." Billie wasn't asking, and Mike knew why. She'd already seen that one.

"Yes, it is." John entered the office again.

"And the others?" Billie lifted her head and met Mike's gaze.

"The second one is Eugene Wilks." Billie's expression didn't change as John continued. "The third one is the fire at Abbie's real estate and that body is photoshopped into the picture."

"The last one?" Billie stared down at that picture.

"I don't know." John's voice came out like a growl, and Billie's head snapped up.

"You haven't found this woman yet?" Billie sounded as if she was about to pass out and Mike moved next to her.

"No." John met Mike's eyes.

The hair on the back of his neck prickled because from the way John's brow furrowed he had a feeling the last picture was what this sicko had planned for Billie.

# *Chapter 22*

Her body trembled as the contents got carefully placed into evidence bags. The last photo burned into her brain, and she couldn't shake the feeling that the reason John didn't know about the fourth crime scene was that it hadn't happened yet.

Mike's secretary sat with John to give her statement. Mike kept his arm around Billie, and she'd never been so glad to have someone to lean on.

She did her best to put on a brave front, but inside she was frozen with fear. Her body was numb and cold as she crossed her arms to calm her shaking.

"You've got to be the bravest woman I've ever met." Mike kissed the top of her head and whispered.

"Then why do I feel like my body is vibrating." Billie turned her head into his chest and took a huge breath.

"I think that may be me." Mike squeezed her against him, but she knew that wasn't true.

Billie had never been inside Mike's office, and to distract herself, she glanced around the room. The first thing she saw was the credenza behind the desk lined with pictures. She tried to zone out and take in each photo.

There were several of his brothers and their families, but the one that caught her attention was the picture of Mike in a graduation gown in between his parents. He looked like a kid with the mischievous smile and his arms draped over his mother and father. She loved that grin, and a terrifying thought crossed her mind.

"I can't be putting you in danger." Billie sighed and stepped away from him.

"Don't do that." Mike reached for her, but she shook her head.

"No, think about it. Everyone that was hurt or killed was because of me." Billie shouted.

"This isn't your fault, Billie," Nick said.

"This guy has some sick twisted mind." John moved next to her.

"Yes, and his sick twisted mind is the reason Peggy is dead. I hated Eugene, but he didn't deserve to be murdered because of me. Then there's Abbie and Dana who could have died. Even the big bad Trunk or Ben or you know who I mean. No, I need to get this guy to grow a set of balls and come face me." Billie stomped out of the office, but she didn't get far.

She was brought to a sudden stop just outside the office by two of Keith's employees. One she hadn't met before but the other she knew they called Bull. The other guy wasn't quite as big as the rest but had the don't screw with me look.

"Billie, this is Cannon." Bull stepped forward.

"What's your real name?" Billie sighed.

"Joel Wiseman," He gave her a half smile.

"Joel, I'm sure your just as good at your job as the rest, but right now I think you need to back off with the Bull here." Billie tried to step between them, but Bull stopped her.

"Billie, let's go back to my place, and we'll figure this out." Billie spun around at the sound of Mike's voice.

"What's to figure out? I'm putting all of you in danger, and I don't know what I did to this guy or why this guy hates me so much that he…" She didn't know when the tears started, but they streamed down her cheeks, and it was hard to catch her breath.

"Sweetheart, this guy is out of his mind. You didn't do anything wrong." She struggled in Mike's arms for a minute, but his last words had her clinging to the front of his shirt.

"Mike's right, Billie." She felt Bull's hand on her shoulder.

"That last picture. It's a warning of what he wants to do to me." Billie pulled her face away from Mike and looked up at him. "He wants to torture me even more than what he's doing now."

"He won't get near you." Mike cupped the back of her head

and pulled her back to his chest.

"What the hell is going on here?" Billie turned around to see a very distinguished looking man with gray hair and an expensive looking three-piece suit. "Where's Stella?"

"I'm here Charles," Stella scurried passed Bull and wrapped her arms around the man.

"Are you okay?" He asked looking Stella up and down.

"I'm sorry about all this, Charles," Mike guided Billie toward the man.

"Why are the police here?" Charles had Stella pulled into his side.

"Charles, someone's trying to hurt Mike's girlfriend." Stella reached out and grabbed Billie's hand.

"I wasn't aware Mike had a girlfriend." The older man tilted his head and gave Billie a friendly smile.

"Charles, this is Billie Carter." Stella squeezed Billie's hand gently. "Billie this is my husband, Charles Bond."

"Charles is my boss," Mike explained.

"I'm glad to meet the woman who finally reigned in this guy," Charles said. "I don't know what's going on but what can I do?"

Billie couldn't believe this man she just met offered to help and he didn't even know the situation. It amazed her how many people had come into her life willing to help.

"Right now, we just need to get back home but thanks for the offer. I'll let you know. I do think Stel needs a little mini vacation though." Mike wrapped his arm around the woman and gave her a quick hug.

"She can have whatever she wants." Charles looked down at the lovely older woman, and Billie had no doubt the two of them were madly in love.

"Can we just go home and you can wait on me hand and foot for the day." Stella cupped his cheek.

"Say no more." Charles turned with his arm around his wife but stopped for a moment and turned back. "You need anything, call me. Got it, Mike."

"Got it, and thanks."

The drive back to Hopedale was quiet. Billie's brain was going a mile a minute as she tried to think of someone she knew that could be doing this. Someone who would hurt others to get to her. She couldn't think of one person. Even when she was in Labrador, nobody threatened her, and she removed several children from their homes.

No, it didn't make sense.

# *Chapter 23*

Everything happens for a reason. That's what Mike always believed and since he's four-bedroom house was now full of temporary residents. He guessed the reason the house had fallen into his lap was that he needed the room for Billie's family and friends.

Keith had supplied the beds from the bunkhouses he used for his employees when they were in town. Billie's parents and grandfather temporarily moved to Mike's parent's place. His mother and grandmother were overjoyed to have a full house for a while. Tom was also there because Nanny Betty figured he'd be great company for Frank.

Philip, Abbie, and Dana were crashing with him. Matt and Chloe were with Ian and Sandy. Of course, Billie felt a little better with everyone close by but she still worried when everyone went to work. Abbie, of course, worked from his place.

Hopedale was probably inconvenient for most of them but considering what his family had dealt with in the past it wasn't beyond crazy to keep everyone close. Billie had asked Philip and Cannon to check on her mother's neighbor whenever they went to St. John's.

Billie's nightmares got worse since the photos appeared which was why she insisted someone check on Rita and Mrs. Fifield. Keith sent Cannon right away.

"Sweetheart, you need to stop." Mike took her into his arms when he saw her pull out the copy of the list she gave John.

"No, I'm missing something." Billie held up the paper.

"You know, I've heard of people being stalked by people they didn't even know." Abbie wasn't using her brain, apparently.

"Thanks, Abs. That helps a lot." Billie grumbled.

"Sorry, I was watching Rex stretch outside. That man … H.O.T." Abbie fanned herself, but it made Billie laugh.

"Jesus, if her, A.J. or Nick ever get together, watch out." Dana chuckled.

Billie's friends had figured out to watch out for his two brothers.

"How about Nick and A.J?" Abbie flopped back on the sofa and moaned.

"What about Nick and A.J.?" Nick sauntered into the house and grinned at Abbie.

"Abbie was just saying that…" Dana got suddenly silenced when Abbie tossed a pillow at her head.

"Two of us Abbie, sorry, I don't cross swords." Nick winked.

"Not all men are secure enough with themselves for that little Nick." Abbie laughed

The little distraction seemed to take the tension out of Billie's body, and she relaxed into his embrace. It seemed like at least one of his brothers would drop by every day to check on things. Apparently, the constant security around his house wasn't enough.

"Rita said to say hi and that it wasn't necessary for you to worry about her. She's worried about you though." Philip said when he and Cannon returned that evening.

"I promised me and the girls would drop over and have a glass of wine with her before all this started." Billie sighed.

"Can't she come here?" Abbie asked.

"No. Rita's the only one to care for her mom, and it's hard to get her out of the house," Billie explained.

Mike felt bad for the woman. If something happened to one of his parents, they had lots of help but being an only child must be hard when a parent got sick.

"Maybe we could go there Friday." Dana seemed to cringe as she waited for a reply.

"We'll see how the next couple of days go." Mike didn't want to forbid it because maybe it was what Billie needed.

"Turn on NTV news," Matt shouted as he burst through the

door.

Mike turned on the television and changed the channel, and all the air whooshed out of his lungs. Being led into a courtroom in handcuffs was Felix Morris. Billie and Philip gasped as the reporter spoke.

"Child Protection Worker, Felix Morris was arrested today for child pornography, child endangerment, as well as fourteen counts of human trafficking. Police say Mr. Morris was taking children from safe foster homes and placing them in homes where the children were put up for auction. Although Mr. Morris was one of fifteen people arrested, he was the only CPS worker arrested. He's being held without bail."

"That's not the same worker …." Mike hadn't heard Abbie's voice so soft since the day he'd met her.

"That's the fucking bastard." Matt looked like his head was about to explode, and Philip's face was close to the same.

"I knew something was wrong with that guy," Philip growled, and Mike agreed.

The day that he'd met with him, something about him just gave Mike an uneasy feeling.

"My God, if Chloe didn't have us…." Billie turned to Mike. "If she didn't have you."

"I did what I was hired to do, but someone was watching over her." Mike glanced around the room at the shocked and angry expressions.

"Peggy," Abbie, Dana, and Billie said at the same time.

"Do you think it's why he tried so hard to keep Chloe away from us?" Billie's voice was just above a whisper.

"It's not something we've got to worry about now." Mike hugged her. "I do wonder what his snooty supervisor is saying about him now."

"I never got to meet him." Billie stood up.

"You wouldn't want to the guy was a complete ass and tried to assure me that Morris was only acting in the best interest of the child." Mike rolled his eyes. "Both of them were only acting in the best interest of themselves."

"Do you think he's involved too?" Philip asked.

"I don't know, but the pencil nose little prick was lucky I didn't punch him when he told me that he would be able to take me more seriously if I'd showed up dressed more professionally." Mike had gripped onto the table to keep from lunging at the guy.

"What's his name anyway?" Philip asked. "All I ever heard him called was, my supervisor."

"Boyd Bassett." Mike couldn't hide the disdain in his voice.

"Sounds like one of those guys who got beat up in school." Nick chuckled. "Then again so does Felix."

"Are you sure his last name wasn't Bastard," Abbie said.

When he felt Billie's body shake at first, he thought she was upset, but when he looked down, she was laughing. Leave it to Abbie to lighten the mood.

Billie and the girls sat in the living room entranced in some chick flick with his cousins. Mike took the chance to catch up with some emails. He had a few days off, but in reality, he still had information that he expected emails from on a weekly or daily basis.

There was an email from Stella with the court schedule for the next month. October didn't look like it would be too busy a month. He checked through several emails he received from other lawyers concerning a few other custody cases. He'd almost cleared his inbox when another email popped up.

It was the last person he expected to receive an email with thank you in the subject line. He opened the email from Yvonne Duffy and read it to himself.

*Mr. O'Connor*

*First, I would like to give you my sincere thank you for all your work with my darling daughter Whitney. She's so happy with her custody arrangement. I was thrilled to be able to see my little girl so relaxed and enjoying life.*

*Her father and I have decided it was best if we hired a third party to do the transfer between us since when we see each other there is nothing but yelling and name calling. My lawyer told me to contact you to see if you had any suggestions or if you would be interested. I promise you it would be worth it.*

*I've enclosed a sample of the perks you would receive if you'd be willing to take on this extra duty. Please, do not hesitate to contact me.*

*Sincerely*

*Yvonne Duffy*

Mike shook his head as he read the email a second time. The email must have been sent by someone other than the bitchy Mrs. Duffy because she wasn't that interested in her daughter in the meetings they had. Mike's curiosity made him click on the PDF file attached to the email.

Mike was instantly sorry he opened it. The first thing to fill his screen was a picture of Mrs. Duffy wearing nothing but a smile. Mike didn't try to scroll through what looked to be several more pictures.

"Porn, bro? Really?" Mike spun in his chair to see John in the doorway.

"Fuck, no. It's from the mother of one of the kids I represented." Mike shuddered. "That woman is a fucking nutcase."

"You must have done a good job from what I saw." John closed the office door and sat next to him.

"Yeah, but it wasn't in her favor. That woman is a barracuda that eats men alive." Mike deleted the email and shuddered again.

"I'm assuming you saw the news." John leaned on the desk.

"Yeah, is that your case too?" Mike leaned back in his chair and linked his fingers behind his head.

"No, I'd probably kill the bastard," John growled.

"But," Mike knew there was one coming.

"I got a call from Steve Parker. You remember him?" John asked.

Mike nodded. Steve worked with the Hopedale PD for a few years but got a promotion and was transferred to the St. John's division. Mike wasn't sure exactly what he did, but he did know he worked with kids.

"Steve told me he's working with the kids that got tangled up with Morris." John pulled out a rolled up piece of paper and opened it. "It's a list of the children that were sold as well as the kids they had buyers lined up for."

Mike shook because he knew what was next.

"Chloe was already bought and paid for. The delivery date is written next to her name here." John pointed to the date, and Mike jumped to his feet.

"Isn't that the…" Mike snatched the paper off the desk and stared at the date.

"Date Peggy Butler was murdered." John finished.

"You're saying Morris killed Peggy?" Mike stared at his brother.

"I can't say, but if you ask me, I think whoever is doing this could be the person who purchased Chloe and is trying to get what he paid for." John stood up.

"So this guy is after Chloe, not Billie." Mike plowed his fingers through his hair. "But why go after Abbie, Dana, and Billie? That doesn't make any sense."

"Maybe he didn't know Billie isn't the one who has custody of Chloe." John shrugged his shoulders.

"Felix knows." Mike still enjoyed the sour face he put on the man when he slapped the paternity papers in front of the asshole.

"I don't know, bro but I've warned Keith, and we need to let Billie's family know." John opened the office door. "I'm also not taking any chances with our kids. If that guy is lurking around trying to get to Chloe, he may just snatch the first kid he can get."

Mike didn't like the thought of that. There were other children in the town that didn't have the security his nieces and nephews did.

"Maybe we should put a warning out there for the rest of the town," Mike suggested.

"I'm already on it. Steve's giving a statement on the news tomorrow." Mike walked out to the front with John. "Do you want me to explain it to Billie and her family?"

"How about you go tell her parents and grandfather? I'll tell Billie and her brothers." Mike gave his brother a quick hug.

"I let Sandy know, and she's keeping the kids in the yard. Keith sent another guy over there with Crash and Trunk." John walked down the steps. "Keep your eyes open, bro."

"Thanks." Mike closed the door and leaned against it.

"What did John want?" Billie walked out of the living room and leaned against the wall.

"Where are Matt and Philip?" Mike held out his hand, and she walked into his arms.

"Philip is in there complaining about the movie we picked, and Matt is out in the yard." Billie snuggled into his chest. "You didn't answer my question."

"I will, but your brothers need to hear this too."

The girls groaned when Billie shut off the television and Philip sighed with relief. Their faces turned to concern when Mike told them he had some news about their situation. He was going to ask Pam, Kristy, Isabelle, and Jess to leave but figured Billie and her brothers needed all the support they could get.

Before he had a chance to start, his front door flew open. John shook his head as he walked into the house. It seemed he hadn't gotten to the end of the road when a parade of vehicles filled with his family turned into Mike's driveway.

"I haven't had a chance…." Mike tried to tell John, but he was interrupted by his grandmother.

"Doncha worry 'bout a ting." Nanny Betty hugged Billie and her brothers. All of which looked utterly confused.

"Nan, I haven't...." She held up her hand and continued.

"We bin here befer." Nanny Betty turned to Mike. "Git on wit it."

Mike waited until everyone filed into the living room and either found a place to sit or stood against the wall. All the kids were held close to one of the adults as if they'd disappear. Mike's gaze went to Chloe. She was scanning the room and looked in complete awe.

"Maybe we should get a couple of the guys to take the kids out to the yard," Kurt suggested.

"This isn't something they need to be worrying about." James nodded.

"Is someone after us again?" James son Mason said it as if it was nothing new. The seven-year-old had seen way more than his share of danger.

"It'll be fine, sweetie." Marina turned the little boy and led him out of the room, but before he was out of earshot, Mike heard him reply to his mother.

"Of course, it will be, Mom. We've got the superheroes to protect us." Mason seemed more annoyed than scared.

"Superheros?" Billie whispered.

"Hulk and a couple of the other guys wear these superhero

shirts a lot. The boys started referring to them as superheroes." James explained and Billie nodded.

Mike sighed as he and John filled everyone in on what the police had discovered. Matt started to pace in front of the window and looked as if he was about to explode. Then again most of the people in the room seemed pissed.

"So this son of a bitch killed our friend because he was trying to get to Chloe?" Dana growled.

"It's what we think, yes." John nodded.

"And nobody knows who this guy is or what he looks like?" Abbie slowly stood up.

"Steve's team is going through the files and records they found on the computers they confiscated from the group they arrested," John explained.

"But they don't have everyone involved with this." Dana shot to her feet.

"Not all of them have been arrested yet, no." John glanced at Mike as if he was about to get jumped.

"Abbie, Dana, sit down." Billie stepped in front of John. "There's something you're not telling us."

"I've told you everything I can." John stepped back.

"John, I don't care what kind of rules or laws you think you're protecting and I don't give a shit that your Uncle is standing over there probably warning you with some look to not tell us what we need to know but I swear..."

"Tell them." Kurt's gruff voice halted Billie's rant.

"Chloe wasn't the only one this guy paid for," John said.

Mike wasn't sure what John was talking about because he hadn't said anything earlier.

"Who else did this guy pay for, John?" Billie growled through gritted teeth.

"You,"

Billie's eyes closed and she turned red. It was almost as if she was trying to calm herself but not because she was scared. Billie was pissed.

Mike knew because the rage was building up inside him that someone out there thought they could buy not only Chloe but Billie as well.

"That last picture delivered to Mike, that's going to be his way to get me to submit to him." Billie hadn't opened her eyes, but her hands fisted at her sides, and she shook.

John didn't answer because Billie wasn't asking a question, it was a statement. When her eyes opened, they were black, and Mike felt a sense of pride that Billie wasn't about to let this guy scare her.

"What can I do to help bring this guy out?" Billie looked John in the eyes.

"Belinda, no." Her mother gasped.

"Billie, not a chance," Philip growled.

"No fucking way, little girl," Matt shouted.

"Billie, you can't put yourself in that kind of danger." Abbie spun Billie around to face her.

"So what do you want me to do? Hide until they find him which might be never." Billie turned to Mike. "Am I wrong?"

"Billie, this is way too dangerous." Mike reached for her, but she stepped away.

"Mike, I love you, and I want to be able to do more than sit in your house or your yard because some sicko thinks he has the right to buy people and use them the way he sees fit." Billie took a deep breath and let it out slowly before she took a step forward and cupped his face. "Are you telling me you want to be worried every time we go anywhere or that you want to have to take Ben, Lane or any of the other guys everywhere you go. I mean I like the guys but no offense to any of them, I like being alone with you."

What was he supposed to say to that? The truth was the only time he and Billie were alone were when they went to bed, and as much as he enjoyed that part, he wanted to be able to just walk to the beach or the park.

"You know if you try and stop her she's going to find some way to do it anyway." Mike glanced over Billie's head at Sandy.

Mike shook his head because when Sandy was trying to draw out the person that was making her life a living hell, she slipped out her father's bathroom window and almost got herself killed.

"Churchie, not everyone would do what you did, and she doesn't need you giving her ideas." Ian pulled Sandy under his arm.

"But she's right." Marina smiled.

"Marina, you're not helping." James narrowed his eyes at his pretty wife.

"I want my freedom back." Billie wrapped her arms around his waist, and Mike gazed into those chocolate eyes. "I want to be free with you, and I want Chloe to be safe."

Mike pulled her against his chest and kissed the top of her head. He scanned the room to see different expressions. The women's showed agreement with Billie. The men had that '*hell, no but we don't have a say*' look.

"I could lose you." Mike hugged her tightly.

"If you keep hugging me so tight, you could lose me now 'cause I won't be able to breathe." Her muffled voice strained.

Reluctantly he released her but grabbed her hands and pressed them to his lips. Billie was strong and determined, but Mike saw too many news reports of women disappearing and never seen again. Human trafficking rings around the world bought and sold people like cattle, and one of them already bought and paid for Billie, that shook him to his core.

"I don't like this, but I'll support you with whatever you want to do." Mike could hardly get the words out as he studied her beautiful face. He just hoped she wasn't about to make a huge mistake. Billie could be about to put herself in the arms of a monster.

# Chapter 24

"There's not a snowball's chance in hell that I'm letting her do this." Matt roared.

"You don't control me, Matt." Billie turned to face her brother and cringed.

Billie's never seen Matt so pissed before, but he directed that fury at Mike, not her. He stalked toward where she and Mike stood, and Billie put herself in between them.

"You. I warned you if she got hurt I'd kick your ass." Matt's voice didn't even sound like him.

"Matthew, back off." Billie wasn't afraid of her brother, and she doubted Mike was but she didn't want a fight in the middle of both their families. "I'll get Jess to kick your big ass."

A chuckle from his cousin had Matt turning around to glare at her, but it didn't appear to bother Jess. She just gave him the raised eyebrow and stretched her arms over her head.

"Trust me, pal. You don't want to go there." Aaron spoke up

for the first time since he'd arrived.

"That's enough." Her father's voice echoed through the house and made almost everyone jump.

It was the first time Mike had heard Bill raise his voice since the day he met him. He stomped across the room and stepped between his son and daughter.

"I've had enough of this. We've all been walking on eggshells around each other because we don't know when someone is going to snap and it's all because we feel trapped. I don't want Belinda or Chloe to be in danger anymore." He turned to Matt. "Son, I'm scared too but none of this is Mike's fault, and you really shouldn't be shouting at him." He turned to Billie and cupped her shoulders. "I don't want you to do this either, but I know you're going to regardless of what anyone says. Promise me you'll let the police put together a plan and do what they tell you."

"I will, Dad." Billie wrapped her arms around her father and closed her eyes to hold back the tears.

"I can't believe this." Matt stomped out of the room, and she heard the front door slam. Before anyone else spoke a voice in the back of the crowd shouted.

"I'm on it." Bull hurried out of the room.

"So what can we do?" Billie turned to John.

"It's not my case, Billie." John shook his head.

"Then call your friend." Billie motioned to the phone in his hand.

"He may not agree to this." John put the phone to his ear as he walked out of the room.

"Bullshit," Nick pulled out his smartphone. "Steve knows if one of our women are putting themselves out there, we're all on board."

Our women.

The statement sounded so chauvinistic, but it made her smile that Mike's family grouped her in with the fabulous females in his family.

"Really, Nick? Could you sound more like a cave man?" Isabelle rolled her eyes.

"First things first," Kurt moved over to Billie. "Have you ever taken any self-defense classes?"

"Umm ... No, but I grew up with two older brothers." Billie chuckled.

"But I'm sure they loved you, so they weren't out to hurt you." Kurt's expression was like stone.

"I wouldn't exactly say they didn't want to hurt me at times," Billie remembered several occasions she would run to her parents because Philip or Matt had hurt her.

"Jess, I want you to show Billie some basic self-defense. I'm sure Keith will give you the time off." Kurt glared at Keith and then turned his attention to Jess.

"I was going to…" Jess began.

"You and I will have a long talk after all this is over and Keith?" Kurt turned to Mike's brother.

"Yes, sir?" It was odd to see a man as big as Keith with the look of a naughty boy on his face.

"I'll be having a long chat with you too." Kurt turned back to her, but she managed to see Keith point his finger at Jess and shake his head.

"Have you ever shot a gun?" Kurt asked.

"No," Billie shook her head.

"Mike, do you keep up with your skills?" Kurt glanced over her head.

"I haven't been to the range in a long while." Mike almost sounded ashamed. Why would he need to know how to shoot? He was a lawyer.

"James," Kurt didn't turn around to look for his other nephew.

"I'll take care of it." James left the room with his phone to his ear.

"Mike, you'll be joining her," Kurt ordered.

"Steve said if we can come up with a plan to draw this guy out, he'll be there with his team. We'll be back up." John re-entered the living room.

"So, now we need a plan." Billie sighed.

"Tom, we gotta go get supplies." Nanny Betty hurried out of the room with Tom behind her.

"Supplies?" Billie glanced at Mike.

"Let's just say, none of us will go hungry." Ian chuckled.

She was scared, but when she looked around the room full of people she loved and grown to love, Billie knew she'd have the courage and strength to get through whatever she was about to face.

"Ugh." Billie slipped on the mat for the fifth time.

"Come on, girl." Jess stood over her with her hand held out.

"I used to like you." Billie groaned and reached for Jess's hand.

"Just be glad, Dad isn't teaching you." Jess laughed.

"You're bad enough." Billie bent over and glared at Mike's cousin.

"Abbie, are you ready?" Jess turned to where Abbie and Dana sat off to the side of the small workout room.

"I don't see why we need this." Abbie stood up. "I mean, I'm a lover, not a fighter."

Before anyone could respond, an arm wrapped around her

friend's neck and Abbie screamed. Dana jumped up and backed away.

"What the fuck?" Abbie struggled with the massive arm. Billie could now see who it was.

"How are you gonna get out of that?" Jess chuckled.

"Ben, for fuck's sake. Let go." Abbie struggled, but it seemed like Trunk was about to give all of them a lesson.

"Do you think an attacker would just let you go if you cursed on him?" Trunk growled.

Abbie sighed and stopped her struggle. Dana stood next to Billie with a grin because she knew as well as Billie that Abbie hated to be wrong.

"Just sing." Jess crossed her arms.

"What?" Abbie threw her arms up in the air, but Trunk still had his arm around her neck.

"Trunk, come here." Jess laughed.

Trunk chuckled when he released Abbie, and she swung her fist at him. Abbie missed, and from the look on her face, she wanted to punch him in the nose.

"Okay, girlies. Sing is an acronym. It stands for solar plexus, instep, nose." Jess pointed to each part as she said them. "and every man's favorite, groin." Jess looked as if she was about to jab Trunk and he covered himself.

"Watch it, little girl." Trunk pointed his finger at her.

"So, watch while I demonstrate on Trunk." Jess laughed when Trunk backed away. "I'm not actually going to hit you. You're such a pussy."

Billie observed as Jess slowly showed each step and Trunk made them laugh by moving in slow motion after each pretend blow. He was quite a character, and he seemed to have taken a liking to Abbie.

"Do you want to try?" Jess asked them.

"Oh, I'll give it a try." Abbie grinned as she stalked toward Trunk.

Trunk looked both excited and scared at the same time. He wrapped his large arm around Abbie's neck and whispered something into her ear. Abbie narrowed her eyes, and for a minute she didn't move.

"What's wrong, Abs?" Trunk chuckled, but that was his first mistake because Abbie came back with her elbow just like Jess had shown them. Trunk didn't expect it, and the air blew out in a whoosh. Abbie stomped down on his instep, and he cursed. When he turned his head to avoid an elbow to the nose, he almost missed Abbie's fist aimed at his groin.

Trunk grabbed her hand kicked his leg behind her knee and knocked her on her back. He sat on her and held her hands over her head the whole while Abbie called him everything but his name.

"You're a real tiger aren't you?" Trunk chuckled, but Abbie

was able to get one of her hands free and quickly used her partial freedom to grab again.

Trunk jumped up before she could and left her panting on the floor with a look that could cut someone in two. She propped herself up on her elbows and turned to look at where Billie, Dana, and Jess stood.

"How was that?" Abbie was a little out of breath, but Trunk clenched his jaw and growled.

"Not bad." Jess laughed. "Anyone else what to give it a go?"

"Not fucking likely. I'll send Smash in. You can beat the shit out of his danglers." Trunk grumbled and left the room.

"Smash?" Dana laughed.

"Gage Hodder, he's another analyst Keith has." Jess helped Abbie to her feet.

The elusive Smash didn't appear, but Jess gave Billie a rough workout. Billie did feel better about being able to protect herself, but that didn't help the sickening feeling she felt every time she thought about being sold to someone.

That evening Billie felt the effects of training with Jess. She had aches where she didn't know she had muscles. It was no wonder Jess looked like a bodybuilder, well not quite a bodybuilder but the woman had no body fat.

"How did it go today?" Mike walked into the room where

Billie lay spread out on the bed. She lifted her head, and he smiled.

"Jess tried to kill us, and Abbie tried to castrate Trunk." Billie let her head drop back and groaned.

"Feeling a little sore?" Mike chuckled as he crawled onto the bed.

"No, a little sore would be fine, but my body thinks I lost my freaking mind," Billie grumbled.

"Roll over." Mike twirled his finger, and she laughed.

"Do you think I could move right now? It was enough of a struggle to raise my hands to wash my hair. Which is why it's still in a towel by the way." Billie sighed.

Mike shook his head and laughed, but he carefully helped her roll over onto her stomach. He pulled the robe she'd wrapped around her, down to her waist and positioned her arms down by her sides as he straddled her legs.

When the heat of his hands touched her skin, she moaned. Then he gently worked his fingers into the sore muscles across her shoulders and down her back. She was sure if anyone were listening they'd think there was more than a massage going on.

"I thought I loved you before but… God that's incredible." Billie sighed.

"I'm glad you like this, but those little noises are making me stiff." Mike groaned when she lifted her hips to tease him.

"I'll massage that for you if you want?" Billie giggled when she heard him curse.

"As tempting as that is, let me do this for you first." Mike leaned over her body and kissed her ear. "Then you can thank me." He sucked her earlobe into his mouth, and she shivered.

Billie's body was vibrating with need by the time Mike worked his way down her back to her ass and the top of her thighs. He ran his tongue down the center of her back while he kneaded the muscles in the back of her legs.

"Fucking beautiful," Mike mumbled.

When his tongue slowly traced between the cheeks of her ass, she gasped. She wasn't sure how she felt about him back there, but it made her core ache with need. He pushed her legs apart and glided his tongue painstakingly slow to where she needed it most.

"Mike. Oh. Yes." Billie raised her hips and fisted the blankets when his tongue slid into her, and his finger made small circles around her clit.

"Come for me," Mike growled against her wetness sending a vibration through her entire body. "I want you to come on my tongue, Beautiful."

Those words were all she needed because her body shuttered as an orgasm exploded through her body. Mike didn't give her a chance to move as he flipped her over, covered her folds with his mouth and drove his tongue deep inside her.

"Oh. Fuck. Mike." Billie's back arched as another climax hit her.

"You. Taste. Better. Than. Anything. I've. Ever. Touched. With. My. Tongue." Mike placed a kiss on her body for every word he spoke as he moved above her.

Billie glanced down between them and saw his erection bulging in the front of his jeans. She bit her lip and looked up to meet his eyes. The blue was darker from arousal, and she was sure hers were probably the same.

"That looks really, painful. He's probably not happy about being confined like that" Billie smiled as she cupped the front of his jeans.

"Oh, he certainly isn't, but I don't trust him when he's uncaged. All he wants is to dive right into that sweet pussy." Mike closed his eyes while she rubbed him through his clothes.

"I don't see the problem with that." Billie popped the button and glided the zipper down.

"It's not a problem. It's just that my mouth likes to have a turn too." Mike dropped his head and sucked a nipple into his mouth.

"I understand that. I like when that mouth takes its turn." Billie pushed him over until he was on his back.

"Condom," Mike gasped as she pulled him free of his jeans and he ripped off his shirt.

"My mouth needs a turn too." Billie didn't give him a chance to answer as she dropped his jeans and crawled between his legs.

"Fuck," Mike growled through clenched teeth when she took him into her mouth and slid her lips down his length. She felt his legs tighten and squeeze against her as she cupped his balls and moved her lips up and down his length.

There was no way she could get the full length of him into her mouth unless she took him down her throat and she knew that made his eyes roll back in his head. She pulled her mouth off and looked up. He was watching every move she made.

"He wants inside." Mike strained when her hands squeezed his balls gently.

"Not yet. I want to watch one thing." The confused look on his face made her giggle.

"What are you up to?"

Billie kept her gaze locked with his and slowly took the head of his cock into her mouth. He smiled as she slowly slid her mouth up and down a couple of times. When she slid down further, she saw the recognition in his face. He knew what was next.

"Holy Fuck." Mike's eyes rolled back in his head, and Billie slowly slid her mouth up and down his length a couple of more times, but she wanted him inside her.

Mike had her on her back in seconds, and the condom rolled on. He grabbed her ankles and rested them on his shoulders. His cock was at the entrance of her sex, and she lifted her hips. Mike grabbed her hips and pulled her onto his length.

"Baby, you feel so fucking good around me." Mike thrust in and out of her.

"I love the way you feel inside me." Billie panted as his speed increased.

"Billie, Fuck." Mike's hips moved fast as he slammed into her over and over.

She knew he wasn't going to last much longer and neither was she. When he pressed the heel of his hand against her swollen clit and rubbed it in time with his thrusts, she felt it start at her toes and slowly travel up her body.

"Come for me, Billie." Mike panted. "I want to feel you come all over my cock."

Seconds later her body trembled and Mike slammed deep inside her. Behind her eyelids, she saw stars, and she was sure she was floating. She'd never had issues achieving orgasm, but with Mike, they were intense and mind-blowing.

She didn't even notice Mike's weight on top of her until she opened her eyes and he was grinning down at her. He was like the cat who ate the canary.

"You look pretty impressed with yourself." Billie stretched her arms over her head.

"You look pretty satisfied, Beautiful." Mike brushed his lips against hers.

"Hmmm. I'm not sure satisfied is the right word." Billie teased but gasped when she realized he was still inside her and still hard. "You didn't come?"

"Not yet. I just wanted you to enjoy that orgasm." Mike covered her mouth with his, and his hips started to move again.

Billie groaned as he slammed into her over and over. His arms braced on either side of her, and he gazed into her eyes. Two more pumps and Mike's body shook. He pushed himself deep inside her, and she felt his cock twitch and jerk.

"That's it, baby." Billie cooed as she grabbed his ass and kept him deep inside her.

Mike returned from the bathroom and crawled under the covers next to her. She didn't bother to put her nightshirt back on. She liked to sleep next to him with nothing between them.

"Thanks for the massage." Billie turned on her side and tucked her hand under her cheek.

"Anytime, Beautiful." Mike kissed the tip of her nose and pulled her into his arms.

"Jess is Satan by the way." Billie laughed.

"Not really, maybe the spawn of Satan. Uncle Kurt is truly evil." Mike swirled his finger into her hair.

"I doubt that." Billie tilted her head back so she could look at him.

"Let me give you an example. When Uncle Kurt taught us Karate, he would have us stretch. We would have to do splits against the wall." Mike shuddered.

"Wouldn't that help support your back?" Billie didn't understand.

"You don't get it. We were facing the wall with our legs spread and if he felt we weren't stretching enough, he'd push us further into the wall." She felt him squeeze his legs together.

"Ouch," Billie cringed.

"Yeah, to this day if I'm near a wall and Uncle Kurt is around I move." Mike chuckled.

Billie curled her body into his and closed her eyes. Lately, the only time she felt at peace was in his arms. She decided to try and lure this guy out, but she had no idea how she would do that or whether she even should.

"James is meeting us at the range tomorrow." Mike yawned.

"I'm not sure about the gun thing." Billie had never liked the damn things.

"It's only to make sure you know how to use one. You may never have to touch one again." Mike kissed the top of her head. "Trust me." And she did.

# *Chapter 25*

James was impressed with how well Billie could shoot. Mike was as well. Considering she'd never even held a gun in her life, she seemed to be a natural. At first, she was nervous, but his brother helped ease that worry.

He rolled his eyes a couple of times when James encouraged her with how much better she was than Mike. Not that his brother was wrong, once she stopped closing her eyes every time she pulled the trigger, she did very well.

"I'm still not sure I like shooting." Billie turned in the seat to look at him.

"Not everyone enjoys it," Rex said.

Rex and Crash had been their escorts to the range. Mike didn't argue because it meant he could sit in the back and hold Billie in his arms.

"Do you enjoy it, Caden?" Billie asked the gruff man. Like his sisters-in-law, Billie refused to call any of the guys by their nicknames. To Billie it wasn't Crash in the front passenger seat, it was Brent Adams, and Rex wasn't driving, Caden Dixon was.

"Darlin', I spent my childhood hunting and most of my adult life in the military." Rex chuckled. He was the only one of Keith's security guys that wasn't Canadian. Rex was from Georgia.

"What about you, Brent?" Billie leaned forward and rested her chin on the seat in front of her.

"I enjoy it when I'm hunting or on the range but when I have to use it for work, no." Crash turned to look at her. "People learn how to shoot and handle weapons for lots of reasons. Mine was initially a hobby. I still enjoy the hobby aspect but when I've got to kill some asshole because he's about to hurt someone. I don't enjoy that. You're learning to handle a gun for protection. Maybe after we get this dick, Mike here can bring you back to the range and show you the fun side."

Billie sat back and dropped her head on Mike's shoulder. Crash was right; this wasn't a trip to the range for fun. They were there to teach the woman he loved how to handle a weapon in case she got into a life and death situation. Mike pulled her tighter against him.

"I'm okay." Billie took his hand and gazed up at him. It was as if she sensed his fear.

"You're a trooper." Rex glanced at Mike in the mirror. "Mike's one lucky bastard."

Mike stepped into his front door and immediately wanted to turn around and run. His dining table contained piles of papers and folders. It looked like a command center with the number of people around it.

"What's going on?" Billie whispered.

"I've got no idea." Mike took her hand and walked into the room.

"Good, you're back." John motioned for them to come closer.

"Can you explain why my house is full of cops?" Mike realized that she knew most of the men and women scurrying around his place.

"I'm not a cop." Keith glanced up from something he was reading

"Okay, why are Keith and a bunch of cops in my house?" Mike turned toward John but rolled his eyes when he heard another voice.

"I'm not a cop either," Smash shouted from where he was set up next on the center island separating the kitchen from the living area. Sandy was next to him, and there was a line of computer equipment in front of them.

"For fuck's sake, why is everyone here?" Mike groaned.

"You remember Steve?" John motioned for the blond man to join them.

"Yes, nice to see you again," Mike shook the man's hand.

"Steve Parker, Billie Carter." John didn't look up from the paper as he did introductions.

"John," Mike shouted to get his brother's attention.

"What?" Mike could only laugh when John's head snapped up.

"Why. Are. You. Here?" Mike spoke slowly.

"Steve wanted to make sure we had all the information we needed to pull this off." John turned to Billie. "Steve got a question for you."

"Okay," Billie smiled.

"Did you have a break-in at your house or your parents before Peggy died?" Steve asked.

Billie shook her head.

"What about at your job?" Steve glanced down at the folder he had.

"Not that I know. There was the fire, but that was after." Billie shuddered when she mentioned the fire and Mike squeezed her hand.

"This is what makes me wonder if it's the same guys." Steve looked at John. "If you look down through that list, every one of them had a break-in just before they were abducted."

"I see that." John's finger was sliding down the paper.

"Wait, Billie the night that stupid cat got in your house." Mike spun around. Matt was sat on the couch behind them a bunch of papers on his lap.

"What's he talking about?" John asked.

"I left the kitchen window open a while back, and Cougar got into the house." Billie shrugged her shoulders.

"I don't get it." Steve looked at Matt.

"Someone was outside her house. We called the cops. There should be a report about it." Matt started shuffling through the papers.

"I forgot about that." Billie covered her mouth with her hand.

"That crazy cat is the reason we heard the guy. It's like a fucking guard cat." Matt continued to shuffle through the papers.

"I got it," Sandy shouted.

"What?" John turned.

"Here's the report." Sandy pointed to the computer screen in front of her.

"Kurt's gonna kill you." Smash shook his head.

"What? I'm a police officer, and I've got access to the database." Sandy shrugged her shoulders.

"Aren't you on maternity leave?" Aaron laughed.

Mike hadn't even seen his youngest brother until he popped up from behind another computer.

"Aren't you supposed to be watching the screen to see if the computer recognizes one of those faces?" Sandy grumbled.

"Anyway." John sighed.

"Yeah, there's a report of a prowler. Let's see…" Sandy

clicked a few more keys and stopped. "Blake Harris was the reporting officer."

"That's Greg's younger brother," Aaron dropped his head when Sandy growled at him.

"Call him." John turned around.

"Why would you call him?" Matt asked.

"Because he took the report and I want to know if he remembers anything that he didn't write down." John glanced at his phone and dropped his head.

"What's wrong?" Mike asked.

"Three, two, one." John counted and then motioned to the door.

"I got lots a food fer ya." Nanny Betty scurried into the house. "I know yar busy but if ya can take a spare one a lads fer a second to carry da stuff in, me and Tom will git out a yar hair."

Before anyone asked, at least four of the men and women jumped up and ran out the door. Nanny Betty pointed to the long counter next to his stove. Aaron ran over and moved some of the boxes that lay there.

"Doncha worry, none a dis got to be heated or anyting. Gotta keep ya strent up." John shook his head and turned around.

"Thanks, Nan." Mike tried not to laugh at his brother's sigh. "I'm sure everyone appreciates it."

"Yes, Mrs. O'Connor, we do." Steve grabbed a sandwich off

one of the trays she'd uncovered.

"Oh dear." Billie covered her mouth when Nanny Betty glared up at the man.

"Mrs. O'Connor was me mudder-in-law, and she was a witch. Yar here ta help our girl?" Nanny Betty asked.

"Yes, umm...ma'me." Steve stammered.

"Den ya call me Nan or Nanny Betty like everyone else." Nanny Betty touched his arm and nodded. "I'm off. If ya needs any more food, text me."

With that statement, she scurried out with poor Tom following behind her. All eyes in the room watched as his bigger than life grandmother disappeared through the door.

"Wasn't that Tom Roberts, the business mogul?" One of the other officers asked.

"Yep," Smash laughed.

"And he's driving around your grandmother?" Steve's expression was one of shock.

"Well, no. Nan's probably driving." Sandy laughed.

"Is he retired?" Steve asked.

"Since he found Nan again, yes." Aaron chuckled.

"I'm not even gonna ask." Steve laughed. "Let's see that report, Sandy and get Harris here."

Billie sat next to her brother and helped him look through the pile of papers for any reports of break and entries they'd missed. Mike helped John mark out points where the abductions and break-ins occurred.

"Why exactly are you using my house as a command post?" Mike finally got a chance to ask.

"Because it's big." Steve chuckled.

"Not enough room at the station?" Mike shook his head.

"There is but haven't you noticed not all the people here work there, and they wouldn't be able to help if we did this there." John raised his eyebrow.

"Uncle Kurt's idea?" Mike knew that Kurt tried to keep to the rules, but when it came to family he allowed them to be bent but if asked he knew nothing. After all, he was now Chief of Police of the Newfoundland Police Department.

"I can't comment on that." John chuckled.

"Wow, you really will make a great superintendent." Steven laughed.

"What?" Mike didn't realize his brother was about to be promoted.

"Yeah, he's taking over the end of the year." Sandy grinned.

"Jesus, bro. Will this fuck that up?" Mike didn't want his brother to ruin his career.

"I don't give a fuck if it does. That girl over there is family."
John grabbed Mike on the shoulder and squeezed. "You were there for
Steph and me and the rest. It's our turn to help you now."

Mike wasn't an emotional person, but that statement from his
brother had a huge lump form in his throat, and he had trouble
swallowing it down. The fact that his house was full of people who
were there to protect the love of his life. It hit him straight in the heart.

"If this Kumbaya moment is over, can we get on with it?"
Steve circled his hand in front of the map.

How could they have been at this until almost midnight? Mike
was exhausted, and Billie was curled up on the couch next to her
brother. Matt's head dropped, and he snored softly. Most of the people
had left except Steve, John, Aaron, and Smash.

"By the way, where's Abbie, Dana, and Philip?" Mike felt
sorry he hadn't realized they weren't around.

"They're staying at Kim's place tonight. Kim and Emily are at
some conference in Montreal for a few days. Keith suggested it.
Trunk's staying with them." John explained.

"Why didn't they just stay here?" Mike didn't understand the
change in arrangements.

"Philip said he was getting a little uncomfortable with the night
noises." Aaron chuckled.

"Fuck off," Mike snapped at his brother.

"That's not a joke, bro." John raised his eyebrow. "Seems you guys were a little enthusiastic last night."

"Damn," Mike wasn't embarrassed, but he knew Billie would be. "Keep that little bit of info to yourselves please."

"At least her parents weren't staying here." Aaron grinned.

For the next few days, Mike dealt with his house full of people. The only time he got alone time with Billie was at night when they went to bed. By that time they were both so exhausted, they'd do little but fall asleep in each other's arms. Not that he was complaining about that aspect.

"Steve's been in touch with the head of the Human Trafficking Taskforce. They gave him the number to the liaison here in Newfoundland. Apparently, they have a couple of people here doing surveillance. The guy said when we're ready to let him know and he'd help with whatever we need." John explained as he and Mike finished their map layout.

They'd found almost twenty missing children over a ten month period who'd fit the parameters they'd found. From what they could figure out, the children were all between the ages of six and thirteen. All transferred from one foster home to the next, and every one of them dealt with Felix Morris.

Steve was also investigating three missing women cases. All women lived alone, had no family, and reported a break-in several days before they disappeared. The other issue was, all three names were on the list they'd retrieved from Felix Morris's computer, and that terrified Mike. Chloe and Billie's names were on that list, and they were the only ones that hadn't vanished.

"I don't understand why they'd go after me. I've got a family which includes two very intrusive brothers." Billie glanced at Matt.

"Intrusive, no. Protective, yes." Matt poked her.

"Either way, I don't fit that profile." Billie tapped her finger on the paper.

"By the way, we went to talk to Boyd Bannister yesterday. He's out of the office for a couple of weeks." Steve raised an eyebrow. "I asked if it was possible to get in touch with him, but the office told me that he was not able to be reached."

"Really? The supervisor of Child Protection Services can't be reached?" Mike chuckled.

"Have you ever heard of that happening?" John asked.

"Never." Mike had dealt with CPS many times. Especially, during a custody case when the child was at risk.

"Who do you deal with when you contact them?" Steve asked.

"I deal with the office on Elizabeth Avenue regularly, but when I had the meeting about Chloe, they wanted to meet at the foster home," Mike said. "I thought it was weird at first and I called my contact on Elizabeth, and they do that sometimes for the convenience of the child."

"You never met at one of the homes before?" John asked.

"I have but usually the foster parent was there but the only ones there that day was me, Chloe, Morris, and Bannister." Mike turned to Steve. "I do remember getting an uneasy feeling, but I figured it was because I didn't like the way they were glaring at Chloe."

"So, you think this Boyd guy is involved, don't you?" Billie linked her arm into his.

Steve looked at John and something about the way they exchanged glances, Mike knew there was something they hadn't told them.

"We think Boyd could be the buyer." Steve leaned back in his chair. "We believe that day you got Chloe; they were prepared to tell you she was staying in foster care and as soon as you left they were taking her."

Billie's grip on his arm tightened, and he felt someone's hand on his shoulder. When he glanced behind him, Matt stood over him, and his face was white as a sheet.

"If Mike hadn't had those papers, Chloe would have vanished?" Matt stumbled over his words, and Mike could feel the man tremble.

"Yes," Steve glanced up at Matt.

"I need to go." Matt turned and hurried from the room.

"I'll be right back." Billie jumped to her feet and went after her brother.

"I can't imagine what that man is going through." John leaned his elbows on the table.

"I think he's dealing with a lot of guilt but he shouldn't. It wasn't his fault." Mike glanced back to see if Billie had returned. "I don't think he's faced losing Peggy either."

Mike sat up in bed. He was exhausted, but he wanted to wait for Billie to return. She'd been outside for the last hour talking to Matt. Mike didn't mind because it seemed like the man needed to talk. John was right. It was hard to know how Matt felt. To lose the woman he loved had to be excruciating because even the thought of something happening to Billie gave Mike a sick feeling.

It had to be even worse when the death was so senseless, and there was no closure. He prayed everything they'd put together over the last few days would work. They'd catch Peggy's killer, give Billie and her family back their lives and make sure the evil bastards responsible were put away for a long time.

# *Chapter 26*

Matt was next to Lane hunched over and vomiting. Lane looked as if nothing was wrong as he glanced at Billie heading toward them. He stepped aside when Billie got close.

"I think it's just nerves. Happens to Ian all the time." Lane handed her a bottle of water, walked away and plopped down on the front step.

"It's not fucking nerves." Matt gagged. "It just makes me physically sick to think of what that fucker wanted to do with Chloe and Billie."

"But he didn't, and he's not going to." Billie rubbed her brother's back as he heaved again.

"I didn't know you were there." Matt wiped his sleeve across his mouth and stood up.

"I couldn't let you take off when you looked about ready to kill someone." Billie opened the bottle and held it out to Matt.

Matt took a mouthful of water, swished it around and spit it out. He stared at her for a moment before he wrapped his arm around her neck and kissed the top of her head. She'd spent so much time over the last few days practicing with Jess and getting comfortable shooting that she hadn't thought about what all this was doing to Matt.

He was on board to help but to think about what could have happened to his daughter had to be killing him. It terrified her.

"You know Nanny Betty's food don't taste quite as good coming back up." Matt's attempt at humor made Billie step back and stare up at him.

"Don't tell her that." Billie smiled.

Matt stared at her, and she didn't miss the unshed tears in his eyes. She just didn't know why they were there at that moment.

"I don't want you to do this," Matt whispered.

"I have to, Matt." Billie linked into his arm, and they walked to where Lane had sat a few minutes earlier.

"You don't have to. They could use a decoy or something." Matt sat on the step and leaned his elbows behind him.

"I want to be the one to help catch this guy." Billie sat next to him.

"You know, Mike doesn't like this either." Matt glanced at her.

"I don't like it either, but I have to do this." Billie would have a chat with Mike about not being honest with her.

"I need to buy that fucking cat a full salmon." Matt smiled.

"Why?" Billie laughed.

"He's the reason that guy didn't break into your place, and it's as if he watches over Chloe." Matt tilted his head to look at Billie. "He lays at the foot of the bed Chloe sleeps in, and as soon as anyone enters the room, he jumps to his feet. It's like he knows."

"Maybe he does," Billie said.

"Animals do have a sixth sense." Billie turned her head because she'd forgotten Lane was still there. He sat on one of the deck chairs with his feet propped up on the rail. "My mother grew up on a reserve. She was Metis. I'm ashamed to say I don't know a lot about my ancestors but she always said animals could sense things that people couldn't."

Lane hadn't raised his head, but when she or Matt didn't speak, he looked up.

"Sorry, I didn't mean to listen, but hey when you do this job, you can't help it." Lane smiled, and Billie had to admit the man was quite handsome. She did see a resemblance between him and Sandy as well.

"It's okay. I also think you may be right." Matt stood up and stretched. "I think I'm going to crash here for the night if that's okay?"

"I'm sure Mike won't mind." Billie stood up.

"I'll make sure I wear my headphones," Matt chuckled, and Lane snorted.

"What?" Billie glanced back and forth between the two men.

"Nothing." Matt opened the door and motioned for her to go ahead of him.

Billie walked into the bedroom and smiled. Mike sat against the headboard softly snoring with a book on his lap. He'd obviously been waiting up for her, but like her, he had to be exhausted. She couldn't believe she could get so tired and not even work every day.

She made her way to the bathroom and got ready for bed. She caught her reflection in the mirror and stared at herself. She looked tired but what she was trying to see is if she had what it took to do this. Matt didn't seem to think it was a good idea and from what he said neither did Mike.

She returned to the bedroom and flicked off the light. Mike hadn't moved, so, when she crawled on the bed, she removed the book and tried to ease him down. The man was not easy to move.

"What?" Mike's eyes opened, and he stared at her.

"I was trying not to wake you." Billie smiled.

"I'm sorry I didn't mean to fall asleep."

"It's okay." Billie slid under the covers and took her usual position tucked into his side with her head on his chest.

"Is Matt okay?" Mike kissed the top of her head.

"He will be. I think we all will when this is over." Billie turned her head and kissed his bare chest.

"We will be." Mike murmured.

"Do you think I don't have what it takes to get this done?" Billie whispered.

"Huh? What makes you say that?" Mike placed his finger under her chin and lifted her face, so she had to look at him.

"Matt said you didn't want me to do this." Billie cupped his cheek.

"I don't, but that's not because I don't think you can't. Jesus, Billie, you can do anything you put your mind to." Mike kissed her forehead.

"I don't know if I've got the guts to go through with this." A tear rolled out of her eye and down the side of her face.

"I want you to know if you don't want to do this, you don't have to. They'll find another way to draw this fucker out. As for you not having the guts, Billie you've got more courage in your little finger than any of those cowards who are stealing kids and turning them over to God knows what." Mike stared into her eyes, and she let herself get lost in his blue gaze.

"I love you," Billie whispered.

"I love you too, Beautiful. More than I could ever say." Mike brushed his lips against hers, and she pulled back.

"By the way, Matt is staying here tonight." Billie giggled when Mike leaned in to kiss her again. "Can you tell me why he thinks he needs to wear his headphones?"

"Maybe because Philip has a big fucking mouth." Mike chuckled.

"What?"

"I wasn't going to say anything but apparently the reason Philip decided to move over to Kim's for a few days was because…" Mike laughed.

"What?" Billie pushed him.

"We were a little noisy." Mike wiggled his eyebrows.

"Oh my God." Billie laughed. "Oops."

"I guess it's awkward to hear your sister scream with pleasure." Mike moved above her and pressed his growing erection against the apex of her thighs.

"Hmmm… I'll try to keep it down for Matt's sake." Billie raised her hips to meet his.

"This should be interesting." Mike leaned down and pulled one nipple into his mouth, and Billie gasped.

Yep, it was going to be interesting.

******

Billie stood in the window of the small house across the street from her parents. The plan set in place, and although she knew she had security, she was nervous. Her parents were back in their house as well, and she could see her mother peek through the curtain for the tenth time in as many minutes.

Mike was with her, but he was supposed to leave at eight in the evening and leave her alone. Not that she was because there were four other men hidden in the back room. It was a good thing the house was up for sale, and Abbie asked the owner to rent it for a few weeks. They didn't know the real reason they needed the place, but Abbie convinced them, or maybe it was because Truck was with her.

They told the owners Truck was in St. John's on business, needed a residence close to his office, and money was no object. The cash wasn't an issue because Tom Roberts offered to finance the whole operation. He wanted Billie and Chloe to be safe and wouldn't take no for an answer.

"Tom has more money than he could ever spend," Mike told her. "He offered. No, he demanded they take the money and shut up about it."

Billie laughed when she thought about the quiet man that followed Nanny Betty around yelling at Steve. They were cute together. Mike told her the story about how they'd been in love as teenagers and how a series of unfortunate events separated them for years. When they found each other again, they knew they were meant to be. It was a beautiful story about long lost love.

"If that cat growls at me once more I'm going to castrate it," Hulk grumbled as he made his way to the kitchen to grab a drink.

"Too late for that." Billie laughed. "He's been fixed."

"Well, no wonder he's such an ass." Hulk gulped down the bottle of water.

"Nah, he was like that before he was neutered." Mike moved over when Cougar jumped up on the couch.

"Billie, you probably shouldn't be staring out the window." Hulk closed the dark curtains and returned to the room in the back.

"Smash said all the video is up and working around the house and your parent's place." Hulk opened the door. "Keep that thing out here."

When Cougar jumped down from the couch and headed toward the room, Hulk slammed the door.

"Ha cat, I'm smarter than you," Hulk shouted through the closed door.

"That's not something to brag about," Mike called out.

Billie plopped next to Mike on the couch and watched as he scrolled through the guide. Neither of them spoke, but she could feel the tension in his body. He'd argued with Steve and John about leaving her. They'd told him nothing would happen if the guy thought Billie wasn't alone.

At eight that evening she walked Mike to his car and kissed him. He held her for a few minutes and whispered how much he wanted to stay and told her how brave she was. She was glad he couldn't read her mind because she was terrified.

She watched him drive off as she sat on the front step. She scanned the street for anything odd or unfamiliar, but there was nothing. She grew up in the neighborhood and knew everyone that was in all ten houses. The only houses she didn't know were the two at the very end. They were rentals and always had different students moving into them each September.

Billie glanced across the street at her parent's place. Her father was in the window watching her. She waved, and he blew her a kiss. According to the plan, the first couple of days they'd restrict her parents to only coming over in the day. She knew inside the house were four men, but she didn't want to go inside.

She jumped when she saw something move out of the corner of her eye. Relief took over when she saw Rita walk across the street.

"Hey," Billie smiled.

"I heard you moved in here." Rita stopped at the bottom of the steps.

"Yeah, I couldn't go back to the other place." Billie didn't lie. She really couldn't go back to the other house. Not just because it had been gutted by the fire, but her best friend brutally lost her life there.

"You'll have to drop over once you get settled." Rita glanced down the street. It was almost as if she was looking for something.

"Of course, I've still got so much unpacking to do, but in a couple of days, I'll give you a call. How's your mom?" Billie felt the hair on the back of her neck stand up when Rita looked back at her.

"She's good, but I need to get back. Call me." Rita waved as she ran across the street and disappeared into her house.

Billie backed up the steps being very careful to check in every direction. Something didn't feel right, which made her hurry into the house and slam the door behind her. She held her hand against her chest to slow her heart rate. How was she going to do this?

"Something seemed to spook your neighbor." Billie jumped at the sound of Steve's voice.

"Something spooked me." Billie sighed.

"You'll be fine." Steve smiled and sat next to her on the sofa. "Mike's going to drive right back to Hopedale. It's just to see if anyone is watching him, but I don't think they are. I've got a feeling this guy knows you're not in Hopedale anymore."

"Why do you think that?"

"Smash is watching a chat room that's mentioned you a few times or the code name they use for you." Steve held out a piece of paper.

"What's this?" Billie opened the paper and scanned the columns.

"That is a list of code names for all the kids and women these guys abducted. It took a while and three of my men to figure it out. Each code has their initials and street name. Your code is BC

Penetanguishene."

"Because I lived on Penetanguishene Road." Billie sighed as she scanned the paper for Chloe's code.

"It's CB Midland." Steve seemed to read her mind.

"This is real." Billie's vision blurred and she tried to blink back the tears.

"It's extremely real." Steve nodded.

He was about to speak when his phone buzzed, and Billie glanced at the screen. It was an unknown number.

"Inspector Parker." He answered.

Billie didn't want to be rude and eavesdrop but damn what else did she have to do. She pulled out her phone and pretended to scroll through Facebook as she listened to the one-sided conversation.

"Yes," Steve said. "Billie felt a little uneasy outside a little while ago."

Cougar nudged Billie's hand and stared up at her. Did he understand fear? Mike asked Chloe if it was okay for Billie to borrow Cougar for a few days because she needed him to help her. Chloe had taken ownership of the cat.

"You've seen our set up. There are no windows." Steve referred to the small room that now contained three huge men and a table full of electronic equipment.

It was a good thing it was Fall because if it were Summer, they would suffocate in the tiny room.

"Mike's on his way back to town, but he's going to be staying with Billie's parents." Steve rolled his eyes. "He won't interfere. He knows what's at stake."

Billie chuckled as Steve slapped his forehead. Whoever was on the other line didn't like the idea of Mike being so close.

"Would you like the person you loved being in danger?" Steve shouted, and after a few minutes, he calmed. "Exactly."

Billie turned the television to the country music channel and sat back. Steve shoved his phone back in his pocket and shook his head.

"That was the director of the task force. Did I mention I hate when people doubt me?" Steve squinted his eyes and wrinkled his nose.

"No, but I could see that." Billie chuckled.

"Anyway, Mike's going to text you when he's with your parents," Steve said.

"What if someone sees him?" Wasn't the reason he left to make the guy think she was alone?

"He's driving Philip's car and wearing your brother's jacket." Steve glanced at his watch. "Since it's cold as hell outside. It won't look weird for him to have his hood up."

Billie waved as Steve disappeared into the back room again. She was alone. Not alone, but it felt that way. The cat had abandoned her to curl up on the back of the chair next to the window, so she didn't even have Cougar to keep her company.

Billie wondered how she ever lived alone for three years. She used to enjoy it, but spending so much time at Mike's place spoiled her. She even missed the constant bickering between Abbie and Trunk. Those two were like oil and water.

Her phone buzzed in her hand, and she saw Mike's face appear on the screen. She tapped the screen to answer it and lay back on the couch.

"Hey, Beautiful." His voice soothed her frayed nerves instantly.

"Hi," Billie sighed.

"Are you okay?" Mike asked.

"I miss you, and I doubt I'm going to sleep tonight." Billie turned on her side and curled her hand under her cheek.

"Me either but your mom said I could sleep in your room." Mike chuckled.

"Maybe you can sneak over and take advantage of me." Billie smiled.

"Very tempting but I think I'd probably get shot." Mike sighed.

"Sing for me," Billie whispered.

"What do you want to hear?"

"The one about angels." Billie closed her eyes.

Mike began to sing, and Billie lost herself in the words of the song. She relaxed as she always did when she was curled up in his arms. He was with her there on the couch singing that beautiful song as he lulled her to sleep.

*Angels Brought Me Here.*

# Chapter 27

Three days he'd had to sleep in a single bed across the street from the woman he loved more than life itself. Three damn nights he had to listen to her quivering voice as he tried to make her feel better by singing that stupid song. He felt useless.

Now he was in the tiny room of the house because he'd managed to convince John and Steve to let him stay a little later that evening. It was supposed to look as if Billie was living in the house and at some point, her boyfriend would spend the night too. Right now he was just happy to be staying later than eight.

Mike had no idea what scrolled up on the screen in front of Smash. It all looked like another language to him, but from the 'ah ha and got ya' from Smash, Mike assumed it was good.

Hulk sat with his chair leaned back on two legs against the wall with his eyes closed. Lane stood in the corner watching the video monitors, and Steve sat with his phone to his ear waiting for the person on the other end to answer. Billie was in the shower, and Mike wished he could join her, but considering the house was so small it probably wasn't a good plan.

"Answer the fucking phone," Steve grumbled.

"What's wrong?" Mike asked.

"This here." Smash pointed to a jumble of letters and numbers on the screen.

"That would be?" Mike asked.

"Watch." Smash tapped a few keys on the keyboard, and the gibberish started to make sense.

"That says tonight." Mike pointed to the first word to pop out.

"That says they are making their move tonight to get BC Penetanguishene," Smash growled.

"And that's Billie." She told him about the codes.

"Yeah and this," Smash pointed to another line.

"It's this address." Mike's body shook. They were going to try and take Billie.

"Answer the fucking phone God damn it." Steve pounded the phone on the table and then put it back to his ear.

"Yeah, that should help," Hulk said without opening his eyes.

"Don't start, Hulk," Steve growled.

Mike left the room to find Billie. He wanted her to know what was going on but before he got to the bathroom, he heard the cat growling and spun around. Cougar stuck his head between the curtains, and hunched his back as if he was about to attack.

Mike peeked out through the side of the window making sure not to move it too much. He didn't see anything. The cat was crazy, but as he was about to step back, he saw an older man walk slowly down the street. He looked like he could barely move as he pushed his walker ahead of him and took two steps.

"You, crazy cat. That poor man can hardly move." Mike shook his head and stepped away from the window.

Billie was dressed and brushing her hair when he walked into the room. She gave him a huge smile and dropped the brush on the dresser. She'd relaxed a little since nothing had happened over the few days, but he was about to ruin that for her.

"Hey, Beautiful." Mike rested his hands on her hips and brushed his lips against hers.

"What's wrong?" Billie must have seen the tension in his body.

"Billie, we need you out here. Now." Steve shouted.

Mike clenched his teeth together because he didn't like the wave of fear that came over her face and erased her smile. It was wrong for her not to smile.

In the living room, Steve stood next to the window where Cougar still growled at the old man.

"Look out the window and see what that cat is growling at."

Steve was on the side of the window, but he couldn't seem to see anything.

Billie pulled back the curtains and looked up and down the street. Cougar continued to hiss and growl even after Billie put her hand on the cat's head to try and calm him.

"I don't see anything." Billie shrugged her shoulders. "Just Mr. Thompson."

"So you know him?" Steve asked.

"Yes, he's lived on this street ever since I can remember, I think he just turned ninety."

"Well, what is wrong with that fucking cat?" Steve seemed about to jump out of his skin.

"Maybe he doesn't like old people." Smash chuckled.

"The cat senses something." Lane said.

"Yeah, okay." Steve rolled his eyes and stomped back to the room in the back.

"What's wrong with him?" Billie asked.

"His contact on the task force is not answering." Mike wrapped his arms around her and pulled her back against him. They stared out through the window and watched as Mr. Thompson disappeared from view. Cougar seemed to settle down once the man was out of sight.

"Guess he doesn't like Arthur." Billie chuckled.

"Mr. Thompson?" Mike laughed.

"Yes, he always tells people to call him Arthur."

"Should you be standing in the window with me?" Billie sighed.

"I'm staying until ten tonight, remember." Mike tucked his face into the crook of her neck and inhaled. "You smell so good."

"So do you," Billie whispered.

"Fuck, I miss you." Mike kissed her neck and hugged her tightly.

"I miss you, too." Billie turned into his arms and tucked her head under his chin.

A few minutes later Steve walked out of the back room and slid around to the window. He told Billie to close the curtains as she did every evening. Cougar sat up staring out through the opening and didn't seem pleased when Billie closed them.

"They're waiting for the boyfriend to leave." Steve motioned for them to come back into the room.

"What're you talking about?" He hadn't gotten a chance to tell Billie, and she was now entirely in the dark.

Steve explained while he moved behind Smash. Billie tensed beside him, and he wrapped his arm around her shoulder. Hulk and Lane had gone to take their place in the house. They'd set up specific spots in the house to hide when they knew everything was about to go down.

"Mike, I know we said you could stay longer but…" Steve shook his head.

"No way. I'm not leaving." Mike wasn't about to run out when Billie was in danger.

"Mike, it's okay. I'll be fine." Billie cupped his face, but her voice quivered.

"No, I… can't leave you." Mike shook his head.

"You've got to go." Billie tugged his hand and pulled him out of the room.

"Billie, you can't ask me to leave when I can stay to help protect you." Mike pushed away his coat she held up.

"You can protect me by letting these guys do their jobs. I know you've helped your brothers in the past, but they're waiting for you to leave. If you don't then this drags out longer. I want to be able to sleep next to you again, and that'll only happen if we get these guys tonight." Billie pleaded with him.

God, he knew she was right, but it killed him to leave her. He was supposed to be her hero. Her knight in shining armor but here she was the brave hero and putting her safety on the line.

"I fucking love you." Mike pulled her into his arms.

"I love you too, with everything in my heart and soul." Billie wrapped her arms around him, and he kissed her as if she'd disappear the minute he stopped.

"See you soon." Billie opened the front door, and Mike stepped outside. She blew him a kiss just before she closed the door with the loudest click he'd ever heard.

# *Chapter 28*

Billie leaned against the door and took several deep breaths. This was really about to happen. Belinda Margaret Carter was about to use herself as bait to catch a monster who bought and sold people like they were nothing. Could she do this?

Billie, you've got more courage in your little finger than any of those cowards who are stealing kids and turning them over to God knows what.

Mike's words echoed in her head. It had been days since he'd said those words to her, but they gave her strength to know he believed she could do this.

*I can do this. I can do this.*

She repeated those words to herself as she made her way into the bedroom where she slept. Steve had gone over what she was to do so often that Billie could hear it in her head.

Put the earpiece in her ear. Go into the bedroom, turn on the light and look out the window. If they're watching, they'll see you're about to go to bed and believe you're alone.

She didn't want to be alone at the moment, and technically she wasn't, but she felt more alone than she thought possible. She pressed her head against the window when she saw movement in the bushes of the next house. Her heart began to pound in her chest, and she gasped. Then a voice came through her earpiece.

"It's just me, Billie," Nick whispered, and she relaxed.

"That's enough time. Step back and close the curtains." Steve's voice buzzed in her ear.

Billie did what he said and plopped down on the bed. Cougar curled up next to the pillow and gave a little meow when she lay up next to him. He purred and rubbed his body against her hand.

"Why does he growl at me and purr for you?" Smash chuckled in her ear.

"He's a typical male. Only likes beautiful women." Leave it to Aaron to say something like that.

Billie listened to the men chatter in her ear and closed her eyes. She suddenly didn't feel so alone. Cougar lay next to her and Billie's body relaxed. She couldn't understand how the hell it happened but it did.

"What the hell is going on?" James growled in her ear.

"I don't know." Steve snapped. "Why are they coming up the steps?"

"They must be part of the task force," Nick said.

"They don't answer the fucking phone all evening and then show up probably blowing this." Steve sounded pissed.

"They're wearing NPD Police vests," James said.

"They're knocking on the door. Really?" Steve snapped. "I should let that fucking cat answer the door but Billie I need you to come here and answer it."

Billie walked out to the front door and couldn't help but laugh at the pissed off expression on Steve's face. He looked like he was about to rip the guys at the door a new one. Billie opened the door and stepped back. Four huge men blocked the doorway.

"Can I help you?" Billie asked the guy sneering at her.

"Step back into the house and don't say a word. Tell the assholes hiding in the corners to come out where we can see them, or I'll shoot you right between the eyes." The man growled, and Billie finally knew what it was like to see pure evil.

"I'm sorry, I'm alone..." Billie tried to act dumb but the click of the gun pointed at her made her not finish the sentence.

"Okay, we're here." Steve stepped out with his weapon pointed at the men on the front step.

"I see three. Where's the fourth one?" The man growled.

"I'm here." Smash stepped into view holding a weapon.

"Do you think it's a good idea to have this sweet thing in the middle of all these cocked guns?" A voice spoke from behind the mean looking guy.

"Then maybe your guys here should drop them first." Steve snapped.

"I don't think that's going to happen until we're safely away from here with this beautiful creature." Billie stepped back as a tall, elegant man stepped around the four men.

If Billie had seen the man anywhere else, she'd have thought he was relatively handsome. A little on the skinny side but not horribly so. Dressed in an expensive suit, he appeared to have just come from a business meeting.

"It seems we're at an impasse because we aren't dropping ours and I assure you there's a hell of a lot more pointed at you then at us." Steve grabbed the back of Billie's shirt and pulled her closer to him and the rest.

"But you see, we have the advantage here." The man grinned.

"I don't see how." Steve chuckled.

The man pulled out his phone and tapped the screen a few times. He waited a few minutes before his phone rang and he touched the screen.

"Show our brave police officer what will happen if I don't return with my purchase." The man held his phone up.

Billie gasped. In front of her was a woman stripped naked

except for panties tied to a post. A man stood next to her with a stick and jabbed her with it. The woman screamed, and Billie felt Steve and Hulk stiffen behind her.

"Oh, and just so you know. This lovely treasure isn't the only one in that room." The man sneered. "Show them our training chamber." The man spoke into the phone.

Billie's body shook as the video showed several children and women tied up in the same way as the first. Each of them stripped naked except for underwear, and if that wasn't bad enough, the cruel bastards poked them with the sticks similar to what the first man had. The screams were horrific.

"In case you're wondering what that is, it's like a type of cattle prod but with a little more kick." The man turned his phone back, so he was able to see it. "Incredible collection."

"We'll find them," Steve growled.

"Oh, I doubt that but whatever gets you through the day." The man held out his hand. "Now, let's make this easy with no violence."

"What's your name?" Billie couldn't think of anything else to say to stall for time.

"Treasure, we'll make formal introductions when we're in a more suitable setting." The man smiled and crooked his finger for her to come closer.

Billie wasn't about to make this easy for him, but she couldn't endanger all those poor children any more than they already were. She turned her head to look at Steve, but the man shouted which made her jump.

"I know this is all new to you, but you're my property, and when I tell you to come with me, you need to listen. That way you won't find yourself in the situation that many of my collection is in at the moment." The man took a step toward her, and she backed up.

"I'd like to know the name of the man who owns me." Billie stood up straight and pushed back her shoulders. He wasn't going to see her fear.

"Such a brave one. Fine but only because you're special. I've never had to go through so much trouble to retrieve one of my purchases before." He held out his hand again. "My name is Felix Morris."

"Liar," Steve shouted.

"I don't lie, officer." He almost seemed offended by Steve's comment.

"Felix Morris is in jail as we speak." Steve reached for Billie and pulled her back between him and Hulk.

"Yes, you do have a man with my identification, and that's the way we planned it. Although, right about now he's hanging from a sheet in his cell. The poor man couldn't take the guilt of selling people like cattle." Felix sneered.

"I'll check it out." A voice shouted through her earpiece. She wasn't sure, but it sounded like James.

"Now, I'm losing my patience. Belinda, it's time to go." He stepped forward, and Billie heard the clicks of the guns next to her.

"Billie isn't going anywhere." Steve and Hulk pushed her behind them.

"Do you want to be responsible for the unnecessary torture of innocent women and children?" Felix laughed. He appeared thrilled by the thought of inflicting pain.

"We aren't responsible for their pain. You are, Morris." Steve snapped. "You're going to spend the rest of your life in jail with people who don't take kindly to men like you."

"Men like me don't go to prison, officer." Felix lifted his finger and the men behind him raised their guns higher.

"No, don't." Billie stepped around Steve and Hulk. "I'll go with you. Just don't hurt any of these men."

She couldn't be responsible for the deaths of the people that were there to do a job. Yes, she was the job, but she wasn't going to allow them to risk their lives anymore.

"Billie, don't do this." Steve reached for her.

"I'm not going to be responsible for so many people getting hurt." Billie turned to the men behind her. "You guys mean too much to me. I just need you to do one thing for me."

"Billie, no." Lane shook his head.

She hoped Felix would fall for her plan and she prayed it

would work.

"Please, tell Mike I love him, and I'll never stop." Billie stepped back toward Felix. When he wrapped his arm around her neck, she smiled. "Can you do one more thing too?"

"Billie," Hulk growled.

"What is it, Billie?" Steve swallowed, but his eyes locked on the man behind her.

"Always remember to…" Billie took a deep breath. "Sing."

With that Billie slammed her elbow back into Felix's stomach and he grunted. She stomped down on his foot, and he yelled but still kept his arm tightly around her neck. When she lifted her arm and slammed her elbow into his nose, she heard a crack, and he released her with a scream.

"Oh, I forgot one thing." Billie grabbed Felix by the shoulders and slammed her knee hard into his groin. "That's for every woman and child you've hurt."

Felix dropped to the floor and rolled around shrieking. The burly men behind him looked confused but by the time they figured it out they were surrounded and handcuffed.

"I love the way you sing." Aaron laughed as he cuffed the last of the men and dragged him off.

Felix was on the floor but handcuffed. He cried as one of the officers read him his rights.

"Not so brave now are you, Felix?"

"Rita?" Billie gasped when she saw her neighbor saunter into the house holstering a gun.

"Hi, Billie." She smiled and motioned for a man to take Felix.

"You're a police officer?" Billie dropped down on the chair in the living room.

"I'm with the human trafficking task force, but I work with Public Safety Canada." Rita smiled.

"But your mom?" Billie had seen Rita push her mother in and out of the house in a wheelchair.

"Mom is perfectly healthy and living with her sister in Gander for a while." Rita sat next to her.

"Who was the woman you were taking care of?" Billie couldn't believe what she was hearing.

"That would be me." Billie looked up to see a man leaned against the doorjamb.

"Bannister," Steve sighed.

"Boyd Bannister," He reached out to shake hands with Billie.

"So, you were undercover?" Billie sighed.

"Yes, we've been working on this for months." He gave Billie a shy smile.

"Mike didn't like you." Billie stared at the man.

"I sensed that." Boyd laughed.

"Billie," Mike shouted as he appeared behind Boyd. "You're okay."

"She's just fine and a very courageous woman." Boyd slapped Mike on the shoulder.

"What the fuck?" Mike's eyes looked like they would pop out of his head.

"He's with the task force." Billie giggled and then she started to laugh hysterically.

"Is she okay?" Mike glanced at Rita, and it made Billie laugh more.

"She's perfectly fine." Rita stood and held out her hand. "I'm Rita Fifield, and Boyd is right. Billie's a brave woman."

"The neighbor?" Mike smiled.

"The very same." Rita gave Billie a quick hug.

Billie couldn't speak because she couldn't stop laughing, and it felt great. It was finally over, and she could go back to her life.

"Let's get you out of here." Mike chuckled as she stood up and bent over to catch her breath.

"Yep, she's definitely gone." Smash chuckled.

"I... need....ha.... I need to.... Oh my God." Billie tried to catch her breath and stop, but it was no use. "Cat." She finally shouted and dropped down on the couch holding her stomach as she laughed.

It felt good.

# *Chapter 29*

Mike rested his cheek on his fist as he watched Billie sleep on the other side of the bed. He couldn't believe how close he came to losing her. There was no way in hell he could go home after he left the house. After his car was parked two streets down, he doubled back and hid behind the bushes with Aaron.

Aaron gave him one of his earpieces so he could hear everything going on and he almost lost it when Billie allowed herself to get close to Felix.

When she told Steve to remember to sing, Aaron pumped his fist in the air because, like Mike, he knew exactly what that meant. It might have been made famous by the Sandra Bullock movie, but they'd learned it a long time ago.

"Are you going to sleep at any point tonight?" Billie's eyes didn't open, but she turned her head toward him.

"Nope, I'm just going to make sure you don't vanish." Mike leaned down and gave her a quick kiss.

"My stomach hurts." Billie giggled.

"Laughing can be a good workout for the abs." Mike pulled her closer.

"I don't know what was wrong with me." Billie opened her eyes and smiled that beautiful smile he loved.

"It happens I guess. Some people cry, some faint, and apparently, you laugh." She cupped his cheek, and he turned his head to press his lips to the palm of her hand.

"That's never happened to me before." Billie ran her fingers through the hair on the top of his head.

"You've never been in that situation before." Mike slid the sheet down from her breasts and placed soft, quick kisses across the top of each one.

"I'm pretty sure I never want to be again," Billie whispered and closed her eyes when he circled her nipple with his tongue.

"Never again." Mike sucked her nipple into his mouth, and all thoughts and conversations turned to how much they loved and wanted each other.

Mike paced in his office as he waited for his next appointment. Mrs. Yvonne Duffy had called and demanded a meeting with him about the custody arrangement. Mike wasn't sure what she was bitching about because the papers were signed and she'd agreed to all of it.

The fact that she'd sent him nude pictures of herself in emails made him wonder if there was more to her sudden call. Stella agreed to sit in on the meeting because Mike didn't trust the woman.

A soft knock on the door made him spin around. Billie leaned against the door a beautiful smile on her face, and he forgot all about his upcoming torture with Mrs. Duffy.

"I didn't know you were coming by." Mike pulled her into the office and closed the door.

"Stella called me told me to dress like a lawyer and gave me these notes to study." Billie shook the folder in her hand.

"Where's Stella?" Mike narrowed his eyes.

"She's about to bring Mrs. Bitchface… oops, I mean Mrs. Duffy into a meeting with you and your sexual harassment lawyer." Billie grinned.

Mike laughed. Only Stella would come up with a plan like that. He'd learned that the email he'd received was one of many ways Mrs. Duffy had sent him racy photos of herself.

"Well, Ms. Carter, are you ready." Mike smiled as he pulled her into his embrace.

"Mr. O'Connor. You don't want a sexual harassment charge against you too, do you?" Billie teased.

"Baby, it would be worth every charge just to get a taste of those sweet lips." Mike leaned forward and was about to press his lips against Billie's when Stella opened the door.

"Not now Casanova. Mrs. Duffy is waiting in the conference room and might I say she's dressed like a hooker." Stella rolled her eyes.

"Great," Billie stood up straight and walked out ahead of Mike. He took her in from head to toe. She looked fucking hot in the power suit and stilettos.

"Stop drooling and let Billie do the talking." Stella shoved him after Billie.

Billie stopped just outside the door to the room and allowed him to go in first. Apparently, the plan was to let Yvonne think she was alone with Mike. At least for a few seconds.

"Mrs. Duffy," Mike wasn't about to say it was nice to see her because the truth was the woman scared him a little.

"Let's drop the formalities, Mike." Yvonne dipped her finger between her cleavage and traced her long nail across the top of her breasts that looked about to pop out of her too tight shirt.

"What can I do for you, Yvonne?" Mike sat on the furthest chair away from the barracuda.

"I never got a response from any of the gifts I sent you." She pouted and leaned forward but before Mike could respond the door opened, and Billie walked in followed by Stella. If Mike didn't know better, he'd say Billie was a lawyer.

"We're in the middle of a private meeting here." Yvonne huffed.

"I see that." Billie glared at the woman. "Sorry I'm late, Mr. O'Connor."

Mike had to admit the way Billie referred to him made his dick twitch. He was never into roleplaying, but at that moment he had plenty of them rolling through his head.

Stella walked behind him and not so subtly slapped the back of his head.

"Focus." She whispered as she sat next to him.

"What is she doing here?" Yvonne whined. "I asked for a meeting with Mike... I mean Mr. O'Connor."

"Mrs. Duffy, I'm Belinda Carter, and I'm Mr. O'Connor's lawyer." Billie reached out her hand, but Yvonne looked at it as if it was something foreign.

"Okay, then. Anyway, we were in the process of filing a sexual harassment suit when you called for a meeting. So, since Mr. O'Connor doesn't want to cause you any embarrassment we thought we'd try to work this out before we do that." Billie sat next to him with her elbows on the table and her fingers steepled in front of her chin. He had to bite his lip to keep from laughing at Yvonne's reaction.

"What are you talking about?" Yvonne snapped as she adjusted her shirt to cover a little more of her breasts.

"Well, that there is one." Billie pointed a finger toward Yvonne's chest.

"I can't help if I'm heavy chested. Maybe Mr. O'Connor should learn to keep his eyes up." She sat straight in her chair and crossed her arms.

"Maybe so but when you send a man this type of thing, it's kind of hard for them not to notice." Billie slapped printed copies of the pictures on the table and slid them in front of Yvonne.

"My goodness. Where did you get these?" Yvonne's attempt at shock was amusing, and Mike dropped his head to avoid laughing. Stella didn't and laughed out loud.

"You know where they came from, Mrs. Duffy. So I will say this one time. Stop sending Mr. O'Connor suggestive notes, emails, pictures or anything else for that matter. If you don't, we will file a sexual harassment suit and make sure it's very public." Billie sat back in her chair, and Mike watched in awe.

"I..." It seemed Yvonne didn't need a second warning. She jumped to her feet and stomped out of the room letting the door slam behind her.

"Are you sure you aren't a lawyer?" Stella laughed. "I'll be keeping this stuff on file just in case she doesn't get the hint."

Stella grabbed the papers and pictures on the desk as she made her way out of the room.

"That was fun." Billie laughed.

"You were incredible." Mike stood up and pulled her to her feet.

"I wanted to scratch her eyes out." Billie fisted the lapel of his jacket.

"I think she may have wanted to do the same, but you know how to sing." Mike brushed his lips against hers.

"Yes, I do. Now kiss me." Billie demanded.

"I just did." Mike laughed.

"That wasn't a kiss. That was a peck." Billie pressed her body against him.

"Your wish is my command, Ms. Carter." Mike dipped her and covered her mouth with his. He kissed her hard, and she met him with every thrust of her tongue. By the time he pulled her upright, they were both panting.

"Now that was a kiss." Billie sighed and gazed into his eyes.

He really loved this woman, and at that moment he knew it was time to take the next step. The first thing he needed to do was talk to her father.

Mike sat in Tim Horton's coffee shop staring into the hot cup of coffee he'd just purchased. He'd asked Bill Carter to meet him there because he needed to talk to him.

Mike glanced out the window when he noticed Billie's father's truck pull into a parking spot. He took a couple of deep breaths and closed his eyes. The nervousness was completely stupid because the one thing Mike was sure about was he wanted to marry Billie more than he wanted to breathe. He just wasn't sure what her father would think about it.

It was old-fashioned to ask for the father's blessing, but he and his brothers were taught to respect the family of the women they loved, and asking Billie's dad was his way to show how much he loved and respected Billie and her family.

His heart dropped when Bill got out of his truck followed by Philip and Matt. Why were her brothers there?

"Hey, Mike." Philip waved as he made his way to the counter.

"I hope you don't mind, but I figured we'd join you." Matt grinned, and something told Mike Billie's brother knew precisely why he'd wanted to meet with Bill.

"Don't mind at all." Mike grinned back.

"Pop wouldn't come because he said we were asses." Matt laughed.

"You being an ass? I don't believe it." Mike feigned shock.

"I know. I'm an absolute pleasure to be around." Matt sat back in the seat.

It was good to see him laugh considering what he'd dealt with over the last few months. Billie told Mike that he'd started to see a therapist to deal with his loss and anger. It looked like it was working.

"Felix is pleading guilty to all charges." Matt's smile faded.

"I heard." John had filled Mike in on everything.

Felix Morris agreed to plead guilty but only if he was kept in protective custody away from any other inmates. The crown Attorney agreed to the deal as long as she was satisfied with his confession.

The imposter posing as Felix Morris was found dead in his cell the same day they brought Felix into custody. One of Morris's cohorts managed to overpower a guard and take his place. He killed the fake Felix and staged it to look like the man hung himself. Luckily the guard was not seriously hurt, and the other man was in custody.

Felix confessed to hiring someone to murder Peggy. Eugene didn't deliver Chloe like he was paid to do so Felix had him killed. He arranged the fire in Billie's house and Abbie's office as a distraction to get Billie. Thank God it failed. He also gave the location of where he held the children and women he'd purchased as well as the names of all of his associates.

He'd spend the rest of his life in prison with no chance of parole, and it was where he belonged. Mike was glad the man didn't put everyone through a long drawn out trial.

"So, what's up?" Bill asked when Philip joined them at the table.

Mike took a deep breath and glanced between Philip and Matt.

Did he really want to do this with these two there?

"What the hell?" Mike sighed. "Bill, I'm pretty sure these two know why I asked you to meet me here which was why they probably suggested they join us."

"I've got no idea what you're talking about." Philip chuckled and sipped his coffee.

"Yep, what he said." Matt laughed.

"Will the two of you shut up and let the man ask me to marry my daughter." Bill slapped both men in the arm.

"Ahh.. well." Mike dropped his head and laughed.

"Well, go ahead." Matt nudged him with his foot.

"Bill, I love your daughter more than I could ever tell you. More than I ever thought I could love someone. She breathed life into me the day I met her. I want to marry her and have a family, but I want your blessing. I want the family's blessing." Mike glanced at the three men.

"I say let him take her off our hands." Philip shrugged.

"She's a real pain in the ass at times." Matt grinned.

"I don't care." Mike laughed.

"You'll take care of her?" Bill met his eyes.

"Yes," Mike didn't hesitate.

"You won't raise your hand to her in anger?" Bill continued

and Mike wasn't offended considering what they saw with Peggy.

"I'd never hurt her." Mike knew that was something he'd never do no matter how angry he was.

"She's my baby girl." Bill's eyes were wet with unshed tears. "She's got a big beautiful heart and a smile that melts me."

"I know the feeling." Mike smiled.

"I'll give you my blessing on one condition." Bill sat back in the chair.

"Anything," Mike said confidently.

"Can you take these two off my hands too?" Bill chuckled and hitched his thumb at Matt and Philip.

"If it means I get to marry your beautiful daughter, I'll take them too." Mike smiled.

"No thanks." Philip laughed.

"I'm sure Billie would love that." Matt smiled.

"In all seriousness, I wholeheartedly give you my blessing to marry Belinda." Bill shoved out his hand and Mike grabbed it. Philip and Matt slapped their hands down on top. "Welcome to the family ."

# *Chapter 30*

Over the last couple of weeks, Mike acted strangely. He was attentive, but something was on his mind, and she couldn't figure out what it was. She asked him about it several times, but he shrugged and said it was work.

She wasn't going to worry about it tonight though because for the first time in months she was going out with her friends. Her circle had gotten larger since she met Mike and the girl's nights now included Mike's cousins, sisters-in-law, and Rita.

They were going to the same club she'd met Mike almost a year before. They were all meeting at Abbie's new office and heading out from there. Mike was relaxing at home with his brothers and friends, but he was driving her to town and picking her up afterward.

The club hadn't changed much in a year, but they rarely did. It was Stephanie's first night out since she had her baby boy and obviously ready to enjoy herself. Emily joined them as well, but since she was five months pregnant, she was the designated driver.

They joined Sandy's sister, Kim. Emily's sister, Elaine and a couple of girls who worked with Kim and Emily. They had five tables pulled together for the large crowd of women.

"This is so awesome," Dana shouted in her ear.

"Yes," Billie laughed as Sandy, Marina, and Stephanie downed tequila shots.

"I swear those girls are party animals." Jess sipped on her beer.

"I never got a chance to thank you for teaching me to sing." Billie leaned into Jess.

"Don't mention it." Jess smiled, but it didn't go right to her eyes the way it should.

"Is everything okay, Jess?" Billie had become close to Jess since everything happened.

"Have you ever wanted to do something but everyone tells you that it's not a good idea?" Jess sighed.

"Yes," A few people told her that it wasn't a good idea to use herself as bait.

"I've had an application filled out for the police academy for five years." Jess looked down at her hands.

"Why haven't you turned it in?" Billie could see Jess as a great police officer.

"I don't know. I ended a relationship because he told me he'd leave if I turned it in. I kicked his ass out, but I still didn't do it." It looked like this was killing her.

"Are you afraid to disappoint your dad?" Billie knew she'd hit the nail on the head when Jess's head snapped up, and she looked at Billie.

"Yes." Jess sighed.

"From what I've seen, I think your dad is proud of you. I've seen him watch you when you're not looking. The pride in his expression when he looks at you and your sisters is obvious." Billie wrapped her arm around Jess' shoulder.

"Really?" How did she not see it?

"Turn it in Jess. Do what you want to do. Life is way too short to have regrets." Billie hugged her.

An hour later her group took up half the dance floor. They all danced to some pumping song she didn't like, but it was fun just to let loose.

Billie was headed back to the table when she heard her name announced over the speakers. She turned around to a bunch of grinning women.

"Billie, could you come here to the front of the stage." The man pointed to a chair sat facing the dance floor.

"What's going on?" Billie whispered to Abbie as she walked by her.

"I'm sure I don't know." Abbie fluttered her eyes.

She stood next to the chair and looked at it as if it was going to bite her. The room got quiet, and she turned around to see Mike's brothers, all the guys from Newfoundland Security Services, Stella, and her husband as well as her own family.

"Could you please sit down, Billie." The Deejay chuckled.

"What's going on?" Billie mouthed the words to her mother, but the woman just stood there grinning.

Billie was about to stand up when she heard the music. Mike's voice echoed through the speakers, and she slowly turned to see him walk out of the crowd.

"Billie I wrote this for you and the guys helped me set it to music. I hope you like it." Mike stepped in front of her and started to sing.

*Here we go, girl, I'm here for you, girl.*

*And the one thing that you need to know is no one else will do.*

*My heart is yours, girl, as well my soul, girl*

*And as long as there's breath in me I only have one goal.*

*That's to put a smile upon your face and kiss you every day*

*I'll never stray,*

*won't ever go away*


*Here we go girl, just look around girl.*

*Everyone is here to celebrate the beauty that is you.*

*It's all for you, girl. You're my life, girl.*

*There's nothing I won't do for you,*

*And on that, you can depend.*

*Trust your heart with me my love, and I will keep it near.*

*You'll never fear.*

*I'll dry every tear.*


*Here we go, girl, you're all I need, girl.*

*And the only other thing I need is you right by my side.*

*It's not for show, girl. I need to know, girl.*

*If you'll make me smile and tell me that you will be my bride.*

*I love you with all my heart,*

*And I'm here on bended knee.*

*You're everything to me.*

*Please say you'll marry me.*


Mike dropped to his knee and held out a small opened box in his free hand. The other held the microphone that he pointed toward her.

Tears streamed down her cheeks, and she had trouble focusing on the ring in his hand.

"Answer him." Billie glanced over Mike's shoulder at Matt.

"You've got to be the most romantic man in the world," Billie cupped his cheeks in her hands. "You were right."

"Right about what, Beautiful." Mike smiled.

"Angels brought us here." Billie leaned forward and made sure she was speaking into the microphone. "Yes, Mike O'Connor. Yes, I'll marry you."

The room erupted with cheers and shouts as Mike slipped the ring onto her finger. It was a white gold band with a single diamond set between two smaller diamonds. It was simple and the type she would have picked for herself.

Mike stood up and pulled her into his arms, and she kissed him with every bit of love she felt in her heart.

Her fiancé. Her lover. Her life.

"I love you," Mike whispered into her ear.

"I love you too." Billie pulled back and gazed into his glistening eyes.

"You've just made me the happiest man in the world." Mike brushed his knuckles against her cheek.

She knew exactly how he felt because there was nothing up to that moment in her life that could have made her happier.

# *Epilogue*

"I think we should just buy one of these monkey suits," Aaron complained. "Every time I turn around I'm getting shoved into one of these fucking things."

"You should be happy your brother found the woman he wants to spend his life with." John shoved the youngest of the O'Connor brothers.

"I'm happy for him, but it shouldn't mean he gets the right to make me unhappy." Aaron pulled at the tie around his neck.

"Think of it this way, when that little tart you brought sees you in that tux she'll want to rip it off later." Mike fixed his tie and chuckled at the change of expression on Aaron's face.

"Good point." Aaron grinned.

They were all lucky bastards. Four of them married now and another about to take that plunge. The other two probably wouldn't be far behind them.

Dean Nash turned around and gazed through the window as she

leaned into the man at her side. She'd brought a date, and it killed him, but he told her there was nothing ever going to happen between them.

"Bull, thanks for the night at the hotel." Mike stood behind him, and he turned.

"You're very welcome." Dean smiled.

The seven O'Connor brothers were like his own brothers, and he'd die for any one of them. He was sure they'd do the same for him but considering what they'd dealt with over the last few years. The last thing they needed was to dive headfirst into his shit.

Keith wouldn't like him taking off again, but he had to make sure she was safe. He'd promised her nobody would ever hurt her and that was one promise he'd keep. That and he'd never stand in the way of Kristy O'Connor finding happiness in the arms of another man.

No, that's how much he loved her. He'd made her believe that he wasn't interested and he should receive an Oscar his performance. Her tears had almost brought him to his knees, but Kristy deserved to be with someone without baggage.

Plus, Kristy O'Connor was so far out of his league that he shouldn't even be in the same room with her. She was better off with the pretty boy next to her.

*Be happy, Kitten.*

Dean nodded to the guys as he left the room and disappeared before anyone asked any questions he couldn't answer.

# About the Author

What does someone say to describe themselves? You could start with giving what others say about you. Scratch that. It doesn't really matter what others think about you. It matters what you think of yourself. So here we go.

First of all, I'm a wife and mother. I'm also a grandmother. That alone would fulfil any woman's life and to be honest it does. But.....

I'm also a writer. Someone who loves to tell stories of love, suspense, heartache and of course happily ever after. For most of my life, I've written those stories for myself. A type of therapy, I suppose. I love the characters I create. They become part of who I am because there's part of me in them.

So.... Now that you know this about me. I hope when you read my books, you fall in love with them.

You should also know that I'm a Newfoundlander. What is that you ask? Well we're a proud people who live on an island, off the east coast of Canada. Some people believe Canada ends with Nova Scotia. It doesn't. If you keep going east, there is a beautiful island full of amazing people and magnificent scenery. That is where my stories are set because let's face it. The best stories always come from the places you know and love.

If there is anything else you would like to know about me. Ask me!

*Coming Soon*

# O'CONNOR GIRLS

*Book 1*

*Available February 15, 2018*

*Will she finally get the man of her dreams or*

*Will his secrets destroy them both?.*

# O'Connor Brother Series

Book 1, 2, 3 & 4

Available on

Amazon and

Kindle Unlimited.

# Also Available

## Dangerous Therapy

## Book 1

Officer John O'Connor is giving up on life after a terrible accident. His family are at their wits end when he refuses any kind of therapy. The only thing keeping him sane is his dreams of a beautiful woman he pulled in for a traffic violation months before.

Physical Therapist Stephanie Kelly is healing from a broken heart. When she is hired by Nightingale's personal care and physical therapy, she's ecstatic, but she's shocked when her boss asks her to take on a new patient. Shocked because the patient is her boss's nephew and he's not exactly keen on therapy. He's also the cop who's been heating up her dreams.

As Stephanie helps John get back on his feet, they grow closer, but someone is out to hurt Stephanie, or worse. After multiple attempts on her life, John's family tries to figure out who's after the woman he loves and stop them before it's too late.

# Dangerous Abduction

## Book 2

Widower James O'Connor has been fighting his growing attraction to his brother's sister-in-law for four long years, but when someone breaks into her home, destroying everything she owns, James takes her and her young son into his home. The break-in wasn't random. Marina and her son are in danger, and James swears to protect them, but can he keep them safe?

Marina Kelly dedicates her life to caring for her sweet little boy, Danny. Since she broke free from her abusive husband, she's sworn off men, but when James O'Connor keeps entering her thoughts and her dreams, it takes everything she has to keep her feelings hidden. Now, her sister and parents are out of the province, and she's in danger, Marina has no choice but to accept James's help and try to hide her attraction and growing feelings.

The attraction between them impossible to resist. Only her ex's family secret may tear it all apart. Can Marina and James unravel the family's hidden mystery without losing each other?

# Dangerous Secrets

## Book 3

Ian O'Connor has everything going for him. He's got the O'Connor drop dead good looks, an incredible body and to top it off he's a doctor. Why wouldn't anyone want the man but none of that was the reason Sandy Churchill was head over heels in love with the man. After he had stood her up for their first official date, she was weary of taking another chance. When she ends up in the hospital because she turned her back on a criminal determined to get away from her, Ian admits that he loves her and wants another chance. A secret from his past throws Sandy into a tailspin, but she has a secret that she's hiding from everyone.

Ian's on cloud nine when he finally takes a leap of faith and tells the woman he's loved for four years how he feels and wants a chance to make up for his screw up. They have two weeks of bliss, but a murder and secrets come back to haunt him. Sandy's reaction tells him there's another reason why she's avoiding him. She's hiding something, but he has no idea what and to make matters worse there's danger coming from her past that could hurt the people he loves the most.

# Dangerous Beauty

## Book 4

When you come from a privileged family, you're expected to follow a particular path in life. Unless you're Emily Bradshaw. Defying her father, Emily turned down a full scholarship to Dalhousie University. Instead, she followed her dream and opened her own salon in the small town of Hopedale with her friend. She's happy. Then her mother vanishes. Her father receives threatening messages and hires Newfoundland Security Services to protect his children. Emily doesn't like the idea, especially when the man that walks into her salon dressed in a black leather jacket makes her weak in the knees. Emily knows she's in danger but not the kind her father is worried about.

Keith O'Connor isn't expecting his newest security job to be anything out of the ordinary. Then he walks into Snippy Gals, a beauty salon in Hopedale. Keith gets the shock of his life when an auburn haired beauty turns to face him. Emily is defiant, sassy, and her sexy curves have him in a complete spin. Fighting his feelings for her becomes almost impossible, but when Emily's mother is found, a family secret is revealed turning Emily's life upside down. Can Keith help her cope and keep her out of the clutches of a vengeful stranger?

# Rhonda Brewer

Keep up to date on all things new.

Follow me on

Facebook

Twitter

Instagram

Sign up for my newsletter and never miss another release!

http://www.rhondabrewerauthor.com/talk-to-me

www.ingramcontent.com/pod-product-compliance
Lightning Source LLC
Chambersburg PA
CBHW071203250626
47159CB00001B/184